The House on the Beach

The Texas Pan American Series

The House on the Beach

A Novel by Juan García Ponce

TRANSLATED INTO ENGLISH BY
MARGARITA VARGAS AND
JUAN BRUCE-NOVOA

University of Texas Press, Austin

Copyright © 1994 by the University of Texas Press
All rights reserved
Printed in the United States of America

First edition, 1994

Requests for permission to reproduce material from this work
should be sent to Permissions, University of Texas Press, Box
7819, Austin, TX 78713-7819.

(∞) The paper used in this publication meets the minimum
requirements of American National Standard for Information
Sciences— Permanence of Paper for Printed Library Materials,
ANSI Z39.48-1984.

Library of Congress Cataloging-in-Publication Data

García Ponce, Juan.
    [Casa en la playa. English]
    The house on the beach : a novel / by Juan García Ponce ;
translated into English by Margarita Vargas and Juan Bruce-
Novoa. — 1st ed.
        p.   cm. — (Texas Pan American series)
    Includes bibliographical references.
    ISBN 0-292-72763-1. — ISBN 0-292-72764-X (pbk.)
    I. Title. II. Series.
    PQ7298.17.A7C313 1994
    863—dc20   93-28451

Contents

Acknowledgments

This translation is the product of a senior project begun at Yale University in 1979 under Juan Bruce-Novoa's supervision. Thanks to a Fulbright Fellowship I was able to revise the translation in conjunction with the author and Juan Bruce-Novoa. The translation remained dormant between 1980 and 1985, during my graduate studies at the University of Kansas. In 1988 Bruce-Novoa and I submitted it to the Letras de Oro contest (sponsored by the University of Miami and American Express), where it received an honorable mention.

We would like to thank Diane Forrest for putting most of the typescript into WordStar and to Olga Valbuena-Pfau for entering two of the chapters. Among the many people who generously responded to questions concerning idiomatic expressions, we would like to include Lois Beery, Cele Cook, Arlene Murawaki, Stephanie Ortega, and Sue Vitello. Special recognition to Cecelia Wallin for reading the entire translation.

Thanks to David for driving me to California so that Juan and I could revise the translation together one last time, to Mary Ann and Juan Carlos for patiently enduring our work marathon, and to my mother (María M. Vargas) for taking care of Isaac and Christopher. The trip to California was made possible by the Nuala McGann Drescher Leave Award.

A final note of appreciation to the editors, Theresa J. May and Carolyn Cates Wylie, for their indispensable suggestions.

Margarita Vargas

Juan García Ponce in Context

by Juan Bruce-Novoa

CONTEXT

While from the outside, from United States or Europe, Latin American literature seems to be dominated by a few writers—García
Márquez, Vargas Llosa, Borges, Isabel Allende, and, in Mexico,
Octavio Paz, Carlos Fuentes, and Elena Poniatowska—the scene
changes dramatically when viewed from within. It should come as
no surprise, then, that when it is created by the Mexicans, the history
of contemporary Mexican literature—the record of its thematic
interests, stylistic trends, and benchmark publications—highlights
writers unfamiliar and even unknown to foreign readers. This is the
case with Juan García Ponce, one of Mexico's major writers and most
influential intellectuals of the last four decades.

García Ponce was born in 1932 in Mérida, Yucatán, and moved in
1944 to Mexico City, where his parents had established their
permanent residence. At the age of twenty-one he decided to become
a writer and dedicated himself first to drama. His *El canto de los grillos*
[The Song of the Crickets] won the Mexico City Prize for best new
play in 1956 and a year later it and another work, *La feria distante*
[The Distant Fair], were staged with moderate success, leading to his
being awarded a fellowship to study in New York. More significant,
however, is that both his writing and social activity placed him in the
center of what in retrospect must be seen as a youth movement that
changed the Mexican arts scene in a radical fashion and determined
its character for the entirety of the second half of the twentieth
century.

Coming into the 1950s, Mexican arts, like the society in general,
were still influenced by the most important historical event of the
century, the Mexican Revolution (1910 to 1920). The oligarchy that
arose out of the violent military and political struggles that extended

sporadically into the decades following the Revolution had as one of its guiding principles the need to pacify and manage social forces on all fronts. Since the early support of muralism under President Alvaro Obregón (1920 to 1924) and later the financial stimulation by the Plutarco Elías Calles regime (1924 to 1928) of the literature about the Revolution, postrevolutionary Mexican leaders have furthered their aims by the subvention of a national program of the arts—with the emphasis on "national" since the function of these programs was to build a sense of shared nationality. We can speak of an officially sanctioned and promoted postrevolutionary cultural production as one facet of the ruling party's strategy of embracing all social discourse across the spectrum of ideologies. This explains how there was room for differing voices, from the propagandistic depictions of populist nationalism to the controversial avant-garde alternatives, although at times the government's embrace was more a suppressive grasp than a nurturing caress. Yet even when a particular regime was at odds with certain artists, like the Communist muralist David Alfaro Siqueiros, it never abandoned the arts in general. On the contrary, support for all forms of expression, from popular to elite, was institutionalized, especially when the products reflected a clear "Mexican" image in flattering harmony with the ruling party's interests.

By the fifties, however, this production had solidified, if not ossified, along the thematic and technical lines called the Mexican School, characterized by the figurative depiction of typical (whether stereotypical or archetypal is a matter of debate) indigenous or proletarian images in monumental style. Especially admired were artistic productions that could be read as allegorical renderings of revolutionary political ideals. Similarly, in literature and film the Revolution and its aftermath remained the central theme, with a focus on rural or proletarian settings, colloquial speech, and picturesque detail. Undeniable masterpieces of this process still impress us, like José Clemente Orozco's murals at the Hospicio Cabañas in Guadalajara or Diego Rivera's frescoes at the Ministry of Education or the National Palace, Francisco Zúñiga's sculptures in the Secretariat of Communications and Public Works or Juan Olaguibel's monumental sculptural tribute to petroleum expropriation, Carlos Chávez's and Silvestre Revueltas's symphonic music, or novels like Mariano Azuela's *Los de abajo*, Martín Luis Guzmán's *La sombra del caudillo*, and Agustín Yáñez's *Al filo del agua*. As this ideological and aesthetic tide peaked at mid century and began to ebb, new artists with different ideas rushed in to reclaim and cultivate the territory formerly held by the stagnant Mexican School. Art critic Teresa del Conde, although speaking of painting, summarizes well the general situation:

> Social realism became folkloric nationalism, utilized as an affirming tool of a stereotyped identity which was supported and financed as official art. It was necessary to maintain an image of Mexico through the plastic arts, but the one maintained for many years is a falsified image.[1]

The sublime moment of triumph was the construction of University City initiated during the administration of Miguel Alemán, the president who renamed the ruling political party Partido Revolucionario Institucional [Institutional Revolutionary Party], accurately reflecting its sense of permanence. The new university campus on the southern outskirts of Mexico City was a monument to institutionalization, in this case the solidification of a one-party rule, a glorification of both the populist educational ideals and social ideals of the triumphant Revolution with which the ruling party disguised its pragmatic economic and political liberalism. Just as the old university, with its buildings and faculties scattered around the city's ancient center, evoked the image of the traditional European university, the new concentration of buildings in one area with all university functions centered around a focal point marked a shift to a modern concept of a campus, reminiscent of both U.S. style and Spanish educational ideals from the late nineteenth and early twentieth centuries. But again, the new campus was to symbolize this government's characteristic manner of structuring its authority: a 360 degree field of apparently unlimited possibilities promoting the coexistence of a variety of well-discerned and discrete groups of participants, but all within a unifying panoptic design of centralized power. Also, it blatantly signaled the government's ability to remake at will both the physical and intellectual Mexican landscapes.

With this ideological purpose in mind, the construction, from the spatial layout to the decorative details, was laden with political significance. The murals ensconced on the walls of buildings and sports facilities bespoke the myth (ideals symbolically represented) of the Revolution and its seizure of the power centers of Mexican culture, while at the same time they reminded the world of the government's ability to enlist for its own purposes the country's most representative artists. Siqueiros's leftist mural fronts the administration building, Rivera's reliefs festoon the stadium, and on the library tower Juan O'Gorman's mosaic pays homage to the pre-Columbian indigenous tradition; throughout the campus are found numerous smaller works by disciples of muralism. Only Orozco's death kept him from adorning a prominent facade. The results were impressive, yet not all was as it seemed on these much celebrated, multicolored, and variegated surfaces.

Although the project seemed imposingly uncontested, a battle raged on those surfaces, or, perhaps more accurately, the surfaces became one side's weapons. Mexicanist images may have covered the walls, but the underlying architecture bespoke a greater debt to Bauhaus and U.S. modernism than to any indigenous Mexican style of construction or to Soviet or Nazi massive traditionalism. This produced intense contradictions: the deep structures signaling the future were masked by surface appliqués recalling a fading past. The former reflected the truly progressive design techniques utilized in postrevolutionary buildings, while the latter constituted an aging though still powerful generation's determination to turn a concrete national project into an idealized monument to the image of its dreams, reprises of social ideology betrayed by the political pragmatism that turned those ideals into cynical populism. Those contradictions, held in tension on the university's walls, were being less peacefully disputed in the streets—miners' marches, taxi drivers' protests, railroad workers' strikes, and so on, all violently repressed, then silenced, in public media—as well as in the more restrained, though no less disputed spaces of the elite: art galleries, theater stages, newspapers' cultural pages, and the major intellectual publications. Another art critic, Rita Eder, gives us an enlightening summary of the situation of those who desired new answers for the future but faced repression by an intransigent institutionalized cultural program that defined the mid century:

> *The central axis of this way of thinking arises from a search of an*
> *ontological nature concerned with what and who we are. It*
> *attempts, in the face of the rhetorical onslaught, to find*
> *Mexicanness outside the folkloric and the anecdotal. . . . In public*
> *life, the consequences of this critical attitude—on the intellectuals'*
> *part—would be the rejection of cultural policies imposed by the*
> *dominant power. Those policies professed, though by then*
> *passionlessly, art's public function, desiring above all to prolong*

the golden age of muralism, symbol of the success of a particular cultural politics, but which, having already declined, had transformed itself into a new academic school.[2]

If Rufino Tamayo best represented painters in whose work this struggle between the contradictory impulses of mid-century Mexican cultural production was being played out progressively, one literary figure epitomizes the intellectual process: Octavio Paz. His *Labyrinth of Solitude* (1949 to 1952) begins with the depiction of the United States' assumption of post–World War II global hegemony as a threat to Mexican identity. After a pessimistically grotesque representation of cultural miscegenation incarnated in the Chicano Pachuco, an image intended to frighten Mexican readers into retreating from the United States and into themselves to seek an alternative response to modernity's challenge, Paz leads his audience on a pilgrimage into the darkness of its past to confront the monsters of its archetypal origins in hope of leading them toward a different version of the future.

Paz's review of Mexican history recalls the playing out of similar historical forces and figures in the muralist movement, but his method and conclusions approximate more closely the substructure of the new university buildings rising at the same moment. As in the avant-garde Bauhaus, Paz seeks the essential, abstracted figures underlying specific situations, using them as foundation blocks of an edifice for human survival in an era of international technological culture. He shares modernism's invocation of universal archetypal imagery applicable to any locale in a dialectic between essential deep structures and contingent surface imagery or symbols, similar to those of Carl Jung's psychology, Joseph Campbell's studies of myth, Northrup Frye's genre criticism, or Noam Chomsky's transformational grammar. He also shares a disenchantment with political messianism—right or left—and a profound faith in artists as the last heroes of civilization.

For many young Mexicans Paz's book and example, coinciding with the years of construction of University City, were liberating, but not always in the same way. For those now most popular in the United States, like Juan Rulfo and Carlos Fuentes, Paz's project, the critical review of Mexican history played out in terms of archetypal mythical figures culminating in the denunciation of a bankrupt contemporary political system, became a model repeated in their works. They focused on the body of Paz's text, recasting it in their own works. Another group took the *Labyrinth* as a declaration of independence from its contents and allegorical method, both closely associated with official culture. They saw no need to repeat the project, but rather concentrated on taking up Paz's concluding challenge to explore the essential areas of human interaction free from the Mexican folkloric code of national representation. As Paz claimed, Mexicans in 1950 found themselves the peers of contemporary men everywhere. These young artists heard Paz call for a turn away from the official rhetoric and back to the basic experiences of mythic encounters, like love, sex, and dreams, and to the way the essential ingredients of life, male and female forces, work themselves out in particular examples. Both groups were concerned with the ontological question of existence and identity, but while the former still saw the answer in terms of the present as a product determined by national history, the latter treated the present as something to be forged creatively toward the future.

In the mid 1950s both camps found themselves, however, collaborating in a common struggle against the entrenched and fully authorized forces of the Mexican School of cultural production. They attended the same openings at new galleries like Prisse or Proteo, where young painters like Pedro and Rafael Coronel, Lilia Carrillo, Alberto Gironella, Enrique Echeverría, Cordelia Urueta, Vlady, and José Luis Cuevas were displaying canvases that tended toward avant-garde techniques, including abstraction. They were fortified in their rebellion by the presence of immigrant artists, like the surrealist Leonora Carrington or the Danzig-born Mathias Goeritz, who applied his theories of emotional architecture to erect in 1953 the artistic space *El eco* [The Echo], the first in a series of monumental abstract constructions that have spawned multiple offspring all over Mexico City's urbanscape.

In the climate of rabid political correctness, these first breaths of renovation were attacked by the establishment as antinational and even as a Central Intelligence Agency plot of cultural colonization. In response, young artists formed coalitions with their literary peers to defend their freedom of expression and their right to participate in officially sanctioned international exhibits from which they were excluded. They published reviews and essays in the major newspapers and journals, engaging the establishment in furious debate while working out their aesthetic positions. They centered their activity, first, at *México en la Cultura*, the cultural supplement of *Novedades*, moving later to *Siempre*'s supplement *La Cultura en*

México. Simultaneously they began *Revista Mexicana de Literatura*, *S.N.O.B.*, and tangentially *Cuadernos del Viento*, and took control of *La Revista de Universidad* for ten years. Later, members of the inner circle, like Juan García Ponce and Salvador Elizondo, would form the core of the editorial board of *Plural* (in the first period) and then *Vuelta*, the most influential cultural publications of the last three decades.

Among the young rebels were such future luminaries as Emmanuel Carballo, José de la Colina, José Luis Cuevas, Carlos Fuentes, Jodorosky, Juan Vicente Melo, Elena Poniatowska, Tomás Segovia, and, of course, Juan García Ponce. The most famous piece to come out of this period was Cuevas's "The Cactus Curtain," a manifesto of frustration with the cliched Mexican School's control of the arts that accurately reflected the position of his peers. Together they mounted a forceful and finally convincing assault on the entrenched establishment.

The Mexican School refused to die without a struggle, so confrontations were unavoidable. Some bordered on violence, as when Siqueiros threatened to close an exhibit by force, or when protesters attacked the judges—including García Ponce—who awarded the national prize for art in 1965 to two painters of the new abstractionist generation. But by the time the government began planning the 1968 Olympics, the one-time rebels found themselves running the official cultural program. Their triumph can be symbolized in yet another public construction, Goeritz's *La ruta de la amistad* [The Route of Friendship], the centerpiece of the Olympic artistic project. The eighteen monumental sculptures, arranged along the freeway leading to the Olympic Village, by regulation had to be abstract pieces. The modernist substructure from the university had thrown off the shackles of its ideological disguise to display itself as glorious surface, flaunting its triumph.

Literature underwent a similar process, although without the highly visible public monuments capable of focusing our attention in such dramatic terms. Yet we could say that a group of works, from Revueltas's *El luto humano* (1943) and Yáñez's *Al filo del agua* (1947) to Rulfo's *Pedro Páramo* (1955) and Fuentes's *La región más transparente* (1957) and *La muerte de Artemio Cruz* (1962), functioned in an analogous way to the University City project. They represented a shift to a modernist foundation in technique and even world vision, but a surface fidelity to that same Mexican populist and folkloric imagery and thematics. The surface thematics had taken on the value of iconography, whose power of signification relied on the repetition of authorized clichés. These works traded on social "truths" reinforced by the government's populist rhetoric, which included even those oppositional voices that continually appealed to the ideals of the Revolution as contrasted to contemporary society's betrayal of them. Each new presidential regime assumed the position of critical realism—a term applied to works that displayed a social consciousness—and claimed to reincarnate the revolutionary program in its purity. Against this situation the same forces of renovation battled, focusing their efforts on the elimination of the worst clichés, the thematic programs, and the concept that a work's significance lay in easily comprehended surface anecdotes.

THE AUTHOR

Juan García Ponce is one of the leading figures among those who took Paz's work as a starting point instead of a model for repetition. Like Cuevas, with whom he sympathized, he detested the control exercised by the old school. Rita Eder acknowledges that among the young critics García Ponce was both the most prolific and the most supportive of the new tendencies in art. Therefore, she can legitimately extrapolate from his writings the aesthetics of the young artists at the start of the second half of the century: "He openly rejected the *Mexican School of Painting*. His articles call for an art subject to its own laws, and all narrative aspects identified with a concept of social utility are . . . apparently condemned."[3] He countered the aesthetics of national representation and ideological rhetoric with a phenomenological orientation that proclaimed the work's right to define its code of signification on its own terms, and hence the observer's need to allow art to exercise its effect without preconceived expectations. Even more, in the face of a dominant ideology in which the individual was sacrificed to the ideals of populism, community, and external experience, García Ponce responded with a call for the exploration of the personal, individual meaning of existence in an urbanized, sophisticated society, and, most significantly, the essential importance of inner experience, of the hidden and mysterious undercurrent of life that flows below the apparently calm, normal surface. In contrast to the Stalinist leftist rhetoric of the likes of José Revueltas or Diego Rivera, he preferred, for instance, Marcuse's fusion of Marx and Freud that produced sexually liberating utopian writing like *Eros and Civilization; A*

Philosophical Inquiry into Freud.[4] To the Jungian archetypal my-
thologizing of Paz and Fuentes, he preferred Norman O. Brown's
Nietzschean reworking of Freudianism. And instead of the stylistic
pyrotechnics of Joyce, he was more inclined toward the subtler
renderings of the human dilemma found in Thomas Mann, Cesare
Pavese, and Robert Musil. They all share, on the one hand, a concern
with human fulfillment in the face of massive institutionalized
repression and, of course, a focus on sex and eroticism as one, and
perhaps the major, source of liberation, while on the other hand their
style resembles the calm, normal surface of everyday life, with the
focus on inner experience. The work should function beyond its
informational surface, creating emotional and even spiritual effects
on the reader. García Ponce became infamous for his call for a
literature in which nothing happens—we must take this in the
context of the anecdotal writing of the Mexican School—because in
"nothing," literally within it, vibrates art's inner emotive power. In
a key essay in which he combined the visual and the literary arts as
if they were one and the same, he called this "the apparition of the
invisible."[5] He made his own work, regardless of the genre, the
obsessive exploration of these thematic, aesthetic, and philosophical
concerns.

THE NOVEL

The House on the Beach is the crowning work in the first phase of
García Ponce's career. In later works he would explore love relationships to the mystical extreme of annihilation of individual identity
as a counter to the limits of alienating consciousness. The erotic
undermining of the socially constructed person has become central
to his later writings. More and more his characters function in
private spheres, with little time and space given in the narrative to
the social context.

Prior to *The House on the Beach*, however, García Ponce's works
were marked by the culminating frustration of the characters. Social
mores and traditional customs truncate desire, making the love
encounter impossible. A strong nostalgia exists for the joy of
freedom and oneness with nature characteristic of childhood and
youth, but it is tinged with the numbing recognition that adult
maturity demands an abandonment of that spirit of uninhibited
movement. Especially poignant is the conflict between individual
desire and the demands of family and work. The characters are

sacrificed to social demands, delivering themselves to what we might call the common good within the context of the greater social system.

The House on the Beach marks the transition between these two phases. Its female protagonist, Elena, a young lawyer from Mexico City, narrates her trip to the provincial state of Yucatán to spend a few weeks with Marta, her best friend from high school and college. Though they are so physically similar that they can be mistaken for each other, they are radically different in their social orientation; Marta yearns for traditional family life and social values while Elena tends to resist both. Yet the two are poised on the brink of major decisions that will determine the rest of their lives. The motif of the vacation frames the narrative action, creating a temporal space during which characters are freed from the usual social order to swim or drift in the uncharted waters of life's possibilities normally kept at a distance by custom, habit, and the demands of a social work schedule. The beach house, with its position on the edge between land and sea, assumes more significance when we learn that it has been used as a permanent residence by Marta and her husband, Eduardo. That is, within the house there is a shifting presence of the normal world, with its work and societal timetable, and the vacation world, with its suspension of those concerns. The house is really like a beach, the strand between opposing spaces that participates in the nature of both, yet is neither. Elena, as we might expect, falls in love within and actually with that space in its fluid character of free movement, but social forces keep trying to define her into a more acceptable identity. Marta, who has maintained her outsider status by living at the beach house, is also caught in between, desiring the freedom to shift and redefine her position while also being pressured to support her husband in a more customary way by moving to the city and accepting a set social identity. The women's relationships with their male counterparts, Eduardo and Rafael, boyhood best friends, will be the field of play and crisis. How they both come to terms with desire and social demands is continually in question; the answer is suspended and played out in the carefully constructed plot, with its constant shifting of focus from one seductively beautiful scene to another. García Ponce's expertise as one of Mexico's leading art critics comes to the fore, and his novel at times seems like a gallery in which we stroll from one canvas to another, admiring each for its particular design and use of color and materials while always conscious of the entire exhibit within which each piece is but one facet meant to reflect and tone our final experience of the whole.

As a product of García Ponce's first phase, *The House on the Beach* allows social forces to intervene in the plot to an extent not found in later works. However, the protagonist's eventual manipulation of those forces to her own ends signals the author's imminent shift to the next phase of his writing. In other words, the novel shares the shifting, contested nature of the major elements in the narrative—the house, the beach, the lovers, the protagonist. And if this opposition of forces struggling over a shared space is anywhere more intense than in those elements, it would be in the act of narrating. In the flow of the creation of the narrative the protagonist's character is continually washed and reshaped by the waves of discourse. Significantly, the protagonist is also the narrator. Elena is not simply the product of setting, plot, and other characters, but also, and perhaps more importantly, of her own self-reflective and retrospective act of narrating. In the end, her true space is the narrative itself. Her ultimate identity and the text are one, or perhaps García Ponce would prefer to say that they fuse to become many possible constant re-creations, because she rejects the identity that others would impose on her. By choosing to be the constructed-constructing site between zones, like a house on a beach or the beach itself, to be a worker always on vacation, to make vacation the site of production, to jettison social identity, Elena becomes much more than herself while never becoming entirely separated from the loveliness of her own body. She takes her love to a space with ever-shifting qualities—literature—a space floating between fluid life and static death, between unpredictable desire and the demands of order, between personal identity and erotic selflessness.

García Ponce, as one of the leading exponents of the aesthetics of his peers and his time, has brought to Mexican literature a renewed focus on the mystery of the most fundamental myths of existence. He takes the question to the heart of freedom or repression, the traditional assumptions of identity. In *The House on the Beach* more than in any work before, he recognized that social repression depended for its power on the desire for personal identity within the code of social values. So he began here an assault on identity itself that his later works have developed full force. Here the balance is more subtle, while later it would be blatant to the extremes of the sublime. Behind what to some readers may seem a traditional style—deliberately kept unobtrusive—the author undermines the pillars of the social construct in favor of literature, in favor of living in literary space . . . of taking, not literature to life, where social values and physical limitations inevitably win out, but life to literature, where anything is possible.

CONCLUSION

To keep faith with García Ponce's vision of art, readers ultimately must be left on their own, alone with the work, to feel its impact in that inner space of experience so dear to the author. It is there where it must be judged.

Juan Bruce-Novoa

NOTES

1. Teresa del Conde, *Un pintor mexicano y su tiempo: Enrique Echeverría (1923–1972)* Mexico City: Universidad Nacional Autónoma de México, 1979), p. 17. Translation, Bruce-Novoa.

2. Rita Eder, *Gironella* (Mexico City: Universidad Nacional Autónoma de México, 1981), p. 19. Translation, Bruce-Novoa.

3. Ibid., p. 25. Translation, Bruce-Novoa.

4. Herbert Marcuse, *Eros y civilización* (Mexico City: ERA, 1965). Translation, García Ponce.

5. Juan García Ponce, *La aparición de lo invisible* (Mexico City: Siglo XXI Editores, 1968).

The House on the Beach

I

We were sitting facing the sea. The children moved around us, splashing their feet in the waves' last surge, constantly picking up shells, small snails, flat rocks, dry algae, and bringing them time and again to show Marta. She would respond with a few words, revealing, more than attention, a desire to be rid of them, and kept staring blankly out to where the sky—stained green by the sea's reflection and reddish yellow by the lingering sun—stretched infinitely.

I felt uncomfortable and annoyed. At the beginning, I had attempted to attract the children to me again and I even tried taking them by the hand to walk along the shore so Marta could have a moment to herself, but as soon as they noticed how far we had gone, they asked me to take them back to their mother, and I had to agree, aware that I didn't know how to make them obey me. I also knew that Marta wasn't going to speak to me and I would have preferred to wander off alone, but when they made me return, I felt compelled to stay by her side, and after sitting down, I couldn't find a way to leave without my action appearing to be another betrayal.

That morning, when I went out to the beach, I had found the sand covered with dead fish—a very unpleasant surprise. I ran back to tell Marta, but she didn't give it too much importance. She kept feeding Eduardito his breakfast and commented, "The sea was rough last night. It happens every year. You'll see how different it is from now on."

The real difference was in us, and the best proof was that before, I would have told her straight out instead of keeping it to myself, but when I went back to the beach, I realized that, in a way, Marta was right about that, too. It was almost ten, but yet, unlike previous days, the beach was deserted. The boats, which a few days before swayed on the sea anchored a few yards offshore, were now beached—resting awkwardly on palm tree trunks in front of the houses, having lost the gracefulness and balance that distinguished them on the water, or hidden under canvas—indicating their readiness for a long rest. It seemed impossible that people could have left so quickly, without my even noticing, in spite of the good-byes, amid the confusion of the last days, but that is how it was, and now, to justify their furtive escape back to the city, the sea was gray and choppy, and along the shore, besides the endless string of dead fish, different kinds of algae, rotting under the heat of the sun, stained the sand, giving it a dirty and repulsive appearance.

Even so, I didn't feel like going back to the house to be with Marta. I walked along the shore as far as the small wooden pier, where the beautiful launch that had excited me so much the first day was still tied, and I sat at the very end to watch the sea, although the sun was starting to burn and my mouth was dry. Later, one of the boys from the town, barefoot, shirtless, with his faded and patched jeans rolled up above his knees, arrived and sat down to fish a few yards away, turning once in a while to look at me. Now they owned the beach again, although I was almost as tanned as he. I remembered the day we went fishing with Rafael. My hook had gotten tangled on something for the umpteenth time and he, impulsively, stripped off his shirt and dove into the water before the fisherman and owner of the boat could finish warning him that it was dangerous. I still had the line in my hand and when I felt him pull it, I let out a scream that made the fisherman and Eduardo laugh. A moment later Rafael came up to the surface. He swam toward us, and when he reached the boat, his hair covering his eyes and out of breath, I instinctively went over to him and reached out my hand to help him up, and as he climbed aboard, I let him embrace me almost completely, although I knew Marta was watching.

I felt tenderly sorry for myself and went to sit next to the boy. He kept staring at the spot where his line sank into the sea. My presence and, above all, my closeness seemed to bother him, but I pretended not to notice and after a short while stupidly asked him if they weren't biting.

"They should bite," he said without taking his eye off the line. "The sea is rough."

"And is that good?" I insisted.

"Yes, of course," he said with authority.

"I'm not from here," I explained.

He turned for a moment to look at me.

"I know. You're from Mexico City. I've seen you around," he added.

I would have liked to continue talking, but he didn't seem to want to say anything else, although I noticed how, once in a while, he would stop staring at the line to steal a glance at my legs, and for a moment I felt the urge to place one of my bare feet on his. But instead, I just stayed next to him without saying anything, feeling a tinge of envy at his ability to concentrate on the line's soft movement over the waves, until the sun began to burn me unbearably on my legs and through my blouse; I felt like putting on my bathing suit and jumping into the sea.

I stood up. The boy turned around again and tilted his head to look at me.

"You're leaving already?"

"Yes. I'm going for a swim," I said.

"Ah . . . ," he said.

There was such disappointment in his voice that I regretted having moved.

"Don't you swim?" I asked, to linger on a while longer.

"Sometimes," he said. "But I don't like to."

I smiled and lightly caressed his head, but he quickly jerked it away, upset, and went back to staring at the line. He couldn't have been more than nine or ten. From the shore, after having walked the whole length of the pier conscious of his presence, I turned to look at him. He had pulled in his hook and stood with the coiled line in one hand, getting ready to throw it back into the sea.

The sun had completely dried the algae, stripping them of color, and over their salty iodine odor drifted the smell of the dead and rotting fish, but not even that was truly unpleasant, just natural.

In front of the house, Marta and the children were already in their bathing suits. Celia, one of the few people still at a beach house, was with her. Marta and her children were playing, lying on the sand, in the place where the waves' power gave out. I greeted her curtly and sat next to Marta, without speaking.

"You're not going to swim?" Celia asked me after a short while, leaning forward to look around Marta's body, which blocked her view of me.

She alone persisted in addressing me formally, treating me like an outsider, in spite of Marta's, Rafael's, and even her husband's insistence that she stop.

"Yes, right this minute," I answered, also leaning forward.

"I thought the sea would have surely bored you by now. We always end up sick of it," she went on.

"No, I still like it," I said. "Maybe it's because I won't be able to come back every year."

"No, of course," she said. "But you will go to Acapulco, or some other place, won't you?"

"Yes, sometimes. But it's different," I answered, almost mechanically, tired of such small talk.

"I can imagine. People go there year round. Whereas here . . . Except for these months it is horrible, and then the north winds begin. I've always believed Marta is the only one who can tolerate them, but we'll see what you think. The breeze makes many people hysterical."

"She's leaving in a few days. You don't have to frighten her with that awful image," Marta broke in.

"You're leaving? So soon? Why? You should at least wait till the rosaries are over, to keep Marta company," Celia said, feigning surprise and leaning completely forward again to see me.

"I'd like to. But I have to get back to work," I answered.

"But I thought you were going to stay longer. Rafael . . ."

She stopped without finishing the sentence, as though she had suddenly realized she was being indiscreet, but Marta broke in immediately as if nothing had happened.

"Rafael can go to see her in Mexico City if he wants. After all, it's not all that serious either."

For a moment I felt we were on the same side, but then I understood that she also had to defend herself and what united us was that necessity more than our relationship. Nevertheless, Marta turned, looked at me, and—with the voice and the complicity of years before, which we'd used at the university with other friends or when we wanted to needle some guy—started talking about Mexico City, about her father and my family, knowing that by doing so, she excluded Celia from the conversation, limiting her to asking an occasional question in an effort to go back to the topic of the funeral.

Finally, bored, Celia got up, called her oldest son, and carried him into the water, without taking off her eternal straw hat. I got up too and told Marta that I was going to put on my bathing suit. She looked at me, smiling.

"Don't pay any attention. It's a matter of getting used to handling them."

"I know," I said. "But I'm not going to."

"You'll have to," she insisted.

"Don't be stupid," I said, trying to keep the same tone, but she looked away.

I put on my bathing suit and went straight into the water. Its astonishing clearness of the previous days was gone and the bottom was no longer visible, but it was still warm and gentle. Besides, now that the noises of the boats, the children's shouts, and, above all, the constant presence of the others a few yards away had disappeared, it was much more pleasant to swim farther out and see the empty beach from a distance—the endless line of summer houses, with their shutters closed till the next season, almost caressed by the murmuring coconut palms to one side, and on the other, the low, pink church tower, surrounded by the town's thatched houses and the nets and boats of the fishermen, owners once again of everything.

Later, lying on the beach, my eyes closed and my head burning, drowsy from the sun's terrible heat and happy to be able to enjoy it freely at last, I thought that if I had arrived now, instead of during the summer, perhaps things might have been different, although I don't know if that was what I wanted. Rafael was coming by in the afternoon and I wanted to talk to Marta before I saw him. Thinking about him, I remembered Pedro for a moment. Right now, in Mexico City, he should be at the office, working. I still hadn't answered his letters and knew I wasn't going to. It was impossible to think about it now; he was too far away and too different, if not him, then me, and I didn't know if I could talk to him and explain everything, assuming there was something to explain. To forget that, I tried to think about Eduardo's father, but that, too, was impossible, and I turned on my back without opening my eyes. Marta, perhaps from the water, was calling one of the boys. Eduardo wasn't coming home for lunch and in the afternoon I would have to talk to her so I could settle things in my mind before leaving.

Much later, Marta sent the maid to tell me it was lunchtime. From the dining room the sea was clearly visible, almost white and sparkling under the sun, full of hues and secret signs. We ate together, with the children. I liked the way Marta knew how to make them obey, keeping them within the limits she had set without resorting to violence, without ever losing her patience, insisting that her orders be followed simply by using love and a surprising power of persuasion. It had surprised me the first day and continued to surprise me now. I told her and she smiled: "It doesn't take much effort. After all, if we're not smarter, at least we're supposed to be craftier."

Nevertheless, at the same time, the constant attention she had to give them, even with the maid's help, kept us from meaningful conversation. In fact, it was always the same since the day I arrived—either Eduardo was always there, or someone came to visit, or else she had something to do. We could never speak freely, talk like we used to when we were both single, in Mexico City. Perhaps that is the fundamental change that comes with marriage: your friends stop being your friends because something always comes between you, something contrary to the essence of friendship itself, but it seemed almost impossible that it could happen to Marta and me. Although now I was aware that more than anything else, I was waiting for Rafael, and talking to Marta seemed more a duty than a natural need.

Before we finished our coffee, Celia and Lorenzo showed up "to keep us company" and it was useless to think that Marta and I would have a chance to be alone. In front of her husband, Celia was much less aggressive, but it was impossible for her to abandon the tone of aloof curiosity with which most of Marta's and Eduardo's female friends always talked to me, a tone that made me feel like a ghost from a past that everyone considered nonexistent just because they had not shared it with Marta.

On the other hand, with the men, the same curiosity took on a different meaning. Almost all of them spoke to me using a kind of double entendre, as if each one of their words wanted to convey more than they could say in front of their wives, aspired to create a supposed secret language even when they were only referring to their jobs or trying to answer one of the silly questions I had asked just to make conversation. In this sense, and in spite of the occasional affection he had showed me, Lorenzo was not an exception. He took advantage of the difference between his wife's exaggerated formal etiquette and his casual, almost intimate manner to try to create a feeling that a higher level of friendship existed between us, that in some way he "knew" and "understood" more about me than he could say. But what was definitely strange was that the women also seemed to like this naive game. They felt a kind of pride that their husbands—"also"—knew how to treat women like me, but still preferred them.

Maybe, at the start, all of this seemed entertaining; I was discovering Marta's world first, and later, Rafael's, but now I no longer had enough energy to continue the game. Lorenzo had sat next to me, while Celia, to accentuate the difference, helped Marta make more coffee, but she kept reappearing to take part in our meager conversation about the end of the "season," what had happened, and the heat that still lingered in the city.

After coffee, Celia suggested we play bridge. In spite of her insistence, I said that I was very sorry but I was too tired and wanted to try to sleep for a while, and I locked myself in my room without bothering to acknowledge her objections. From there, naked on the bed, trying not to perspire, I heard them talking for a moment longer before I fell asleep, vaguely thinking about returning home, about how difficult it would be to say good-bye to Eduardo's mother, about Rafael's presence, and also, a little, about Pedro . . .

Marta's knock on the door woke me up; still half asleep I asked her what she wanted.

"Nothing," she explained. "But it's almost six. Don't you want to go to the beach for a while?"

"Come in," I said.

She sat on the edge of the bed and looked at me.

"You're really tanned . . ."

I smiled.

"Yes, it's been a long time. Did those two leave?"

"A minute ago," she said, shrugging her shoulders in a gesture of disgust. "They don't want to miss one single rosary."

I kept quiet for a moment, wondering whether I should tell her she was tanned, too, or anything else that might indicate that she also looked very attractive, and then, instead, I asked her if she thought Eduardo would be coming home to sleep.

"I don't know. If he comes it won't be before eight," she answered.

"Rafael is coming, too," I said then, without thinking.

"I know," she said.

"Do you want to see him?"

"Why not? Anything else would be absurd. We've been friends for a long time. Truthfully, I think he's the only male friend I've ever had. And I really love him, as a friend."

I sat up because I felt uncomfortable talking to her lying down, but when I did, all of a sudden I felt I also loved her very much, and I took her hand.

"It's me, Marta. Don't be foolish. Why can't we talk? I came here to be with you. Nothing else. And I really wanted to. I always thought we mattered more than anything else. Don't you remember?"

She remained silent, then said, "I don't know. Everything seems different now. I mean, from the start, since you arrived. It didn't happen just now; it's just too different. I don't think I have anything to tell you, or if I do, I don't know how to say it, but in any case, everything's the same. Don't you think so?"

"But we're still friends."

"Yes, of course. I know it perfectly well, and I believe it. Maybe what's wrong is that we can't be friends the way we used to."

"Why? I've thought about it, too, and I can't completely understand it. I know there's something between you and me, apart from everything else. Why?"

"I can't understand it very well either. But I want to find out what it is, today. We're not the same anymore, we've changed without knowing it. It's no use talking about it, in any case we'd have to talk about other things, not about our friendship. To me it's always there." She paused and added, "Let's go to the beach, the children are waiting for us."

I got off the bed, put on my shorts and blouse again, and started to fix my makeup in front of the mirror. Marta didn't move.

"Do you think I'm a whore?" I asked suddenly, turning my back so as not to face her.

"Of course not," she said. "And you? What do you think about me? After all, what I've done is much worse. What do you think?"

"I'd rather not say," I said, laughing.

She laughed too and then said, "We don't have to talk this way. It's absurd."

I turned to look at her, serious again, and asked what she planned to do.

"Nothing," she said, averting her eyes. "I don't want to talk about it. Not with you or anyone else. I don't like it. There's something offensive about it. We shouldn't have brought it up."

I knew it was useless to insist, and we went to the beach with the children, separated again even more deeply this time.

Rafael arrived before the sun had disappeared completely and called to us from the road, waving his hand out the car window.

"Heeey!"

His smile was pleasant and contagious, even at that distance, from which, more than seeing it, I imagined it. Instinctively, I looked at my legs and was glad I had come out barefoot. I thought Marta might be examining herself in the same way and I avoided looking at her. It was strange that what I felt was not jealousy but something else, impossible to define, that derived from the assumption that by rights, some part of him belonged to her, a part that could never be mine and that I probably didn't want either.

Marta stood up after me and mechanically took the hand of Eduardito, who was sitting next to her when Rafael arrived, but neither of us moved until he was a few steps away.

"It's so deserted, isn't it?" he said then, not addressing either one of us in particular; we both smiled at the same time.

Then Rafael bent down to kiss one of the boys, and as he straightened up, he added, "Eduardo will be here later. He had several things to take care of. He has a surprise for you," he added with an ambiguous expression, then turned to the other boy.

"Aren't you going to say hello to me?" he said, lifting him up in his arms.

The boy kissed him on the cheek; still holding him in his arms, Rafael turned toward me.

"Hi."

"Hi," I said.

Once again he addressed the two of us.

"I'm dead tired and bored, too. All this can be so boring." He set the child on the sand once again and went on. "It's been terribly hot. Would anyone like to swim? There's still light."

"Not me, that's for sure," Marta said.

Rafael hesitated for an instant and then turned to me.

"What about you?"

"If you want my company, yes," I said.

"Maybe it's not worth it. I'd have to change clothes and I don't feel like seeing Celia," he said slowly.

"They're going to the rosary," Marta broke in.

"Oh, good," Rafael said, pensive; then he changed his tone and asked, "Shall we go for a ride, then?"

"Do you always have to be doing something?" Marta asked, half smiling. "I don't see why we can't stay here peacefully. I can't leave the boys."

"I'm bored," he said, also half smiling.

"Take Elena," Marta said, with no aggression, and then, addressing me, added, "If you want to..."

"Shall we go?" Rafael asked.

"Yes," I said. "Let's go."

"Are you sure you don't want to come?" he asked Marta again. "We can take the boys."

"No, if Eduardo's coming I'd rather wait for him," she answered.

"Whatever you want," Rafael said. "We'll be right back, then. See you later."

He took my arm and we walked to his car.

"Where do you want to go?" he asked me before starting the car.

"Wherever you want. It doesn't matter."

"We can go get some ice cream. Or go to the marsh. You haven't been there yet, have you?"

"No."

"Let's go, then. It's terrific. At this time of day the salt marsh looks fantastic."

He started the engine and before pulling away he turned to really look at me for the first time.

"How are you?"

"Fine," I said, somewhat disturbed.

Eduardo was home when we got back. Marta had put the children to bed, and he was fixing himself a drink.

II

When Marta wrote inviting me to spend a few weeks with her, almost a year had passed since I had heard from her. As he does every year, her father phoned to wish me a Merry Christmas, and thanks to his call I remembered to send her a card, promising to write soon, but I never received a reply or kept my promise. In the daily routine of work, time loses its continuity and the days become one, without the small differences that occur during the hours lived outside of it ever managing to break the monotony. Marta's letter made me realize, with surprise, that it was already April and I had been seeing Pedro for five months.

Marta wanted me to spend the month of May with them, assuring me that it was a splendid time to be at the beach. Her letter was written with a strange timidity, which seemed the result of trying to hide something she did not even want to think about. So she turned the invitation into a spur-of-the-moment idea, unexpected but particularly significant. Although after such a long time it was impossible to take her invitation casually, I liked the idea of finally visiting her and finding out how she lived. I answered right away that I would try to arrange things at the office. She wrote back immediately, urging me to do it. In her second letter she confessed to being very lonely and said that I would do her a great favor by coming as soon as possible, but the best I could do was move up my September vacation and add a few days to it. I left in the middle of August. Pedro took me to the airport, and as we said good-bye, after kissing him with a sincere feeling of regret for having caused this brief separation, I promised to write every day.

The plane left almost an hour late. I had to wait alone at the airport, without knowing what to do or how to kill time, having told

Pedro to leave just minutes before they announced the delay. When we finally took off, I had the sensation of having started the trip long before. Nevertheless, during the flight I was not able to sleep as I had intended, or read either, because in the seat next to me a young man, about eighteen years old, talked constantly. He was returning from the United States to spend the last weeks of his vacation with his parents and insisted on telling me everything about Mérida when he learned it was my first visit. Of course, he knew Eduardo and the whole family; although he said he did not remember Marta, he assured me that he would recognize her immediately, as if not being able to place her represented a failure on his part. He was pleasant, but in all his conversation there was an air of security, excessive in relation to his youth, that made him seem somewhat pedantic. Listening to him, I tried to compare him with the boys I knew in high school, and though he differed from my memory of them, I realized, with a certain nostalgia, that I, too, had left that period behind long ago and would never be able to recover it, or return to its tone and significance. Now I could listen to him talk without his naïveté and false security, implicit in every statement, awakening in me the old need to make fun of men like him. This upset me a little, not with him, but with myself.

After giving me all the information he considered pertinent and repeating several times how very rich and well known Eduardo's family was, he asked me if I, too, was married. I told him a few things about my work and life in Mexico City, and for the first time he kept quiet for a moment, obviously disconcerted. Then, unable to hide his embarrassment, he confessed with a smile, "You're the first woman lawyer I've ever met, although in the United States lots of women work."

"In Mexico, too," I said.

We had left the sea behind—which until then I had glimpsed once in a while, green and peaceful, through the white clouds—and were again flying over land. The plane turned suddenly, tilting to one side, and in my surprise I instinctively grasped the young man's arm. He looked at me for a moment and explained, "We're about to land. We have to fasten our seat belts. There are always wind currents over the peninsula and the ride gets choppy."

I followed his suggestion, and a little later the plane jolted even more, the "fasten seat belt" sign lighting up over the cabin door. From then on, I noticed how he casually tried to rub his arm against mine, and when he felt them touch, he would press lightly to make it more evident. Fortunately, we arrived soon after.

As we got off the plane, still on the stairs, he pointed out Eduardo. "There they are, waiting for you."

I saw Marta next to him with a little boy in her arms and I happily waved hello. At the door the young man returned my bag, which he had offered to carry; he told me his name was Jorge Rendón and he hoped to see me again. We shook hands and I lost sight of him among the people greeting the travelers.

It was terribly hot. Perspiring, I embraced Marta and let Eduardo pick up my bag without exchanging more than three words with him. Still in Marta's arms, the boy stared at me with a startled look, not knowing exactly how to react. Till then I had only seen him in pictures and it suddenly surprised me that he could actually be Marta's son, as if he only now began to really exist for me.

"Is he the oldest?" I asked.

"No, silly, the youngest one," Marta answered.

I did not remember his name and had to ask her.

"Roberto, like my father," she said. "What's wrong with you? Are you losing your mind?"

"I hope not," I said, and both of us smiled somewhat stupidly, aware that we really did not know what to say.

Nevertheless, I was happy to see her again. She was the same Marta, slightly thinner, short hair instead of the long braid and with a child in her arms, but still the same. I hugged her again and she smiled, as if finally recognizing me.

"How are you?" she said.

"Fine. And you?"

"Just fine, really," she said. "We'll talk later."

"Of course," I said. "All the time. I don't want to do anything else. Is it always this hot?"

"Here, yes, a little less, maybe. But at the beach you won't feel it. Don't worry."

For a moment we did not say anything, then I observed, "Your son doesn't look like you."

"No. The other one doesn't either. They both take after Eduardo," she said.

"Where's the other one?"

"At my in-laws. We'll stop by to pick him up." She caressed the child, who kept staring at me in amazement, and added, "I'm very glad you came."

Eduardo was already next to us, with my suitcase.

"Shall we go?" he asked, looking at us happily.

As we left, the young man waved to me from afar, and the couple with him turned to look at me. Eduardo and Marta nodded a greeting to them. She asked where I had met him, and I explained that we had sat next to each other on the plane.

"His parents are close friends of Eduardo's," Marta said, when we were in the car.

She had taken the back seat, with the child, and I sat in front with Eduardo, who was driving. On hearing Marta, he shrugged his shoulders and turned toward me.

"Everybody's a friend of everybody here, so it's nothing special. What do you think of this?" he asked then, surveying the road with his gaze.

We had left the airport and were moving down a tree-lined highway. Through the open window hot air struck my face; the asphalt radiated heat.

"Different," I said, looking at the thin tree branches and the almost-white rock wall behind them.

"Yes, very different. You'll see," he confirmed.

Then Marta started asking about my mother and brothers, and we stayed on the subject of Mexico City, although everything relating to my life there seemed to have become incredibly distant.

Now the car moved down an avenue divided by a row of tall, slender palms. Along the sides the vegetation was amazing; not just because of the colors, but also for the shapes of the trees, which sometimes spread out broadly, their vast tops forming a kind of platter, and at other times rose, delicate but solid at once, while around them grew all kinds of unusually large shrubs and climbing plants. Between the trees you could barely glimpse thatched houses and curving, whitewashed walls. But as we entered the city, I began to see much larger houses, painted white or some other pale color, with terraces, verandas, and well-groomed gardens trying to imitate the French style. When we turned onto a stone-paved street, the gardens disappeared, and the single-storied houses, with their large colonial windows, displayed their austere, shady interiors. Finally, we came to another avenue, even wider than the previous one, with trees bordering the sides and a small median running down the center.

While I talked with Marta, Eduardo had continually followed my gaze, and as we entered the avenue, he commented, "This is Montejo Avenue."

"He's so proud," Marta laughed. "Tell him you like it."

I laughed, too, and asked Eduardo what kind of trees lined the avenue.

"Indian laurels and tamarinds," he explained.

Beyond them, the gardens had reappeared, fenced in behind wrought-iron railings, even higher than the ones before, encircling the homes, which were also enormous. Eduardo finally stopped in front of one of them and got out to open the door for me.

"My parents live here," he said. "We have to go in for a moment."

Through the wrought-iron fence, I could see that the garden, which at one time must have been carefully planned, was now obviously neglected. The plants defeated the intended design and spread freely, invading the paths and mixing with each other. The outer walls showed the same neglect—rain having stained dark lines into the paint—specially around the windows and the decorations of the facade. Nevertheless, this neglect, far from destroying the house's charm, heightened it, giving the long verandas, the columns, the innumerable door and window frames a most intimate mark of times well lived. This feeling won out over the impression of coldness the construction's overly imposing aspect must have originally produced.

We crossed the garden without anyone coming out to greet us, but as we moved down one of the corridors, Marta's oldest son came running out from somewhere—chased by a nanny who to no avail tried to catch him by the hand—his arms outstretched to me. Instinctively, I picked him up, as soon as he was in my arms, the boy stopped smiling and anxiously looked around for Marta, not letting me kiss him, pushing against my shoulders to free himself. Eduardo laughed.

"He mistook you for Marta," he said and then turned to the boy, who was still in my arms. "She's a friend of your mother's. Don't you like her?"

The boy reached out for Eduardo and I had to let him go, but as soon as he saw Marta a few steps behind, he did the same thing, and Eduardo, in turn, passed him on to her, then picked up the other child. Meanwhile, Eduardo's mother also appeared. She had not gone to Marta and Eduardo's wedding, so I did not know her. In spite of the heat, she was wearing a dark dress. From what Marta had told me about her, she could not have been more than fifty years old, but her hair was completely gray. In contrast to the somewhat hard lines of her face, her eyes were gentle and clear, like Eduardo's. When she squeezed my hand, independent of what she was saying, she questioned me with her eyes, as if their truth did not correspond to her words and at the same time she expected me to answer in the same way to that hidden dialogue.

"I'm very glad you have come. Although these months are so lively, I can imagine how lonely Marta must feel, as secluded as my son has her at the house on the beach. I hope you like it and decide to stay a long time. I've always been against the insane idea of living at the beach, but they insisted so much it was impossible not to give in. Now, with you there, at least she'll have company."

Marta broke in to explain that I would only be able to stay a few weeks. Once again addressing me, Eduardo's mother said, "Is that all? What a shame! Couldn't you stay longer?"

"I'd love to," I answered. "But I have to work."

"Oh, I understand," she said. "You must excuse me. I can't get used to the idea that nowadays young women like yourselves also have to work. Everything is so different . . ."

I smiled mechanically, angry with myself, because although long before I had imagined what she was like, her presence was somewhat imposing and I did not know how to answer.

"Take her to say hello to your father, Eduardo," she continued. "I'm sure he will be very glad to see her. He's in the study. I'll stay here with the boys." She squeezed my hand once again and added, "I'm glad you're here. I trust you will come and have dinner with us some night."

Marta assured her we would and she continued talking to me: "They say that the heat is unbearable here during these months, but I don't think it's worse than at the beach. All one has to do is not think about it . . ."

"Shall we go to see father?" Eduardo said, slightly impatient.

"Yes, go, go. I won't take any more of your time," she added immediately.

We crossed through a room with very high ceilings, furnished with sofas and wicker chairs, to reach an enclosed interior patio that also had several huge trees.

"Father's study is on the other side," Eduardo explained.

When we got there, he paused for a moment in front of the closed door before knocking.

"You know he's sick, right? But don't bring it up. He prefers not to talk about it."

"Yes. Fine," I said.

Eduardo finally knocked and Don Manuel told us to enter.

Later on I noticed that the room had three windows, but heavy drapes kept it in shadows. The only light came from a small lamp on the desk behind which Eduardo's father sat. I had met him when he went to Mexico City to meet Marta's father and saw him again at the wedding, but now his appearance had changed entirely. He greeted us without moving from his chair, asking us, in a low and strained voice, to come closer.

Marta crossed the room and gave him a kiss, to which he responded by lightly caressing her face. I stayed next to Eduardo, in front of the desk.

"Pardon me for not standing up," he said, with difficulty. "My children must have explained to you," he said, making an impatient gesture and not finishing the sentence. "I can hardly move, or talk . . . ," he went on.

I did not know what to answer and for a moment we all remained silent. The sound of the fan at one side of the desk became too noticeable.

"Did you have a good trip?" Don Manuel asked me at last.

"Yes, magnificent," I said. "And the city is beautiful. Well, at least the ride from the airport here."

"It's pretty, yes," he said. "Now I almost never go out, but I would've liked to show you some things. You'll have to do it, Eduardo."

"Yes, father," Eduardo said.

His father turned toward Marta.

"Don't let her get bored, show her around . . . Has she seen the house?"

"We'll do it later," Marta said.

"And mother wants us to come for dinner some night," Eduardo went on.

"Fine, fine," Don Manuel said. "Now go outside. This darkness is not good. It's already too hot, isn't it?" he ended, turning toward me.

"Yes, a little," I said, forcing a smile.

"Go on, then. I'm very glad to see you again."

Before leaving, Eduardo asked him if he didn't want the drapes opened, but he answered that it wasn't necessary and once again insisted we go out to the light. I remembered his assurance and cheerfulness when I met him in Mexico City and the ease with which he had won over Marta's father, and it seemed absurd that she had told me so little about his present condition, but I also understood that during the last few years we had hardly written to each other and I did not even remember exactly when he had suffered his attack.

On the veranda once again, I felt compelled to tell Eduardo that his father's appearance had affected me a lot, confessing that I didn't know he was so sick, but he seemed to be used to the situation and told me with complete naturalness that Don Manuel had actually gotten much better.

"What's absurd is for him to be locked up in that room all day," Marta said. "It'd be much better for him at the beach. If we could convince him . . ."

"Yes, if we could. But you know him. It's useless to keep bringing it up," Eduardo answered almost curtly.

His mother was waiting for us in the dining room with the boys. As soon as we reached her, she asked me how I found her husband, and I had to admit that I was unaware the attack had been so severe and it had surprised me somewhat; fortunately Eduardo interrupted the conversation to tell her we had to leave. In the meantime, Marta, with the youngest boy already in her arms, shouted toward the garden, calling the other one. He came immediately, running toward us, and as soon as he was near Marta, he began telling her that he had seen a gigantic lizard in the rosebushes, but his nanny had not allowed him to catch it. Before he finished telling his story, Eduardo took him by the hand and started to walk to the car. His mother insisted on walking us to the gate and, after saying good-bye, still repeated that we shouldn't forget to let her know what day we wanted to have dinner with them.

Before leaving the city, I remembered my promise to Pedro to send him a telegram as soon as I arrived, but I did not feel I could ask Eduardo to make another stop at the telegraph office and decided I would write him the next day. Less than two hours travel, and Mexico City seemed years away from me.

Now, lined with trees whose broad tops were covered with red flowers, the highway opened out in a straight line ahead of us and the vastness of the horizon intensified the strangeness of that limitless scenery, in which only once in a while the dark stain of a patch of trees, next to which also rose the towers of the windmills that Marta had identified for me as weather vanes, broke the prickly monotony of the henequen—its tall, slender beauty, within a radical symmetry, surprised me.

"It's a very harsh landscape, isn't it?" Eduardo said over the noise of the wind entering through the open window.

And he was right. There was something different and beautiful, a harsh and inhospitable beauty, in the regularity with which the henequen fields followed one after another, varying only in the size of the plants, sometimes barely visible among the rocks and at other times grown to full size with the tall, erect stalk exploding into a red flower, signaling the plant's imminent end. The flower's disturbing significance—its birth announcing that the plant had reached its maximum growth and would soon die—was revealed to me much later by Rafael.

Marta, leaning forward to rest her arms and head against the front seat, tried to explain everything to me, but the noise of the wind that blew her hair did not let me follow her words clearly; yet in this way, the smell of the sea became evident even before the beginning of the marsh signaled that we were near it.

"It already smells like the sea," I said.

Eduardo clarified.

"A rotting sea. Look, it's the marsh. At this point we're below sea level."

At that moment, the thick entanglement of shrubs that had replaced the fields of henequen for the last few yards gave way to the mangrove trees and the flowering rush of the marsh. It branched out into innumerable canals interrupted by more patches of flowering rush, producing together a sensation of mystery. Eduardo said that the canals could be traveled in a small boat, and I commented that it must be very pleasant, but Marta immediately added, "There are more mosquitoes in that place than anywhere else in the world. I don't recommend that trip. Only Eduardo can stand it."

We moved along an embankment separating the highway from the marsh and soon the outlying structures of the port appeared, unpainted houses, exposing their walls of stone and cement, instead of the brick I was used to. In front of the opened doors, the owners gathered in small groups, swaying in their swings. After another four or five blocks, in which the people walking freely down the middle of the street made the driving difficult, we arrived at the town square. On the highway we had come across several cars, but only now I noticed that the traffic was much heavier than in Mérida. The treeless square looked too big for the place, but, like the streets, it was crowded with people resting on the benches or walking from one side to the other, carrying on lively conversations. A few blocks ahead, we turned down another street full of small stands obstructing the flow of traffic; from stores and bars within the shady arcades covering the sidewalk, jukeboxes blared. The oldest boy, who had fallen asleep, raised his head for a moment to ask for an ice-cream cone, but no one paid any attention to him and he went back to sleep.

"Do you like it?" Eduardo asked me.

I answered sincerely that I did and asked him why there were so many people.

"It's the peak of the season. Everyone comes to the beach, even those who don't have a place to stay," Marta explained and then asked Eduardo if he wasn't going to drive out to the levee so I could see the ocean.

He directed his answer to me: "We're only two miles away. Do you mind waiting? The traffic is terrible."

I said it didn't matter, although the sensation of being so close to the ocean without seeing it yet made me impatient. He continued down the same street—lined by houses that like the ones on the other edge of the town, replaced the stores and bars—until suddenly it turned back into a highway again.

Instead of henequen to the sides, coconut trees appeared, and among them a few wooden houses. We were passing other cars constantly and Eduardo waved at almost everybody.

"The ocean is there, behind the coconut trees. Watch and you'll see it," Marta told me, and Eduardo commented, "She'll have more than enough of the sea. Don't rush her into it so soon."

A car passed us, its horn blaring, and a woman stuck her body halfway out the window to greet us.

"It's Celia," Marta said. "She's dying of curiosity. I bet she'll be at the house in a minute."

Eduardo smiled without answering. We kept moving between a double row of houses, these much more elegant. The older boy woke up again and asked if we hadn't arrived yet, and Eduardo, easing on the brakes and turning, answered for my sake and his.

"Yes, we're here."

We had entered an interior patio of firmly packed sand, where five or six coconut trees and one with red flowers swayed softly, almost touching the railing of the balcony that circled the second floor of the house. The back faced the patio. It was painted white and, from the car, I could see the side gate that swung out onto the beach. Eduardo got out of the car and opened the door for me, while Marta, with the youngest boy in her arms, also got out.

"Come on, come and see the ocean," Marta said, still carrying the boy in her arms.

Eduardo stayed behind to take my suitcase out of the trunk, while we walked toward the terrace. A maid, dressed in the typical fashion of the region, came out to greet us and took the boy from Marta's arms. As soon as we climbed the four steps leading to the terrace, I saw the ocean. From both sides of the house, the beach reached out infinitely in a straight line, incredibly white and clean, until it blended with the sky and sea at the horizon. The sea's semicircle, its light green edge darkening ultimately into blue, stretched endlessly, changing, alive and mysterious in front of us. Although the sun was already very low, there were a few swimmers, their heads bobbing above the waves, as if bodiless. A little farther away and with a much more pronounced swaying, there were also a few boats and two or three tall sailing craft, but with the exception of several multicolored umbrellas fluttering in the wind, the beach was deserted. The oldest boy caught up with us and took Marta's hand, but she sent him to help his father and he obeyed happily. Then Marta turned to me, smiling.

"It's beautiful, isn't it?"

"It's great," I said. "What marvelous luck to be able to live here."

She did not respond.

I sat on the handrail to take off my shoes; barefoot, I crossed the strip of sand and waded into the sea. The water was warm. Marta stopped a few steps behind me. One of the swimmers waved, and she responded with the same gesture.

"Who is it?" I asked.

"A friend of Eduardo's," she said. "You'll meet them all, don't worry. It's late now, but you'll see what this is like in the morning. You can't move an inch."

It seemed to me that her tone revealed a certain weariness, so I asked her if she wasn't happy.

"Yes," she said. "These months are very lively and now, above all, you're here . . . Look at the sun."

It looked like an enormous ball in the middle of the white sky, which nevertheless was beginning to stain red, along with the sea, but now I wanted to talk to her.

"Your letter surprised me," I said.

She smiled, without joy.

"Forget it. I was depressed when I wrote it."

"And you're not anymore?"

"I don't know. It's not exactly a matter of depression. It's something different, kind of hard to explain. This isn't always as you're going to see it now. Most of the year, Eduardo and I are quite alone. Other people are here only during these two months; they're so absurd they only come during the summer, as if it weren't always summer here. Eduardo has to go to work and I'm alone all day long. Before, we used to say we always wanted to be alone, remember? But I assure you it can be very boring."

"But you and Eduardo are doing okay?"

"Yes," she said, and then added, "Or at least he is. He's so good. I can't complain, I shouldn't complain."

"To me you can. That's why I came," I said and right away regretted it. It sounded false and, above all, premature.

Nevertheless, it didn't seem to bother Marta and she might have kept talking, but at that moment her oldest son came up to us.

"Dad's calling you," he said.

From the terrace Eduardo was waving to us. The boy let me hold his hand as we walked toward the house.

"I've been yelling at you for half an hour. Are you deaf?" Eduardo said when we were close enough to hear him.

"You can't hear anything with that breeze," Marta answered.

He disappeared into the house and came out to the terrace to meet us.

"Do you want a drink? Beer, rum?" he asked me.

"Starting already?" Marta said.

"We have to celebrate Elena's arrival, don't we?" he said, smiling, and asked me again, "Rum and coke?"

"At least let her see the house first," Marta insisted.

"She'll have time for that later," he answered, no longer smiling. "I'll get you a drink, then," he ended, talking to me, and before going back inside the house he turned to Marta. "And one for you, too."

We brought out three wicker chairs from the living room and sat on the terrace facing the sea. The younger boy climbed onto my lap and asked me if I knew how to swim and then what my name was. He spoke with a regional accent that made him even cuter. I told Marta that, in spite of my first impression, he did look like her.

"Don't tell my mother-in-law, she'll kill you," she answered.

Eduardo came back with the drinks on a tray and sat next to us. Marta took only a few sips from hers, then said she had to go and prepare the children's dinner. I offered to help her, but she refused, leaving me alone with Eduardo, who was toying with the ice in his glass, taking a few quick and nervous sips. The sunset prolonged itself infinitely, staining both sea and sky red and yellow, accentuating its immensity and indifference to its own beauty. Most of the swimmers were gone and someone had removed the umbrellas from the sand, but the temperature was perfect. For a moment everything seemed unreal and I couldn't be the one who was here, next to Marta's husband, in a place that had not only proved different from what I had expected, but absolutely unforeseen. I also thought that Marta, more than being different, had turned out to be a stranger, and I realized that I had had to make an effort to talk to her and that I really didn't want her to tell me anything, because under these circumstances it would have been impossible for me to understand her. Here, she belonged to this world and I had to place her in it, in the same way that I needed to see Eduardo with other eyes to be able to recognize him in this person in shirtsleeves, somewhat thinner than the one I had met in Mexico City and, above all, completely stripped of the unknowing look that back there had made him seem insecure and out of place.

In the meantime, Eduardo had finished his drink without saying a word. I felt I had to say something to him and I turned to watch the sea, trying to find a subject.

"Is the water always this warm?" I asked finally.

Eduardo had to look at me for an instant before answering, as if my words had to be thought over, as well as heard, to be understood.

"Yes," he said then. "Always. Do you want to go for a swim?"

"No . . . I don't know . . . The sun has set already. I think I'd be a little scared," I said, a little surprised, too.

"Scared, why? The sea is very shallow here. Nothing can happen. If you want, I'll go with you," he went on.

"I think I'd rather wait till tomorrow," I said.

All he did was smile and once again we became silent. Then, making an effort, he asked me about Marta's father. I told him that I saw very little of him now, but I imagined that he was doing fine or at least was the same as always; he muttered almost to himself, "Mexico City . . ."

Suddenly, I remembered him with Marta on their wedding day. I had thought Eduardo was very handsome, but above everything else it had seemed strange that from then on he would be Marta's husband. Nevertheless, when they returned from their honeymoon and I went to see them at her father's house, where they had stopped for a few days before coming to Mérida for good, undoubtedly Marta was already closer to him than she had been even to me or anyone else in her entire life.

The
House
on
the
Beach

23

"Do you want another drink?" Eduardo asked me then.

"No, thanks, I still have some," I answered and then added, without thinking, "Do you drink a lot?"

"According to Marta, yes. But it's a lie. The thing is, everyone around here drinks. There are very few things to do . . ."

"In Mexico City people drink a lot, too," I said.

"Yes, but it's different here. You'll see. People get bored . . ."

"You too?"

"Maybe . . . A little," Eduardo said. "It's not only that, anyway. Things have changed a lot. Marta and I have to live here and sometimes it exasperates her, and me, too. But this house doesn't cost us anything and it's better than living with my parents. Marta must have told you all about that already, hasn't she? Money's a problem . . ."

"Yes, I can imagine," I said, somewhat disturbed.

"I like this house, but I understand that sometimes it's inconvenient to live so far from everything," he went on. "We don't even have a phone; it's quite isolated. Except for these months, of course . . . And we also have friends who come by all the time. But I don't know . . . Marta was really anxious for you to come," he ended suddenly.

I smiled, without knowing what to say.

"I'm going to get another drink," Eduardo said, as he stood up. "Are you sure you don't want one?"

"No," I said. "I'll wait here."

But when he went in, I thought it was absurd that I had not gone inside the house yet, and I followed him. The living room was large and very comfortable. It was furnished with wicker chairs for the beach and in one corner there was a small bar. Through the window the sea was clearly visible. The dining area occupied the far end of the room; Marta was about to finish feeding the oldest boy. I went over to her and she told me that we could go up to see my room. It was another beautiful room facing the beach; the palms of one of the coconut trees brushed against the side window. Eduardo had left my suitcase on the bed and Marta helped me unpack. Her son, who had come up with us, picked things up constantly and persisted in putting them away himself, until Marta lost her patience and called the maid to put him to bed. I took off my dress and put on pants and a blouse, and before Marta, Eduardo, and I had finished dinner, Celia and Lorenzo showed up.

At first, Celia insisted that we had met in Mexico City and mentioned all the possible names and activities to let me know she knew a lot of people there, but Marta took it upon herself to show her we didn't associate with the same people and so it was impossible for her to have seen me. Then Celia started talking about the children and about their mutual friends, making it almost impossible for me to participate in the conversation. As for Lorenzo, he simply said hello when we were introduced and then talked to Eduardo as if I weren't there. He must have been Eduardo's age, but he was overweight, which made him appear much older. Both of them drank a great deal, and Celia made several jokes about it, in a tone indicating the teasing followed formulas established long ago; neither of the men paid any attention to her. Finally, Lorenzo suddenly remembered that there was a party at some friend's house and suggested we go. Then Celia mentioned that Rafael would probably be there. It was the first time I heard his name and I don't know why I remembered it later, but at the time it didn't mean anything to me and the idea of meeting more people frightened me a little. I said I was tired and suggested to Marta that she and Eduardo go, but she absolutely refused.

When we were alone again, I realized it was only nine-thirty and it was a little absurd to think about going to bed so early. During dinner Marta and I had tried to talk a little about Mexico City and the past, but Eduardo's presence made me feel that I had to include him in the conversation and I kept changing the subject so he could have something to say. Now all three of us were quiet and I felt that he would have preferred to go to the party. From the highway came the steady, low rumble of horns and voices, giving the impression of activity and movement that contrasted with the silence of the dark stain the beach had become. Eduardo poured himself another drink and I asked for one. He gave it to me without speaking, avoiding Marta's reproachful look. It was hot again and when I finished my drink I asked them if they would like to go out to the beach for a moment. They agreed, and we sat facing the sea, in silence, from time to time exchanging a few phrases about the beauty of the night. There was a moon and the sky was clear, but even in the semidarkness, the night turned the sea into a somewhat frightening dark force, whose rhythmic murmur produced a sensation of independent life entirely alien to us.

"It seems unbelievable that you're here with us, but then again, it feels as if it's always been like this, and it's absolutely natural," Marta suddenly commented, but in spite of her words, I felt lonely and could not avoid wondering if I had not made a mistake by saying I could stay for such a long time.

Finally, Eduardo said he was tired and was going to bed. I felt I had to make it clear that I was very sorry I'd made him miss the party, but he assured me it didn't matter.

"We've gone to the same party a thousand times. Don't worry, they're all the same. If you and Marta want to keep on talking for a while I don't mind. I understand you must have a lot to talk about."

"No," Marta said, taking his arm. "I'm tired, too. We'd better go. We have more than enough time to talk."

I followed them to the house. Seen from the beach, the endless line of illuminated houses, with the ghostlike shadows of the palms rising between or behind them, seemed enveloped in the sea's eternal murmur, but, by listening closely, it was also possible to hear the movement of the traffic farther away and even the distant music of a record player.

The breeze had died down and my room was hot again, but I was embarrassed to go to bed naked, as I would have preferred, so I put on my nightgown, unable to stop thinking how ridiculous it was. Before I switched off the light, Marta came in and sat on the edge of the bed.

"It's incredible, but Eduardo has already fallen asleep. It's hot, isn't it?"

"Yes, a little," I said.

"Here everybody sleeps in hammocks. If you want to try it, I'll set one up for you . . ."

"You too?" I asked.

"No," she said. "I haven't been able to get used to it. But they say it's much cooler."

"I prefer the bed, anyway," I said.

She remained silent for a moment, without looking at me, then she said, "It was a bit depressing, wasn't it?"

"What?" I asked, sincerely surprised.

"Everything," she answered. "Eduardo's parents and the ever-so-enchanting evening with Celia and Lorenzo. Don't think they're all like that. There are much better people. What happens is that it's a close-knit group, too close, and they're used to talking about nothing but their own things."

"I felt very comfortable, really. I think the place is beautiful," I said.

"You're telling me?" she answered, smiling without joy. "I admit I've lost touch, but I'm not that bad."

"Anyway, everything is beautiful," I insisted.

"Everything. Except the people," she said. "I have to confess I envy you a little."

"Why?"

"I don't know. You look different. And that's very important."

"You know exactly what I'm like."

"Of course," she went on, with a gesture that made me recognize her again and feel the same affection as always. "But seeing you makes me think I'm no longer that way and I don't like it. I don't know what I want, or what I expect, or why I do things or stop doing them. Especially stop," she added.

"I don't understand. Is something wrong? You have Eduardo and the children . . ."

"Yes. I have all that. It should be enough, right?"

"I don't know," I said. "It's up to you to decide. You have to tell me if there's something wrong."

"Yes, maybe later," she answered. She kissed me on the cheek and stood up. "I'm very glad you came. We must have fun and talk about you, not just about me. I also want to know how you are doing. Good night."

"Good night," I said, and we both laughed.

I asked her to switch the light off on her way out, but I didn't go to sleep for a long time, desiring Pedro and thinking about Mexico City, feeling strange in the room and trying to listen to the murmur of the sea to forget everything.

III

 Marta and I met in high school, a few months after classes had started, and for more than six years we were inseparable. The first time I saw her was at the coffeehouse where students used to meet after classes. I was sitting at one of the tables with a boy I liked when all of a sudden she came over to say hello to him, smiled at me sarcastically, and left before he could introduce us. After that, our eyes met every time I turned toward her table. I thought she was pretty, but not more than I was, and although I had to admit she was well dressed and looked different from the other girls, I decided I couldn't stand her and I tried to pretend I was laughing at her with my friend, although I didn't even dare ask him who she was and why he got so upset when she said hello. But she didn't even notice and, the next day, during a break between classes, she came up and asked if I was going steady with him. Her self-assurance made me feel defenseless and, without thinking how easy it would be for her to find out that I was lying, I said yes. She answered immediately that he also dated one of her girlfriends and she wanted to warn me so that I would not be disillusioned. With false dignity, I told her that I didn't like gossip and went into my classroom, but on the way out she told me she would like to walk home with me. I asked her why and she answered, slightly shrugging her shoulders, "You're alright and I think we could be good friends. Look around and you'll see we don't look as stupid as the rest."

I had to laugh and accepted her offer. On the way home, while we were plotting against my unlucky friend, I discovered that I liked her, too. In those days we all had great intellectual aspirations and she had read many more books than I had; she also had a lot of projects in mind and could talk about them with an assurance that fascinated me.

Back then time meant nothing to us and everything passed by with surprising speed. Without noticing, very soon it seemed I had known her all my life. Every morning we met at school and spent the rest of the day together walking through the city, shuffling dirty books in used bookstores, at the movies, studying at her house or mine, feeling at every moment that we had an endless series of similar days ahead of us and that nothing could keep us from carrying out our plans, which were many.

Marta lived with her father in the elegant Lomas district in a one-story house set off by itself, surrounded by a small garden, which she took care of herself, making out of it all a ceremony somehow related to Omar Khayyám, which to me seemed charming and ridiculous at the same time, like almost everything she did. Although I took her over to my house right away, several months went by before she decided to invite me to hers, but the first time I went, I loved the contrast between her house and mine, and her independence made me feel a kind of envy. In my apartment, with my mother and my three brothers, we could barely take a step without running into each other, while she had the whole place to herself. The two maids treated her like the lady of the house, and she gave orders, demanded and scolded with complete naturalness. Nevertheless, I soon learned that her independence was actually quite relative, because even though most of the time her father only came home to sleep, leaving her alone all day, his authority was constantly present in the house. Marta could greet me as the absolute owner, offer me drinks, and order coffee for us, but before leaving, we had to clean the ashtrays carefully and erase every trace of those endless afternoons when we pretended to be adults, listening to records, drinking, and talking to the point of exhaustion about the boys in school and the pedantry or charm of our classmates. This is probably why, in spite of the relative independence we had at her house, she seemed to prefer the confusion and disorder of mine, and very soon my mother and brothers saw her almost as another member of the family, who went there even when I wasn't in and killed time talking to my mother or just reading in my room.

Nevertheless, our relationship wasn't easy at all. When we were alone, everything seemed simple and natural: we talked about our projects, planned fabulous trips, and, above all, tried to convince each other that our lives would be different from those of the adults we knew. We were sure we would always have more than enough time to study thousands of things, to learn languages and how to dance, and that nothing could make us give up the kind of life we wanted for an insipid and boring security. We would talk about all this for hours on end at Marta's house—lying on the carpet, not even touching the books we had checked out of the library, listening to some record and forgetting to turn on the light when it started to get dark, or walking along the street, while the afternoon light appeared to have stopped forever among the trees. But when we went out with some girlfriend, or especially with boys, in a way that was almost unconscious, but in spite of herself, always unavoidable, Marta set up a kind of competition between us and she kept getting in the way, or she tried to prevent any activity I initiated that didn't completely revolve around her. With the boys, this was particularly exasperating, because she tried to get me away from all the ones I liked, coming between us, attacking or ridiculing them until she managed to make me lose interest. Nevertheless, to me, this seemed just part of her and I didn't give it much thought, because, truthfully, there was no one with whom I felt more comfortable, and our complicity, knowing we supported each other, made us feel much more secure in front of the boys.

Back then we used to go out with anyone who invited us, and we definitely fell in love every week, but even though some afternoons we took advantage of the solitude of Marta's house to dance, and we had parties every Saturday, I still hadn't let anybody kiss me, and Marta could only remember the kisses that years before one of her cousins gave her whenever she visited his home and the two of them would hide anywhere they could find. We also talked constantly of that possibility and tried to choose the best candidate, but our first year in high school ended without either one of us having chosen anybody. Many times, dancing at Marta's house, I felt the moment had come, when in the semidarkness my partner embraced me completely and the contact of his body, with his leg between mine, persuaded me to let him kiss my hair and neck, but at the last moment something told me that it was better to wait, and looking around for Marta I noticed she hadn't gotten anywhere either, and, in a way, that reinforced my decision.

The following year we signed up for the same subjects and started taking French in the afternoon. According to our plans, because we were in the same courses, we should have been much closer that year, but in the French class I met a young man, started dating him, and stopped seeing Marta almost completely outside of class. At first we both liked him; but soon we found out that I was the one he liked.

The discovery made me keep him at a distance for a while. I felt a special pleasure in confirming how he looked at me and tried to find the chance to be alone with me; and, for that same reason, I insisted on prolonging the situation. I avoided him carefully, and when we allowed him to accompany us somewhere, I always made sure that he had to drop both Marta and me off at the same time. Then, alone with Marta, I would laugh about his restlessness and I sincerely thought I wasn't interested in him anymore and only wanted to keep his admiration for the fun of it. But one afternoon we went to Marta's house and she put on some records and set it up so he would dance only with her, forcing me to watch them from one of the armchairs, unable to separate them, pretending an indifference I no longer felt, flipping through pages of her father's books without really looking at them. That night, alone at home, furious at Marta, I decided to make him tell me he loved me.

When Marta found out we were going together, she laughed for a long time and told me I owed it to her, but by then I thought I really liked him and decided to take him seriously, although at the start it made me very nervous to be alone with him, and deep inside, more than love for him, I felt a kind of attraction toward my own fear. A few days later, on one of the streets near my house, he kissed me for the first time. It was a quick kiss, which we both broke off before we really started feeling our lips, more concerned about the action than the pleasure of kissing, but the following night, as if we both obeyed an unstated agreement, we stopped at the same place and I let him embrace me and waited consciously for his mouth, feeling his body against mine and his hands on my back, and I opened my lips, almost without noticing, when his mouth touched mine.

Marta constantly asked me if he had already kissed me, but I didn't tell her anything about it. I wanted to keep it all to myself, and for almost a whole year I managed to do it. His name was Enrique and he was an engineering major. He picked me up every afternoon and I learned to kiss him in his car without any fear; I let him caress my breasts and thighs, probably getting more pleasure from watching him than from feeling it myself, and night after night I thought that if the next day he asked me to go to bed I would accept right away, although the possibility of getting pregnant terrified me and my only obsession was to find someone whom I could ask about the easiest way to avoid having children. But instead of asking me to go to bed, one day he only dared to suggest that we go to a hotel and I let him undress me, but without doing anything. I felt disappointed and disgusted; I knew that deep inside he was as scared as I was.

In the meantime, Marta started dating one of the football players at school who made her completely forget not only her French lessons, but all her old plans. Now she dreamed of becoming part of the university pep squad, she used a lot more makeup than before and styled her hair differently, and the few times I saw them together, her old intellectual pretensions seemed to embarrass her in front of him. I felt a great need to know if she had already gone to bed, but I didn't dare ask her, because now she appeared much more sure of herself and I didn't want to play the naive role, until one night, when classes had finished and the year was again coming to an end—and I was unable to believe it had gone by so quickly—Marta showed up at my house and said she wanted to talk to me.

We locked ourselves in my room and she began to tell me in halting words that her boyfriend had broken up with her, and finally she burst into tears. Inexplicably, I too felt very sad, as if I had to feel defeated also because it was a much more interesting position to adopt. I went to the dining room for a bottle of tequila I remembered having seen in one of the cabinets, and when we finished it, I went back for a bottle of vermouth. Marta hadn't yet slept with anyone either, but both of us felt we had lived a lot that year, and after we told each other in minute detail exactly what we felt when we were touched, how far we had gone, and everything we made our boyfriends do, we were sure we now knew all that could be expected from love. Before we were completely drunk, she called her father to tell him she was going to spend the night with me. I had to talk to him to convince him that Marta was in fact at my house, and finally my mother took the phone to reassure him, and right after the call, she recommended that we stop acting silly and go to sleep. But we were too happy with our sadness to think about obeying her. We went back to my room to finish the bottle of vermouth and talked until both of us had to go to the bathroom; we held each other's heads while we vomited, unable to stop laughing for an instant, in spite of feeling sick. My brother had to help us back to my room. When we were alone, Marta threw herself laughing on the bed and said that she was going to sleep with her clothes on. I leaned over to undress her. After struggling with her dress and managing to take off her slip, I felt her pull me and let myself fall on top of her. She gave me a kiss on the cheek and said, "I love you very much . . ."

Unaware of what I was doing, I kissed her lightly on the mouth and lay next to her, without touching her, a little frightened. A moment later, with her head resting on her hand and her elbow on the bed, she turned to look at me.

"It's a shame we're not lesbians, don't you think? Everything would be much easier."

"Yes," I said, laughing.

Then I was able to undress myself, too, and we fell asleep without even getting under the covers.

We never talked about it again; yet, in a certain way, that brief scene made us understand that what had happened before had only been a game and that maybe now we had to start to get serious about things and try to accept them. But this knowledge was still too obscure for us to be able to express it and we were not even clearly aware of it.

Nevertheless, the first years at the university went by much more slowly and almost without a change. I broke up with my first boyfriend to start a new relationship similar in almost every way to the previous one, but now Marta and I seemed to have reached a silent agreement. We told each other everything we did in the grossest way possible, and always with the same mixture of laughter and excitement; it turned into a mechanical act, but we didn't let those relationships interfere with our friendship, and above all, we accepted that we didn't have the same enthusiasm as before.

In general, we preferred not to talk about our plans, which now seemed too naive and, besides, unattainable. The French lessons were part of the routine, and after five sessions we gave up the idea of taking dancing classes. Ahead of us lay very similar days at the university, the mild excitement and the fear during exams, and the feeling that it had been exaggerated when they were over. If as students we weren't particularly brilliant, the effort it would have taken didn't seem worth it, and the university atmosphere was nothing but a repetition, with slight variations, of high school. It was still fun to hear the shouts and whistles when we walked through the halls and to notice the special attention some professors paid us, as it was to go out once in a while with classmates and let ourselves be desired while we danced, and kissed when they succeeded in getting us to give in to the dangers of the game, only to tell each other about it later. But the feeling that we were repeating something that had lost all its meaning a long time before was inevitable and it tired us.

When I stayed at her house, Marta's father now treated me with much more consideration, as if he suddenly had started thinking that we were somebody and we could be talked to now for real.

Nevertheless, his efforts to show special interest in our careers or to prove that he trusted us—by revealing his loneliness since Marta's mother had died—only made us think that deep inside he was much more naive than we were and his problems were insignificant, as unreal as ours.

Unaware of the hidden meaning of the conversation, he could spend hours on end talking about the resemblance between Marta and her mother, and his whole relationship with her was determined by that struggle between his desire to consider her as something completely his and the recognition that Marta had to have an independent life. She told me that for several years he had not allowed her to bring friends home and he accompanied her everywhere so that she didn't have to go with anybody else. Then he changed his attitude and abandoned her almost entirely, but he kept a constant watch over her, controlling all her actions. Finally, now, as even I could tell, he seemed determined to win her for himself, acting like an understanding friend, suppressing all the instincts that led him to try to exercise his authority, although we were aware of the extraordinary effort he sometimes had to make to maintain that line of conduct.

To Marta, this situation was much more comfortable and it allowed her to lessen the tension that for so many years she had felt and suffered in her relationship with her father.

Observing how he acted around us, feeling that I understood his motives better than he did, I also remembered how much I thought I had suffered at the age of eleven when I found out that my father had a lover and my mother told my brothers and me that she was going to file for divorce. My little brother and I used to lock ourselves in the bathroom to cry together where no one could see us, thinking that the others couldn't understand what we were going through; and in school I awaited with true anxiety the occasions when the other students' parents would visit the school, thinking that I, who could only take my mother, was different, marked with a special stigma. On the other hand, now I felt that if I had the chance to see my father, I could tell him I that understood him perfectly, and I toyed with the idea of tracking him down in order to write him a letter explaining it all and asking if he would let me see him. But that too seemed futile, no more than a sentimental attempt to relive childhood emotions, similar to what Marta and I attempted when, during the endless afternoons, impossible to fill, we tried to remember our first year in high school with an exaggerated nostalgia, unaware, and not wanting to admit, that that life—which now seemed so intense and full of discoveries—was almost the same as the one we were leading at the moment and its only appeal was the novelty of having marked a beginning that time now rendered beautiful.

In the meantime, my oldest brother got married, and at his wedding I met a friend of his, a little older than he, who worked in the same office. His name was Héctor and for the next few months he managed to make time take on a different rhythm for me. From the moment we met, in front of the church, he didn't leave my side, and when we said good-bye, after having been with me throughout the entire reception, he invited me to go out the next day. I accepted because it seemed that it would be interesting to go out with someone older than the men we usually dated, and at first the difference in age made me feel not only that he was different, but that, in addition, he had a kind of authority over me that made me take him seriously. He seemed aware of my feelings and during our first dates he was so agreeable that he seemed condescending, laughing at my judgments and opinions as if in reality the only thing that mattered about them was the witty, and according to him youthful, way I expressed them. To try the same game of approach and withdrawal with him that we played with university men was impossible and from the first date I let him kiss me goodnight and, after that kiss, to treat me as if I was his steady girlfriend.

At the beginning, I didn't know if I really liked him or if it was only the difference in the way he treated me that attracted me, making him seem superior to the rest, but at least I had fun with him and knowing I had to take him seriously made things much more interesting. He lived with his mother and never wanted to pick me up at school or have anything to do with any of my friends or acquaintances, except sometimes for Marta. He picked me up at home and we would go to the movies or out to dinner; then, in his car, we kissed endlessly. On those occasions he seemed to give himself entirely to me and I liked feeling the power this gave me over him, although many times the intensity of his desire overcame the feeling of power and I also gave in to mine. Afterward he would ask me, with an anxiety that made him appear particularly intense, if I could ever love him, and I would respond, believing I was sincere, having no reason to pretend, that I already loved him, but he never seemed satisfied with my answers.

"Sometimes I think you're too young. To you everything can be a game, just something new, and for me it isn't."

"For me either," I insisted. "I already told you I love you, that I think I love you."

"See? That's what's wrong. You have to add 'I think' because you're not sure."

"How can you be sure of anything? I don't do it consciously. Besides, to think I love you is to love you already. I can't see things any other way."

"That way isn't enough for me. I need you to change. I don't think I love you, I love you, I love you all the time, without ever doubting it."

"I love you, too. You're the one who makes me doubt it. You have to accept me as I am."

Then he, who up to then had been serious and tense, would laugh almost paternally, as if suddenly accepting that to argue with me was useless.

"And what are you like?" he would ask, still laughing.

"As you see me. Very old," I'd say.

"I see you very young. And very attractive, incredibly attractive. And I see that I need you and I don't have you."

I tried to study his face to determine if he seemed handsome to me, too. I never could decide, but I thought I liked him anyway and, above all, that his interest flattered me and made me feel a curiosity about him stronger than any feeling I had ever experienced. I would ask him to kiss me and let myself go completely. At first he always stopped at a certain point, as if my age forced him to control himself in order to protect me, but little by little I made him go further and several times he had me almost naked in the car and ready for everything.

Finally, I suggested that, if he couldn't take me home because of his mother, we go to a hotel. He refused. We were already talking about the need to get married, and during those first months I thought I was ready, but only as something far in the future. Yet the need to make love grew stronger and stronger. Though Héctor tried to avoid it, we ended up doing it, in a hotel.

The first night, when he agreed and started the car to drive to the hotel, I felt a touch of fear and for an instant I thought of asking him to wait a little longer. We had been kissing as usual and my blouse was entirely unbuttoned and I was very excited. On the way, overtaken by that feeling of fear, I tried to move away and button my blouse, but he drew me to him and continued caressing me, and I couldn't say anything. As we reached the hotel, I closed my eyes and waited for him to ask me to get out of the car. His voice was hoarse and he too was a bit nervous. He undressed me and led me to the bed. When he moved away to undress, I tried to forget where I was, thinking that I liked his body and how beautiful it was to see him naked. Then he came near again and asked me if I wanted him to turn off the light.

"No," I said. "I like to look at you and for you to look at me."

A moment later, almost talking into my ear, he told me, "If it hurts, tell me. I don't want to hurt you."

But I didn't have to tell him anything. Later, however, I felt embarrassed and uncomfortable there. I dressed hurriedly and asked if we could leave, and in the car I stayed away from him, making him feel guilty for what had happened, but before we said good night, I had already forgotten everything, and even though he promised that we would never go back, that instead we would get married right away, two days later we returned.

The intensity of our relationship erased my guilt, and during those first few months I felt I was truly in love, though when he talked of getting married I always asked him to wait, arguing that we were fine for now and there was no need to hurry things.

When Marta found out I had gone to bed with Héctor, she made me tell her everything, without omitting a single detail, although it made us both laugh nervously. Then, very serious, she confessed that she was jealous, but when she found out I was thinking of marrying him, she tried to convince me to graduate first, and for several afternoons we discussed the advantages and disadvantages of my situation as if we had remained faithful to our old plans until I met Héctor. Shortly after, however, she met Eduardo at a party. She dated him for several weeks before telling me, and the first time she talked to me about him, she seemed embarrassed for liking him. But rather than dulling Eduardo's image, her embarrassment turned into a kind of advantage, because knowing that if she lied to me I would find out when I met him forced her from the start to accept him without illusions. She began by explaining that he was the exact opposite of Héctor and that he gave the impression of being younger than we were, though actually he was three years older. He had come to Mexico City on business for his father and didn't know how long he would stay, but she didn't even want to think about his leaving.

"I think I'm in love, too," she finished, laughing. "Isn't it absurd? We'll end up getting married like everybody else. But it's not bad, is it?"

Then, serious again, she said she wanted me to meet him, and we decided that the four of us would go out the following Saturday. That first day, Eduardo also gave me the impression of needing to be protected, not only because his appearance and his way of talking gave him a provincial air, or at least made him different from most of the men we knew—I understood how that could be attractive—but because Héctor's presence made him feel insecure, and not knowing how to deal with him, Eduardo would turn to Marta, and even to me, for support. From the start I tried to show that I accepted him simply because he was with Marta, but the situation irritated her a little. I sincerely felt relieved when we dropped them off and I was once again alone with Héctor.

I called the next day to tell Marta how much I had liked Eduardo. With a feigned laugh she responded that it had been a horrible evening none of us could have enjoyed, but that Eduardo had liked me too and, for her, everything had worked out fine because now she was sure she really loved him.

Eduardo stayed with Marta two more weeks and when he left, he promised to return in three months to request her father's permission to get married. I saw them again five or six times without Héctor, but the night before Eduardo left, the four of us went dancing. These few times were enough for me to know I liked him, but a few weeks later, when Marta said she was planning to get married and live in Mérida, I repeated the same objections she had made to me a few months before, supporting them, in addition, with the argument that it was too risky to go and live in a place she didn't even know and where life must be very different from the one she had led up to then, although deep inside I felt that I was wrong and maybe nothing could be better for either one of us than to change our environment completely and start over in a different way.

Whether I felt sorry for her or envied her, it was evident she was in love and that was more than enough; I, on the other hand, felt further and further away from Héctor. We kept going to bed, and whenever he succeeded in turning me on, I felt everything was going to be fine, but it happened less and less frequently. His propriety, the staunch seriousness with which he took everything, his steadiness, and even a sense of justice that made him feel somewhat guilty about me, bored me to death. For no reason I tried to hurt him by making him feel, sometimes without believing it myself, that he actually was guilty; at other times, convinced by his constant harping or aware of what I was doing, I emphasized the indecisiveness of my feelings just to exasperate him and provoke a fight. At those times, the impression of stability and authority he had made me feel at the beginning completely disappeared, and he became like the other men I had dated, only more boring. After those fights he would insist more than ever that we get married as soon as possible, but for me each argument made the possibility ever more remote. That's probably why, when I remembered how Marta and Eduardo looked when they were together, I thought that, whatever happened, she was much better off than I and her faith in Eduardo was infinitely more satisfactory than my indifference toward Héctor.

While Eduardo was away, Marta wrote him almost daily, and after three months he returned with his father. A week before, Marta informed her father about her plans and they had an argument. Her father swore he would never give his permission. Marta slept at my house that night, and then I spent the next six days at hers, keeping her company. At first, her father, who had ordered Marta to be home for dinner every day, continually asked me to help him convince her the whole idea was foolish, forcing me to play the role of mediator, and making me feel uncomfortable and annoyed, but little by little he relented and two nights before Eduardo's arrival he requested, more than ordered, that she postpone the wedding for at least one year. But Marta didn't accept even that suggestion, and when Eduardo arrived, her father had already agreed to invite him and his father to dinner one night to talk. When he gave his permission, Marta stood up to kiss him, but her father pushed her away almost rudely and locked himself in his room.

The next day, I went out with Héctor and didn't eat with them. I returned very late and as I was entering our room I found Marta's father, in his robe, standing next to the bed, watching her sleep. When he saw me, he raised a finger to his lips to ask me not to speak, grasped my arm so firmly it almost hurt, and held me for a long while, staring at Marta along with him. Then he murmured almost to himself, "She's so beautiful. I could look at her all my life."

And still holding my arm, he led me to the living room and for more than two hours talked to me about Marta, asking me what she thought of him, wanting me to tell him what she did and what she liked, as if she were a stranger to him. I tried to tell him what he wanted to hear, but none of my answers seemed to satisfy him completely and his anxiety disturbed me deeply. Finally, he asked me to tell him why, in my own opinion, she had decided to get married. Because she had fallen in love with Eduardo, I answered; he assured me that he only wanted her happiness. I felt very tired and told him I was going to bed.

The night Eduardo and his father came to dinner, although I was no longer staying at Marta's, she invited me also. She was happy. She thought Eduardo's father was marvelous and was even more convinced that she would not mind living far away as long as she could count on Eduardo and him. And obviously, he, much more than Eduardo, deserved the credit for the evening's success. From the start, he agreed with Marta's father on everything, and his manner and conversation created a cordial atmosphere in which it seemed possible to solve any problem. He looked vigorous, with no indication of the illness that would leave him partially disabled a few years later. Eduardo let his father do all the talking, which also made Marta's father see him, perhaps unconsciously, in a friendlier light. When we finished eating, Eduardo's father asked the three of us to leave them alone for a moment, so we went to the living room, certain that nothing could upset the harmonious mood of the dinner. While Marta's high spirits made me happy, for the first time I also felt somewhat apart from her and lonelier. Then Eduardo and his father took me home; while I talked to them, I noticed I was treating them as though Marta, in spite of all of our years of friendship, was closer to them than to me, belonging to them in some way.

Eduardo spent another three months in Mexico City, dedicated exclusively to Marta, and I stopped seeing them almost entirely, not only because she had stopped going to the university, but also because I knew they preferred to be alone. Then he returned to Mérida for a few days to arrange things and came back with his father again to get married. Marta expected his mother to come with them, but Eduardo's father explained that she was sick and the doctor had not allowed her to travel.

I felt a little ridiculous at the wedding trying to take the role of maid of honor seriously, and I remembered how many times Marta and I had laughed at ostentatious wedding ceremonies, but, in spite of this, it was exciting to be at her side, and when I had to get close to her during the ceremony, I squeezed her shoulder for an instant and felt like crying when she turned to look at me with a slight smile, making fun of the ceremony and her own excitement. Héctor was there, but as we left the church I felt I should keep Marta's father company for a while and left with him instead.

I saw Marta again when she got back from her honeymoon, her head full of plans and unable to leave Eduardo's side for one second, and then, six months later, when she returned to Mexico City for a few days without Eduardo, already pregnant with her first child. We talked endlessly once again. Her face and words confirmed the happiness expressed in her letters. They were still living with Eduardo's parents but were planning to move to a house nearby once the baby was born, and she loved the life in Mérida, despite some unpleasant aspects. In a letter, I had told her I had broken up with Héctor and wanted to continue studying, but as we talked, I noticed that, although outwardly she approved of my decision, deep inside it was incomprehensible to her. Even though her pregnancy was not too far along, it still made her look different, and she kept bringing the conversation back to the subject of her baby, but despite everything, she was the same Marta as always, capable of laughing to the point of tears for the slightest reason, of getting excited about things, and of arguing to exhaustion when she believed she was right about something. One morning we went to the university, and for a moment, as we walked through the familiar hallways, I felt time hadn't passed and we were still the same friends who together made absurd plans in high school and thought their lives were going to be different, sure of knowing what they wanted before anything had begun to happen to them.

IV

The first day at the house on the beach, the sound of a motor woke me. Light filled the room, but when I looked at the clock, it wasn't even six yet. The sun filtered through the shutters and it was starting to get hot. Thinking it was too early, I tried to go back to sleep but couldn't. I felt a little tired, but my curiosity was too strong, and I finally got up and looked out the window, not daring to fully open the shutter, for fear that someone might see me from the beach. But it was deserted. The sea, even calmer than the previous afternoon, with the sun barely beginning to shine on it, had a variety of different colors and seemed to be awakening also to the brightness of the day. Pale green along the shore, the water darkened gradually into a deep blue that in a certain way made it seem cooler, but somewhat startling as well. It was a sea different from itself and for that reason also more authentic. The launch, whose motor must have awakened me, was slowly disappearing in the distance.

I opened the shutter wide, feeling totally free and happy, then saw—to the left, where the line of summer houses ended and the town started, out near the pier—a group of men in the water trying to drag something out of the sea, while on the shore, women were gathering to observe their efforts. From my window I couldn't tell what they were doing, but the image—the men in their straw hats, with pants rolled up and naked torsos, forming two symmetrical lines reaching all the way into the shore, intent on their mysterious common task, with the women watching—had something ritualistic and truly beautiful about it.

I stayed watching them from the window, hesitating to go down and find out what they were doing for fear that everyone in the house would still be asleep, until I saw one of the maids walk out toward the group on the beach. I washed my face, put on a dress, and went downstairs. Marta was in the living room, in shorts, talking to the other maid.

"It's very early," she said, surprised. "Why did you get up?"

"I wasn't sleepy. A noisy motor woke me up and I couldn't go back to sleep. I've been looking out the window for more than half an hour, hesitating to come down; I thought you might still be asleep."

"Oh, no!" she said. "The motor was Eduardo's; he went fishing with Rafael and Lorenzo. I had to get up to fix him breakfast."

"Fishing? This early?"

"More like late, because today they didn't have anything ready. Rafael came by to wake up Eduardo after you went to bed and convinced him to go."

"Who's Rafael?"

"A friend of ours. Celia's brother. You'll meet him. He's very nice. The best around here," Marta explained to me.

"You don't get up this early every day, do you?"

"Of course not," she said. "The boys are still sleeping. But sometimes you have to. Besides, see, you're up too."

"Yes . . . What's going on at the beach? It's fascinating, those men pulling something out of the sea."

"You saw them? It's really beautiful. They're dragging the nets."

"What's that?"

Marta smiled, as did the maid, who remained next to her, awaiting her orders.

"Fishing with a net, stupid," she said.

"Like that? So close to the shore?"

"They don't start that close; they work their way in. First they cast the nets from their boats. I sent out to get fish for breakfast, if you'd like some."

"Let's go and watch them, can we?" I said. "I've been dying of curiosity."

"Go on. I can't," she answered. "I have to wait for the boys to wake up."

"You don't mind?"

"Of course not. That's why you came. I'll wait for you so we can have breakfast together," she said, pushing me toward the door.

Her attitude was completely different from that of the day before. She seemed to have forgotten whatever was bothering her and looked genuinely happy.

I went out to the beach, delighted, thinking that the vacation was turning out as I had expected; the place was marvelous. I could sense already how life at the house on the beach was so different that you had to see things in a special way, more clearly, from new perspectives.

High above, the sun was already getting extremely hot, and walking with shoes on the loose sand was impossible. I took them off and, carrying them in my hand, walked just along the water's edge toward the fishermen, who were almost completely out of the water now. A moment later I noticed the sparkling fish churning the sea as they jumped within the nets. A few fishermen had gone into the middle of that seething and desperate mass to select the fish, throwing some back into the open sea, where they would disappear immediately, and others out onto the beach, still jumping, while the women went closer to look them over.

I caught the eyes of some of the fishermen watching me when I approached the women, who kept their distance, as if my presence among them was unusual and disturbing, but the fish jumping and squirming in the nets, while the stooped fishermen caught and separated them out by hooking their fingers in their gills, was a spectacle much too fascinating to let their behavior bother me. Marta's maid came over to warn me to be careful because a sharp bone could cut my bare feet, so I moved back a few steps, more than anything to show I appreciated her warning. She stayed by my side and I noticed that by speaking to me, she had, in a certain way, identified me for the rest of the women, who now seemed to resent my presence less. The fishermen finished dragging the nets from the sea and began gathering the catch they had scattered over the beach; awkwardly and painfully, the fish kept trying to leap toward the water. The maid chose three, explaining to me what kind they were and in how many ways they could be prepared, and after paying for them she asked if I was ready to leave. Watching the women select their purchases from among the sand-covered but still living fish continued to fascinate me, but it was no longer beautiful, so I decided to accompany her back. As we walked along the beach the maid, dangling the fish from a palm strip tied through their mouths, asked if "Doña Marta" and I had known each other for a long time.

"Yes, a long time."

"Before she met Don Eduardo?"

"Yes, long before. We went to school together," I said, watching her.

She must not have been more than fifteen, and in her regional dress she looked very pretty.

"I've known Don Eduardo all my life," she commented. "My mother works in his house in Mérida."

"Oh, really?" I said, a bit disconcerted.

"Yes," she answered confidently and with a certain pride.

We walked a few more steps in silence before she asked, "Are you married?"

"No, I'm not," I said, wondering what she was leading up to.

"But you're very pretty," she went on. "Like Doña Marta . . ."

"Thank you," I said, smiling, but the maid still added, "She must love Don Eduardo a lot."

Her tone indicated that she wanted a response to confirm her assumption, but I could only answer, "I guess so . . ."

For a moment she remained quiet, somewhat disturbed, and then she returned to the subject of the fish, obviously trying to make me forget what she had said before we reached the house. She had a natural charm, and in spite of everything, I felt happy next to her. I also realized how hungry I was and liked the idea of eating the fish for breakfast.

Marta was in the kitchen with the boys. She offered me a cup of coffee and I sat there watching how she prepared the fish. Later, the nanny took the boys to change their clothes, and, sitting at the kitchen table together, we ate the freshly cooked fish. When we finished, Marta told me that since it was so hot, if I wanted we could put on our bathing suits and go to the beach with the boys.

"Everyone goes swimming very early here," she explained.

When we went out with the nanny and the boys, the beach, deserted a moment before, had actually filled up with swimmers and it looked different. Some people talked in groups beneath the beach umbrellas they had stuck in the sand, but also, in the sea, others formed small groups to continue their conversations in the water, as if the ocean were only there to cool them off. There were lots of children, most with their nannies right next to them, and countless teenagers running from one side to another, yelling and playing pranks on each other, but all the groups revolved around the adults, who watched from their terraces or seated in canvas chairs under the umbrellas. With the people, the beach appeared happier and more civilized; it reminded me more of other places. In the water, the sailboats and motorboats came dangerously close to the swimmers. The sun shone on everything, flooding it with light.

Marta and I sat on towels spread over the sand, while the boys went to the water's edge, holding their nanny's hand. Soon after,

Celia came over with a couple I didn't know. Marta introduced me to the strangers, who invited us to join their family under one of the umbrellas, but I said that I wanted to sunbathe for a while, so they sat down next to us.

"You should be careful. The sun is very strong here," Celia warned me. "We're used to it, but you obviously don't have much of a tan."

"At least you should put on some kind of cream," Celia's friend's husband went on. "We have some if you want."

His wife glanced at him silently; I answered that I had already rubbed on suntan lotion and showed him the bottle.

"That's a lot better than the cream," the woman said. "It's the kind I used to use."

She was very dark, with pretty features and large eyes, but next to her, her husband looked younger and much more handsome. I thought that, in general, the men I had seen were more attractive than the women, which perhaps explained the women's insecurity. Nevertheless, it was true that even next to Marta I looked very pale, but, on the other hand, considering how long they had been at the beach, nobody seemed especially tanned. Later I found out that in fact they hardly ever sunbathed; they exposed themselves to the sun only when they went in the water or dried off, and returned immediately to the shade of their terraces or umbrellas. In addition, the women protected their faces with hats even in the sea.

For a few minutes, Celia and her friends asked me polite questions about Mexico City and my life there, but soon they tired and began talking about their mutual friends and the events of the last few days, which, from what I could tell, consisted mainly of getting drunk. At first I tried to pretend I was listening, though not knowing the protagonists took away whatever interest the conversation might have held, but when I realized that they were indifferent to my presence, I turned on my stomach to sunbathe.

With my eyes shut, the murmurs from the beach became softer and more muffled, and for a time I managed to feel completely alone, comfortable, half lulled to sleep by the heat and the sense of the sea's closeness, as if only it and the sun were real and everything else had been devoured by the strength of that reality.

In that drowsy state, I heard Celia and Marta comment that Eduardo, Lorenzo, and Rafael should arrive any minute now, and I wondered what he was like. A soft breeze mixed the rustle of the palm trees with the sea's murmur, and between them they erased almost entirely all other sounds, but the sun was burning my back and I sat up to suggest to Marta that we go into the water.

When I opened my eyes, everything seemed to go suddenly dark, as if a thin, purple veil dissolved the outline of objects, making them unreal, but gradually the light invaded everything again, making the sea shine and turning the sky into a dazzling space without limits or color.

Celia and her friends said they had already been in the water and, making us promise to join them after our swim, went back to their umbrella. As Marta and I approached the water's edge, the boys grabbed her arms, begging her to take them in. Holding their hands, she let the waves splash them, while I waited on the shore, aware for the first time of the stares my low-cut bathing suit was attracting; it exposed my back entirely and that proved too revealing compared to the rest. The constant attention Marta had to give the boys made me feel differently toward her, too, creating a new dimension I didn't know how to reach, perhaps because deep inside I had no desire to, either. I had never entertained the possibility of having children and it was hard for me to see them as more than cute objects, impossible to really understand. However, I tried to help her when she brought the boys out of the water and ordered their nanny to take them home and get them dressed, despite their protests.

Before getting into the water, I noticed the young man I had met on the plane standing a few yards away from us, with a group of friends his own age, staring at me insistently. I waved, but instead of just waving back, as I expected, he came over. For a moment I tolerated his stare and naive questions, but suddenly I felt impatient and tired of pretending, perhaps because his conversation added another to all the others that had kept me from freely enjoying the beach. I said I wanted to go into the sea and left him talking to Marta.

The water was almost hot, but after having been under the sun for such a long time, the feel of it proved to be marvelous. Although I had swum away from the shore, when I surfaced and tried to touch bottom, I found the water only waist deep. I swam farther out, but it didn't get much deeper and I understood how people could continue gathering in groups so far from shore. The water's absolute transparency allowed me to see my legs and the sandy bottom clearly; the movement of the waves caused the sun's rays to shimmer on the sand. Marta joined me a moment later.

"That poor child is crazy about you," she said when she came near. "It was impossible to get rid of him. He wanted to know everything about you."

"Did you tell him?" I said, laughing, in a good mood.

"I couldn't," she answered. "I don't know anything either."

"I'm the same as before. There's nothing new," I said.

"That's good," she said. And then she added: "But it's true, you look very attractive," and immediately, as if suddenly wanting to change the subject, she asked, "Isn't the water delicious?"

"Yes. Delicious."

We separated a little, each swimming her own way, and then I saw Marta coming toward me quickly.

"Look," she said, "there's Eduardo and Rafael."

"Where?"

"That sailboat," she said, pointing to a barely visible white sail. "I didn't think it was so late. Let's swim out to them, okay?"

"Sure, let's go," I said, though it seemed impossible to swim such a long distance.

We drew away from the shore, swimming slowly, side by side, pausing once in a while to see how the silhouette of the sailboat was becoming clearer every minute until, much sooner than I had expected, we could make out the shapes of the crew. Marta stopped and raised her arm out of the water to wave. They waved back, and minutes later the sailboat was almost on top of us. Lorenzo had the wheel and couldn't leave it, but Eduardo and the man I didn't know lay down flat along the edge of the deck, stretching an arm toward Marta in a vain attempt to grasp her hand and pull her aboard. But the boat was moving too fast. In an instant it passed between us, separating us and leaving them empty-handed as it continued its trip to shore. Marta and I watched it leave us behind, laughing, excited, and Eduardo yelled, "Come on!"

Everything happened in a moment, but the feeling that the boat was going to pass right over us, forcing us out to the sides, was very exciting. Without saying anything to each other, both of us started swimming as fast as we could toward the shore.

Before I got there, I had to stop to catch my breath and saw that they were lowering the sail; then Rafael and the fisherman who was with them jumped into the water to help the boat overcome the waves' resistance by pushing it toward the beach. I started swimming again, slower. Marta hadn't stopped, and when I got out of the water she was with them, talking to Rafael. She introduced him to me.

"You're Elena . . ." he said, offering me his hand with a smile. "We've been expecting you for months. Glad to meet you."

"Yes, glad to meet you," I said, then remained quietly by his side.

He wasn't wearing a shirt and his water-soaked pants stuck to his legs. Although he was probably the same height as Eduardo, he looked taller, maybe because he was thinner, and he seemed older. I watched him as he talked to Marta about the fishing and thought he wasn't handsome, but there was something about him I liked. Eduardo came up to me with a fish in his hand and held it in front of my face.

"Do you like it?"

Instinctively, I moved back, and Eduardo and Rafael laughed.

"They're pretty, aren't they?" Rafael said. Then, talking to Eduardo, he continued, "Should we make soup? We had bad luck," he explained to me. "But at least there's enough to make soup."

Marta said they could make it at her house and Rafael turned to Lorenzo.

"Shall we join them for lunch?"

"Yes, that'll be perfect," he said. "I'll go tell Celia."

The children who were nearby had circled the boat and were watching the fisherman clean the fish. Rafael went and told him to take them to Eduardo's house when he finished and then rejoined us.

"I'll see you in a while, then. I'm going to take a bath."

"Don't take too long," Marta said. "I want you to help me."

"Of course," he said, and turned toward me. "See you later. And again, nice meeting you."

As he walked toward his house, Marta asked me, "He's nice, isn't he?"

Later I noticed how she, as well as Rafael, constantly turned statements into questions, but I didn't want to attribute any special significance to it and I forgot it right away.

In the meantime, the beach had been emptying slowly; most of the umbrellas had been picked up and only a few swimmers were left, most of them very young. It was extremely hot and the sun, apparently motionless directly overhead, made the sky shine so brightly that it was impossible to look at it.

"Shall we go?" Eduardo said. "You're really burned."

"Yes, let's go," I said.

But Eduardo again stopped for a moment at the boat, picking up hooks and instructing the fisherman to take the outboard motor to the house, and the sight of the boat's benches stained with the scales, blood, and guts of the fish repulsed me.

Back at the house, Marta went to the kitchen to get things ready and watch the children eat; I went up to my room to shower. Eduardo went up with me and we talked for a while outside my door. I asked him what Rafael did for a living.

"He's a doctor," he answered. "I hope you like him. He's my best friend. We've known each other for as long as I can remember. Imagine. Even longer than you've known Marta. And he's a good doctor, too. He's the kids' doctor."

"He must be very intelligent," I said stupidly, somewhat embarrassed by Eduardo's intensity.

"Yes," he said smiling, also embarrassed. "I'll see you downstairs."

I went into my room and, as I took off my bathing suit, I noticed that I was actually quite sunburned. I knew my skin was going to sting that night, and it bothered me to have to admit that after all, Marta's friends had been right. Later, while I showered, I remembered Rafael again. It was impossible to imagine him as a doctor without supposing that he must look a little ridiculous in his office. For some reason the profession didn't fit him, but I couldn't imagine him working elsewhere either, in my law office, for example. I could only see him as he had appeared to me that first moment, coming back from fishing, his hair caked with salt and his pants soaked. I didn't realize, however, that I had been thinking about him until I started getting dressed, because first I put on a pair of shorts and then changed into a skirt, knowing I didn't want him to look at my red, burned legs. For the same reason, after trying on some sandals, I decided to go barefoot.

Celia and Lorenzo were already in the living room when I got downstairs. Seeing them made me stop for an instant on the stairs. In Mexico City I had always acted as if Marta's house were also mine and now I didn't know whether I should greet them like guests or act like a guest myself, but Lorenzo cleared up any doubt by offering me a beer as soon as he saw me and getting it from the bar himself.

I sat next to Celia; Lorenzo gave me the beer, then went back to his place next to the bar.

"How was the beach?" he asked from there, smiling amiably.

"Very nice, splendid," I said.

"She and Marta were off alone the whole time," Celia broke in, not addressing either one of us in particular. "Marta is so monopolizing. Everyone wanted to meet her and she disappointed them."

"Good for her," Lorenzo said. "Everywhere you turn, you'll find parents, grandparents, and uncles, all of them with one thing in common: they're all boring. Try to avoid them."

"No," I began to explain, "I didn't know . . ."

But he interrupted me: "Don't pay any attention. It was a joke. Is your beer cold?"

"Yes, perfect," I said. "Where's Marta?"

"In the kitchen, with Rafael," Lorenzo answered. "The official cooks. But apparently, today they plan to starve us to death," he added, checking his watch.

"I'll see if I can get something for us to snack on," I said. But Celia didn't let me get up.

"Don't bother. I'll go. I'm really much more a part of the family than you," she affirmed, without any bad intentions, with a friendliness she hadn't shown until then.

When we were alone, Lorenzo took a few sips of beer, without talking. Then he asked me what I did in Mexico City.

"Yesterday we didn't get a chance to talk. And I'm sorry," he explained. "We're too used to thinking only about our own things."

I told him about my job in Mexico City; then he started telling me about the economic situation in Mérida and how hard it had become for everyone. With the exception of Marta, it had always been easier for me to talk to men, and now with Lorenzo the same was true. I felt freer, more comfortable, and it seemed to me that in spite of his being overweight and looking unkempt, Lorenzo was much more pleasant than he had struck me the night before. His curiosity proved more natural and I could answer him without effort. When Celia returned with potato chips and a dip, we were laughing. She left the tray next to him, on the bar, and asked what we were talking about.

"Business," he said maliciously, and we both laughed.

Celia glanced at Lorenzo for a moment and asked me if I didn't want something to eat, without the friendliness she had shown before. I went up to the bar, aware of the change in her mood. Lorenzo offered me another beer.

"She's going to get drunk," Celia said, half joking, half serious.

"No; I'm used to it," I said, pretending I hadn't noticed the change in her mood.

Fortunately, Eduardo came down at that moment. He asked about Marta and Rafael and served himself a glass of rum.

"So early?" Lorenzo said.

"I have to take advantage of Marta's absence."

"You're too much," Celia broke in right away. "You're going to make her think Marta doesn't let you breathe."

"Besides, she can tell on you. Remember, they're friends," Lorenzo added, converting Celia's interjection into a joke, as well.

"That's exactly what I'm going to do. And while I'm at it, I'll check and see how long before lunch is ready," I said and took the opportunity to go to the kitchen.

Marta and Rafael, with one of the maids, were frying the fish.

"Will it take much longer?" I asked. "We're starving."

"One more minute," Rafael said. "We're about to start serving."

Marta was still in her bathing suit. She said she was going to change, but not to wait for her, and asked me to stay and help Rafael and the maid. From the kitchen we could hear how the others yelled at Marta when she passed by, teasing her about the food not being ready yet. Rafael ordered the maid to get the plates, went to the stove to turn over one of the fish, and, with his back to me, asked in a surprisingly serious tone, "Do you like the sea?"

"Why so serious?" I said, feeling awkward because I didn't know what to do to help.

"Was I being serious?" he answered. "I didn't notice. But do you like the sea?" he repeated, turning to look at me.

"Yes, a lot. That's why I came."

"Not because of Marta? She's told me so much about you."

"Yes, because of Marta too, of course," I agreed. "I really wanted to see her."

"I can imagine."

He lifted the lid from the pot that was on the other burner and asked the maid to start serving the soup.

"You're going to see what a good cook I am," he said and then added, "If you like the sea, we'll have to go out fishing one of these days. It's marvelous. I could spend my life fishing."

I told him I'd love to go, although the memory of the boat's bloodstained benches didn't make the prospect very appealing, and he assured me he would arrange it as soon as possible. The maid carried out the first course, and he took the last fish out of the pan and turned off the stove.

"You weren't much help," he said. "But you look very nice that way, barefoot."

He said it very naturally, as if confirming an objective fact, and I smiled, knowing I didn't have to answer. The maid came back and Rafael ordered her to continue serving; he told me we should go into the dining room.

Celia, Eduardo, and Lorenzo had opened beers for everybody and they were already eating. We joined them. The soup was really good, but it turned out to be too spicy and made us perspire. I thought I'd never understand Rafael's fondness for cooking and I compared him to Pedro, without knowing why, but already thinking that it wasn't the only difference between them. Although my face and shoulders were burning a little, I was comfortable. From where I sat I could see the ocean, calm, shining under the sun, which seemed to sink everything in a peaceful lethargy, and suddenly I noticed that I no longer felt so much of a stranger among Eduardo, Lorenzo, Celia, and Rafael.

Marta came down a little later and sat next to me, facing Rafael, and to the right of Eduardo, who was sitting at the head of the table. She began to eat her soup while the rest of us waited for the second course, talking; she asked me, "Are you happy?"

I said yes, noticing that the others were listening to me, but I wasn't lying.

As soon as we finished our coffee, Lorenzo stretched his arms and said he was going to sleep.

"I'd advise you to stay," Eduardo answered. "I have a surprise."

He went to the bar and returned with a bottle of cognac.

"Look."

"Not even that can convince me," Lorenzo said. "I only got three hours of sleep. These fishing trips are going to kill me. Let's go, Celia. To the hammock!" he added, laughing.

"Your loss," Eduardo said, somewhat impatient, avoiding Marta's eyes.

Celia stood up, a bit upset by Lorenzo's joke, and asked Rafael if he wasn't coming with them.

"If you're not going to rest, I'll stay," he said, speaking mainly to Marta.

"Stay," Eduardo told him.

He didn't leave until it got dark, and we finished almost the whole bottle of cognac. Marta and I drank at the same pace they did and in the end we were quite drunk, but Eduardo and Rafael were so engrossed in remembering their childhood and talking about themselves that they didn't even notice.

V

During the next three days I met every aunt, uncle, niece, nephew, and friend there was to meet and saw Rafael most of the time. When we went out to the beach in the morning, he was there and would join us immediately. Unlike the first afternoon, whenever he was alone with Marta and me he never talked much. He would lie on the sand next to us or play with the boys—who continuously asked him for things, knowing they could get whatever they wanted from him—and would follow us if we decided to go into the water. Then, after lunch with Celia and Lorenzo and a short siesta, he would return. By then, Eduardo, who had spent the morning working in Mérida, was back home. We would sit on the terrace and, egged on by my questions, they would start talking about their childhood. With a certain fascination, I noticed how different mine or Marta's had been, merely because they had been born here, in the provinces. For them everything seemed always to have followed an old, perfectly determined path, their childhood repeating, with a few minor, superficial variations, other childhoods, those of their parents, maybe even of their grandparents, uniting all of them.

Rafael was very aware of this and talked about the excursions to the haciendas, the first days of school, previous seasons at the beach, and even his required trip to the United States, as if he were talking not only about himself and Eduardo, but of an entire way of life, a system that turned personal stories into something much more general and more important—the history of a city, of several generations, which reflected and repeated itself in each succeeding generation charged with repeating it to ensure its own continuity.

By the third day, my sunburn bothered me so much that I decided not to go to the beach that morning. Rafael divided his time between

Marta, who sunbathed on the sand with the boys as usual, and me; I watched them from the terrace, wishing he would come over to talk for a while and that Celia, who had decided to keep me company, would leave us alone. Then, in the evening, just before the sun set completely, he suddenly asked me if I wanted to go swimming, since I hadn't gone in the morning.

"The sun's almost down and the water must be delicious," he added.

I accepted enthusiastically, and he went home to put on his trunks. When I found myself alone with Marta and Eduardo, I realized that neither one of us had bothered to ask them if they wanted to join us; I pretended that it had been assumed by asking Marta before I went to my room if she wasn't coming up to put on her bathing suit.

"No, I'm not going swimming. I'm tired. Go by yourself," she said.

"What about you?" I asked Eduardo.

"I'd rather watch you from here," he answered.

I went up to my room and put on the black suit I hadn't worn yet. From the window I saw Rafael coming back, running, with a towel in his hand, and for the first time I asked myself if I really liked him, or if he only seemed better than the rest. We had spent the previous nights with several of Marta and Eduardo's friends, and though they had all been equally open and pleasant, and the few bachelors gave me all their attention, I couldn't help getting bored by the conversations and even the jokes, identical to Lorenzo's; equally boring was the obligation to talk to the older people, who imposed their presence with utter naturalness, feeling that they had the right to ask all kinds of questions and always expecting me to answer with the false naïveté I had to learn to use as a defense against their partly unconscious, but nonetheless annoying, impertinence. With Rafael, on the other hand, it wasn't that way at all. He seemed to have an innate sense of tact, and the touch of shyness I had discovered in him during the few occasions we had had the chance to talk alone accentuated his refinement and made him more charming. All this ran through my mind while I watched him run toward the house, and I went downstairs knowing that, if nothing else, I wanted him to like me.

Instead of coming up to the terrace, he was waiting for me on the beach, talking from there to Marta and Eduardo. So it was easier to cross the terrace without stopping to talk to them and walk alone with Rafael toward the sea. Before reaching the water's edge, without warning, he ran in and swam a few yards out. Then, from there, seeing that I had stayed behind on the shore, he yelled and signaled me to come over: "Come on, come on . . ."

I got in the water and swam toward him. When I reached him I felt I had gone to him too directly, and without saying anything, I pretended to have lost my breath. I noticed him looking at me, not knowing what to say either, and I looked away until he asked me, "It feels good, doesn't it?"

"Yes, very," I said.

Then I looked toward the house and saw Marta standing on the terrace, watching us. As if following the direction of my gaze, Rafael commented, "She'll be sorry she didn't come."

"Marta?"

"Of course. Eduardo's too comfortable with his rum to think about the sea."

I smiled mechanically, wondering whether I should ask him also if Eduardo drank too much, but before I had a chance he was talking again, while the rhythm of the waves separated us and brought us together, swaying us softly, but without imposing its presence.

"I love them very much. Both of them. You've probably noticed."

"Yes," I said. "And they love you too."

"It's very strange," he went on. "I can't see that row of houses without seeing myself and Eduardo building sand castles, pretending we already knew how to swim, lying on the shore, or playing cops and robbers on the terrace. We were obsessed by the idea of going to the marsh, or to the cemetery at night, but we never did. Or maybe we never tried. Now it seems to me that we were loners. Maybe because he's an only child and I only have one sister. You've probably noticed how unusual that is around here," he added. "Everything's so strange . . . It seems impossible that time has passed, that things could change so much . . . Everything looks so much the same from here: the houses, the beach, the sky . . . How dumb!" he ended, laughing at himself.

Nevertheless, he had spoken seriously and I felt that standing there in the sea, conversing like that, was also strange. The sun had set and it felt cold out of the water. Instinctively, we tried to keep our bodies low in the water while the waves kept swaying us gently, sometimes forcing us to jump a little to avoid getting washed over.

"You know what?" I said. "I can't believe you're a doctor."

Rafael laughed.

"Why?"

"I don't know. Maybe because I've only seen you here, at the beach."

"Well, let me tell you, I really love medicine," he answered. "Someday I'll bore you with the subject."

Then he asked how long I planned to stay, and I discovered that I didn't want to think about it.

"About ten days, maybe fifteen," I said. "Should we get out? I miss the sun..."

"Whatever you want," he said.

In spite of our efforts, the current had carried us away from the point where we had started. We swam back toward it and when we got out, Rafael picked up the towel he had left on the sand and covered my shoulders.

"The breeze is cold. Dry yourself off," he said, rubbing me lightly with the towel.

Eduardo met us at the terrace with half a glass of rum in each hand.

"The best thing for after swimming," he explained, handing them to us.

Rafael took a long drink.

"How was the water?" Marta asked.

"Perfect, but it feels cold when you get out," I said and handed the towel back to Rafael. "You can use it now."

Marta said she was going to the kitchen, but before leaving us, she asked Rafael if he wanted to join us for dinner.

"Sure," he said. "Do you want me to bring something?"

"No, nothing," she answered. "Tell Celia and Lorenzo, too."

"Okay," Rafael said.

The sea and the beach were fading into the darkness, but we sat on the terrace a while longer, finishing our drinks. The rum warmed my stomach, accentuating the coldness of my bathing suit. As soon as Rafael said good-bye, I went up to my room to take a shower, and before I finished, Marta came in with a bottle in her hand.

"I thought I'd rub some vinegar on your sunburn. Everyone around here says it works really well. Does it still sting?"

"No, not as much," I answered from the shower. "I'd rather not put anything on it."

Then, while I was getting dressed, she lay down on the bed and stared at me in silence.

"What's the matter?" I asked.

"I'm very tired," she answered. "Sometimes the boys exhaust me."

"That's partly my fault. I don't do anything all day. I'd like to help you somehow."

She smiled.

"With what? You still don't know how to be a housewife, fortunately . . . ," she said, with a slightly bitter tone, despite her smile.

"But I can learn."

She followed my movements, looking at me affectionately.

"No. I like you the way you are." She kept quiet for a moment while I finished getting dressed, and when I sat in front of the mirror to comb my hair, she added, "We haven't had a chance to talk at all. What do you think of Rafael?"

"He's very nice," I said. "The best of the bunch. He looks a little like Eduardo."

"I hadn't thought about it," she answered, almost to herself, and went on, "I think you've impressed him. Do you like him?"

I laughed.

"What's wrong?" Marta said. "There's nothing strange about it, is there? Why are you laughing?"

"It's not that," I said. "It's just that we're talking like we used to. It's been years since anybody asked me if I liked someone. And maybe I've missed it."

"It's true," she said, pensive again. "It's also been some time since I asked anybody that."

"It's okay, though," I said, turning toward her. "I like being with you and I'm glad I came."

She said she was also happy that we were together, but then she fell quiet again, and when I finished getting ready, she commented, "It'd be funny if you liked him." Adding right away: "Shall we go downstairs?"

"Yes, I'm ready," I said, without thinking to ask what she had meant.

During dinner Rafael remembered his promise to take me fishing and suggested going the next day. All of them had been drinking as usual and Lorenzo, who was quite drunk, commented, "Fishing with women is not fishing. They just get in the way."

"Call it an outing, then, but we can go anyway," Rafael responded quickly, and then he asked Eduardo if he could miss work.

"Of course," he said. "But I warn you, I refuse to tell Don José. If you want us to go, you'll have to do it yourself. I can't move."

"Obviously," Marta said, irritated.

She had been very nervous the whole time, but her aggressive tone surprised me, a tone I had never heard her use with Eduardo. But he didn't bother to answer. Celia broke in to say that she wouldn't go no matter what.

"It's sheer torture. I get terribly dizzy," she explained to me. "I hope you're not the same."

"A few pills beforehand and there's no problem," Rafael answered.

Later, after supper, he asked Marta if she could fix lunch for the next day.

"Let's go see what there is," she said, getting up. As soon as they left, Celia commented, "I don't know what's the matter with us today. Everyone seems to be out of sorts."

"Don't include me. I'm perfectly fine," Eduardo answered. "What do you want to do, play poker?"

"I'd rather go to bed early if we're going fishing," Lorenzo said.

"Not me, I'm not sleepy," Eduardo said and went to the bar for another drink.

He downed it in one swallow and poured himself another. I didn't move or say anything, uncomfortable because, in some way, the tension everyone felt seemed to be my fault.

As soon as Marta and Rafael returned, Lorenzo said he and Celia were leaving. Eduardo stared at his drink without getting up or answering, and Rafael said he too was leaving to tell the fisherman about tomorrow.

"Should we go with him?" Marta asked Eduardo. "It's still early."

"No, I already said no. I'm quite comfortable right here," he said. "But you two go, if you want."

"Don't worry," Rafael broke in. "I don't mind going by myself."

"Let them go with you," Eduardo insisted. "I'll wait here."

"It's hot. Let's go, if you want," Marta told me.

"Yes, why not," I answered, thinking it was better to get out of the house for a while.

Celia and Lorenzo left by way of the terrace to walk home along the beach while the three of us went out the back to the highway, to walk toward the center of town. The white clothes hung out to dry between the palm trees moved like ghosts in the patio. Rafael had to struggle with the wooden gate, which was stuck in the sand the breeze had deposited in front of it, and then left it open. Only a few isolated street lamps lit the highway, but the moon was out; lights were on in most of the houses along the road and the cars passing in both directions added to the brightness. At first we kept running into groups of vacationers going from one house to another, but as we approached the center of town the traffic died down and, with it, the lights. None of us talked. Rafael, walking between the two of us, hands in his pockets and head lowered, as if wanting to stare at his feet, blocked my view of Marta. Nevertheless, the silence wasn't oppressive. The peacefulness of the night, its mystery full of soft sounds, made me feel comfortable and I supposed Marta and Rafael felt the same way.

Near the town square, it got bright again and we started to run into people, not vacationers, but fishermen, sailors, and dockworkers, some quite drunk.

"No one's going to talk?" Rafael said then. "I might as well have come alone."

"I thought you were the one who didn't want to talk," Marta answered.

"You know I always want to talk," he said, and turning to me, he added, "And you?"

"I'm fine. I don't have a thing to say."

He commented to himself, half joking and half serious, "Darkness calls for silence."

We reached the square, just a small church painted pink on one side, with the remains of a colonnade on another and thatched, wooden houses along the other two sides. In the center, a few benches tried to create the illusion of a park, but there were no plants, and sand invaded the grounds. On our left a paved street led to the pier, but beyond the colonnade, the highway also ended, and one had to walk, as on the beach, over loose sand. The town's only movie house and several cantinas, still open and full, were located along the short stretch of paved street. The music and the murmurs of voices coming from the cars were lost in the square's large, empty space, swallowed by the darkness and the wind.

"We're almost there," Rafael said for my benefit, noticing how difficult it was for me to walk on the sand in my high heels.

"It doesn't matter," I said. "I like it very much."

"What?" he asked.

"I don't know. The town, the deserted square," I answered, a little embarrassed.

He laughed, for no other reason than to join me in my embarrassment.

"It's true," he said then. "At this time of night it's beautiful. I don't know if you've noticed how everything is built between the sea and the marsh. One day they'll reunite and everything will go. The memories will end. Isn't it true, Marta?"

"You know it better than I do," she said. "They're your theories. Explain them to her."

But Rafael didn't say anything else.

When we got to the corner, we turned right and a few steps ahead stopped in front of the dilapidated fence of one of the wooden houses whose shape could barely be distinguished in the dark.

Rafael leaned on the gate and called out.

"José!"

Immediately, barking came from everywhere and one of the dogs emerged from the darkness between the gate and the house, and ran toward us, barking furiously. Marta and I instinctively grasped Rafael's arm, forcing him to step back, and he started laughing.

"It can't get out, it's closed," he explained, pointing to the gate. Then he talked to the dog, who was still barking from between the planks of the wooden gate: "Zape! Get back! Get back!"

The dog retreated a little, made a complete turn, and came back barking, arousing again the chorus of barks.

"José!" Rafael yelled again over the barking.

The front door opened and the fisherman who was with Rafael the first time I saw him came out, an oil lamp in his hand. As he approached, he kicked the dog and it disappeared into the dark, emitting only a slight howl. Immediately the other barks also ceased.

"Good evening, Don Rafael; evening, ladies," the fisherman said when he was near us.

Rafael explained that he wanted him to accompany us fishing the next day, and Don José promised to make sure everything was ready.

"See you at five o'clock sharp, then, José. I don't want the same thing to happen again," Rafael insisted.

"No, Don Rafael, I promise. I'll be there early," the fisherman assured him. "Good night, ladies."

He disappeared back into the darkness of the house, the dog trailing close behind, wagging its tail and ignoring us.

On the way back, excited by the prospect of the fishing trip, Rafael couldn't stop talking, explaining everything about it to me. Marta, who since the dog barked at us had left her arm in Rafael's, added a few things of her own, and between them they communicated their enthusiasm to me, although the possibility of getting dizzy like Celia and making a fool of myself in front of Rafael frightened me a little.

As soon as we passed the square, Rafael suggested that we return along the beach, and we walked toward it down one of the narrow side streets covered with sand and thorny plants. The moon extended a thread of light over the water, but the sea had again become a constant rumble, deaf and monotonous, with something frightening about it. Most of the summer homes were dark already and, in spite of Marta and Rafael's conversation, for a moment I felt that the night's solitude enveloped us completely.

We walked very near the water, because there the humidity hardened the sand and made walking easier, but nevertheless, Marta and I had to remove our shoes. When the lights of the house came into view, Marta took Rafael's hand and said, "Let's leave her alone."

Without letting go of his hand, she pulled him and forced him to run with her. Surprised, I stopped cold and watched them go past the house, where their silhouettes became almost impossible to distinguish, not understanding Marta's joke, but recognizing it as one of hers. I kept walking toward them, choosing not to run, because in a certain sense I felt foolish and out of the game; a little later I noticed them walking back. Before they reached me, Marta started running again, toward me this time, Rafael's hand still in hers; she arrived pulling him along, laughing in an exaggerated way.

"Were you scared?" she asked, still laughing and out of breath.

"You're crazy," I said, trying to laugh, too.

"We were too serious; I had to do something," she explained, talking with difficulty.

At her side, Rafael smiled slightly, somewhat disturbed, unable to laugh. Marta let go of his hand and we continued walking.

"Let's see how the lonely hero's doing," she said when we stopped in front of the house.

We looked through the window and saw Eduardo asleep in one of the armchairs, the glass still in his hand. Marta raised her arm to knock on the window and wake him, but Rafael caught it with a quick, though gentle, gesture.

"Leave him alone."

"Don't you want to come in?"

"I'd better not. We have to get up very early tomorrow," he answered in a low voice, as if wanting to avoid bothering Eduardo, although it was impossible for him to hear anything.

"Okay. See you tomorrow, then. I still have to finish preparing the food," Marta said.

"Yes, see you tomorrow," he answered.

He turned to me and said, "Thank you for going with me."

"Thank you for inviting me to go fishing," I said.

Without adding anything, he gestured "think nothing of it," slightly shrugging his shoulders and moving one arm, then turned and left.

Marta and I entered the house. She went over to Eduardo and woke him up by putting a hand on his shoulder and shaking him, while I waited a few steps away.

"Where's Rafael?" Eduardo asked when he opened his eyes, still half asleep.

"He left."

He looked at her with an empty glance, stupefied, trying to sit up.

"What time is it?" he asked.

"I don't know. It's still very early. Why do you have to drink so much?" Marta asked, without reproach, in a loving, compassionate tone.

Eduardo shrugged his shoulders and moved his arm in a gesture very similar to Rafael's a moment before, but much more helpless and childish, then fell back in the chair with his eyes closed. Marta took the glass from his hand and turned toward me.

"Help me take him up to our room."

Between the two of us we managed to make him climb the stairs and laid him on the bed.

"Go to bed," Marta told me in a low voice, while smoothing back into place a lock of hair that had fallen over his forehead. "I have to undress him."

"Don't you want me to help you down in the kitchen?" I asked in the same tone.

"No, don't worry. I just have to make sure the maids are doing everything right. Tomorrow I'm going to wake you up at four-thirty. These men get furious when they leave late and it's a miracle they invited us."

I kissed her on the cheek, and she turned toward the bed to start undressing Eduardo.

I still hadn't sent Pedro more than a hurried letter, so I decided to write him before going to sleep. But after the first page, even though while I was writing it I had felt I needed and desired him very much, I realized that I was sweating and felt tired, and I got up from the table with the intention of getting undressed and then continuing the letter. Nevertheless, instead, I lay for a moment on the bed and unconsciously began thinking about Rafael. Once I realized it, I decided that it was simply because he was closer and I felt lonely, but instead of getting up to finish the letter I turned the light off and fell asleep right away, without getting underneath the covers.

The next day Marta came in to wake me and was gone before I finished sitting up. It was still very dark and I needed the light, which Marta had turned on when she came in. Sleepy, I went to the bathroom, but the water was cold, so instead of taking a shower, I just washed my face, put on a blouse and shorts, and went down to the living room, with almost no makeup, knowing my eyes must be swollen.

Eduardo was near the bar, leaning over a cooler, filling it with beer. When he noticed me, he looked up and smiled.

"Hi. I believe you had to carry me up to my room last night."

"Yes," I said. "Like a bag of cement."

"How embarrassing. I hope you won't tell anybody in Mexico City."

"Don't worry. I promise. Where's Marta?"

"In the kitchen. Go and have some breakfast. José should be here any minute now."

Marta served me juice and coffee in the kitchen, and I drank them sitting at the maids' table, while she put some sandwiches in a basket. The fact that it was still dark made us talk in low voices and gave the preparations an exciting, mysterious air. I drank my coffee quickly and returned to the living room, more than anything to see what Eduardo was doing, but he had left. So I went out to the beach. Though it was still very dark, a slight glow was starting to insinuate itself far out at sea, over the horizon, gradually becoming more visible, but it wasn't possible to tell how the change was taking place. Although it was cold, I was too excited to think about going back to the house for a sweater. Eduardo was on the beach with the fisherman. He had already brought the boat up to the shore and its silhouette rocked gently more or less where the waves broke, with the same softness. As I walked towards them, I noticed Rafael and Lorenzo, half lost in the darkness.

"Good morning, ma'am," the fisherman said to me when I got near them; then he went on talking to Eduardo.

I stayed next to him, with my arms crossed to protect myself from the cold.

"Where's the motor?" Rafael asked as he came up to us, without acknowledging me.

"We're going to get it," Eduardo said. "Come on, Lorenzo, give me a hand."

They headed toward the house and Rafael turned to the fisherman. "Bring the boat in closer, will you?"

After beaching the boat, the fisherman rolled up his pants and got into the water to make sure the back, where the motor had to be attached, wasn't touching bottom. In the meantime, Rafael came over to me.

"How are you? Sleepy?"

"No. I'm fine."

"Let's see how we do. We have to hurry," he continued, looking toward the place where the sky was growing lighter. "Let's go and help them with the things. Aren't you cold?"

"A little, but I don't mind."

"It's better that way," he said. "You won't be once the sun comes out; then it'll get very hot. We have to ask Marta to give you a hat. I also wanted to tell you how good you looked yesterday in that black bathing suit," he added.

He was wearing light-colored pants and a blue cotton sweater. I thought he was very handsome and it embarrassed me a little to remember that desiring him the night before had kept me from finishing the letter to Pedro.

Walking toward the house we ran into Eduardo and Lorenzo, who were carrying the motor out to the boat with difficulty.

"Bring the cooler," Eduardo told Rafael as they passed.

Marta had brought the basket of food into the living room, where she was waiting for us. Instead of the pants she was wearing when I saw her in the kitchen, she had changed into white shorts. Rafael tried to carry the cooler by himself, but it was too heavy so he asked me to help him. We were about to go out again when he remembered the hat and asked Marta if she couldn't lend me one.

By the time everything was ready, the soft glow that earlier had insinuated itself at the edge of the horizon had extended much higher into the sky, but the sun hadn't come out yet and the light had a delicate, tenuous character that seemed to bloom from nothingness. Rafael had carried me to the boat so I wouldn't have to get wet, and I could still feel the contact of his hands on my legs while, seated next to Marta in the center of the boat, we waited in some suspense for the fisherman to start the motor. Next to him, Eduardo held the wheel. Rafael and Lorenzo were sitting behind us, in the bow. We had rowed out from the shore and now the boat bobbed adrift.

"Now if only this piece of junk will catch," Eduardo said after the fourth attempt to start the motor.

The fisherman kept trying, oblivious to everyone's impatience, his lips broadened into a slight smile of understanding as he finally got the motor to run.

Eduardo set the course, heading the boat straight into the waves, and we started pulling away from the shore. A moment later, the sun started coming out.

"Look," Marta said, "isn't it incredible?"

In the meantime, working between Eduardo and us the fisherman had started cutting bait and preparing the hooks. When Marta pointed at the sun, he raised his head and looked at us for an instant, smiling again. I realized that what to us was exceptional, to him was nothing more than an everyday occurrence he must have viewed quite differently; nevertheless, it was impossible to ignore the beauty of it all. The waves slapped the boat with a measured rhythm, producing a murmur like a soft panting. As the coastline extended itself ever wider and the size of the houses decreased, blurring the sharpness of their outline, the sensation that the sea surrounded us entirely, separating us from the coast and taking possession of us, the same way it gathered all of the sun's light and blended into the sky in the distance, made the boat seem strangely cozy.

Once in a while, a wave bigger than the ones before would spatter us when it crashed against the boat, but it wasn't cold anymore and the water felt good.

I would've liked to go on endlessly moving toward the horizon, while the sun lifted slowly away from the depths of the sea and began to possess the sky; when Rafael suggested that we should stop, I felt disappointed, thinking the best part of the outing was over. But I was wrong. Though Eduardo stopped the motor, the boat kept moving forward a while longer, until the waves turned it sideways, setting it parallel to the coast, now just a thin white and green line rising and falling to one side of us; then Lorenzo threw the huge rock they used as an anchor into the water.

At first, the boat's rocking motion, much more noticeable than when we were moving, bothered me a little, and for a moment I thought I was going to be seasick, but I got used to it right away and after a while it even felt pleasant.

In the meantime, the fisherman had thrown two hooks into the sea for Marta and me and had put the lines in our hands. Eduardo, Rafael, and Lorenzo, busy with theirs, seemed to have completely forgotten about us. They fished without a rod, holding the lines in their hands, with the ends tied to the bench. The intensity with which the three of them stared at the point where the line dropped into the sea seemed exaggerated and even comical.

"You're not going to fish?" I asked the fisherman.

His face, dry, sun-hardened, furrowed by wrinkles, framed by the wiry and tangled white hair, had a strange cleanliness. He answered with the same smile.

"No, today I rest. But they're very good at it. I've been coming with them since they were children. And their fathers too. Isn't that right, Don Eduardo?" he added, with a certain pride, as if he could take credit for a part of their education.

"It's true, yes. For a long time," Eduardo answered, and went right back to staring at the line.

The fisherman started telling me about other fishing trips they had been on together and of those he had made as part of his regular job under more difficult conditions, pointing at other fishermen's boats we could make out in the distance and recalling shipwrecks and even deaths as something natural, something to be accepted as part of his way of life; suddenly my line tugged and I screamed.

"Pull, pull, they're biting!" the fisherman said.

Everyone dropped their lines and turned toward me, excited.

"Faster," Rafael said, standing next to me. "Hurry, or else it'll get away."

I pulled the line in as fast as I could, laughing nervously, and suddenly I saw the fish at the end of the line, just below the water, and an instant later I had him in the boat, jumping in the air.

"Perfect! It's a bass!" Eduardo said.

"And a huge one!" Lorenzo added.

What a marvelous sensation it had been, and now everyone surrounded me, delighted. I hugged Marta, still laughing.

"What luck, making the first catch!" Rafael said, smiling happily; absurdly I suddenly felt I loved him and all I wanted was to be with him.

The fisherman took the fish off my hook and left it flipping on the bottom of the boat, still alive. From then on they started taking all the hooks in an incredible way, as I'd never imagined it could happen, and in what seemed only an instant to me, we had twenty fish in the boat. I caught three more, one of them very large, and was overjoyed. Rafael kept busy casting my hook into the water and I felt I had known him forever and had always liked him, but now, in a different way, I also liked Eduardo and Lorenzo, and the fisherman.

"I never imagined it like this," I told Marta. "It's marvelous."

"Yes, marvelous," she answered. "And you picked it up so quickly."

The scarf she had tied on her head accentuated the perfect oval of her face, and she looked very attractive without makeup and tanned.

Then, in the same unexpected way they had started biting, the fish stopped, and after waiting fruitlessly a while, Eduardo suggested we go somewhere else. The fisherman nodded in agreement and started the motor. I knew it must be very late because the sun was high and it was very hot, but the time had gone by unnoticed.

At the new place, farther away from the coast, while Marta, Rafael, Lorenzo, and especially Eduardo caught more fish, mostly smaller than the first ones, my line kept snagging on something whenever I thought I had a bite. The bottom was rocky, the fisherman explained as he untangled it over and over again, but once, when he couldn't get it loose, Rafael stripped to his swimming trunks and jumped into the water to free it, and when he surfaced, I helped him back aboard, letting him hug me almost entirely with his wet body, although for the first time I noticed that it bothered Marta.

Later we tried our luck again at another place. Marta took out the sandwiches and we started to drink beer, somewhat tired already, but suddenly Lorenzo yelled that he had something big; he leaned over the line, toward the sea. The fisherman rushed to assist him, telling him to slacken the line and then helping him pull it; after a long struggle, they succeeded in bringing to the surface what turned out to be a female shark—"a cat," the fisherman said they called it. It had to be harpooned, bludgeoned, and finally stabbed to death with a knife, before it could be lifted into the boat.

Everyone agreed that after this success we could stop fishing, and Lorenzo turned to me.

"You brought us good luck."

"It's true," Eduardo confirmed. "It's a good catch. Don't think it's always like this; catching a cat is extraordinary."

They decided that there was enough breeze to return under sail and Lorenzo and the fisherman raised it, while Rafael took the wheel. He was still wearing his bathing suit. I sat next to him and let my leg rub against his.

No sooner had they finished raising the sail than the breeze inflated it violently. The boat almost leaped forward; I saw Rafael tighten his grip on the wheel, and we started moving toward the coast. On the floor, the fish squirmed around the dead shark, producing a murmur that blended with that of the waves breaking against the boat. Eduardo and Marta were sitting together up front, his arm around her shoulders.

"Did you have fun?" Rafael asked me.

"Lots," I answered, looking at him.

The heat made the sea around us appear marvelously fresh, alive, and happy. I put my arm in the water and splashed it up to my shoulder, some drops falling on my face and hair; I felt how the sun dried them right away.

Little by little the contours of the coastline became clearer. The green of the coconut trees separated from the white of the houses until it was possible to distinguish them perfectly beyond the almost golden line of the beach. As we got closer to them, sitting next to Rafael, feeling the closeness of his skin and the salty flavor of the breeze, I felt I would like to become part of that world.

VI

Rafael had to spend the next couple of days in Mérida. I saw him again Saturday morning at the beach. Celia and Lorenzo were with us when he appeared on the terrace of their house and yelled for us to wait for him to change so we could go swimming together. Afterward, drinking beer on the terrace of our house, he suggested that we go dancing that night at the open-air nightclub of the small hotel, which was open only during the summer. For two days, Marta and I had languished under the sun, as if time had stopped forever; now, Rafael arrived in such a good mood that we couldn't help but get excited and we started making ridiculous plans for the night, but when Eduardo arrived, he announced that his parents were expecting us for dinner. Marta overreacted and for a moment it seemed as if they were going to fight over it. Celia, Lorenzo, and I sat quietly while they argued, but Rafael, feeling somewhat guilty, intervened to convince her that it was senseless to quarrel and that all of us could go dancing some other day.

"It won't be the same," Marta said, angry, but without speaking to Eduardo, she accepted Rafael's opinion that it was useless to argue.

Without another word Eduardo went inside. However, when Rafael, Celia, and Lorenzo left, Marta's mood changed. She kissed Eduardo and asked him to forgive her.

"Everything you said was true," he conceded, "but we can't refuse the invitation."

Then he turned to me and explained, "They feel they have to do it for you. You know how they are."

He still hadn't changed clothes and had that tired, somewhat dirty appearance that driving twenty-five miles from Mérida under the hot sun always gave him. Marta told him that if he wanted, they could go to the beach together before lunch, and I stayed with the nanny to keep an eye on the boys, who were already eating. From the dining room I saw Marta and Eduardo walking along the beach hand-in-hand and thought that, in spite of everything, they were a couple. Nevertheless, during the past two days, she had been very nervous, scolding the maids for the slightest reason and losing her patience with the boys. Although we had been alone several times, we still hadn't talked seriously and it seemed to me that in reality she no longer wanted to tell me anything; in part, perhaps, it was my fault, because during my first week at the beach, due to Rafael's presence, I had stopped being just the friend who had come to visit her. The last two days—sunbathing on the beach or bored over bridge with Celia and Lorenzo, trying to read during the immensity of those afternoons or finally writing Pedro a decent letter—lying naked on my bed, thinking that at that moment Marta and Eduardo must be making love—I had missed Rafael constantly. When I saw him on the terrace that morning, I realized that I had been waiting for him all along and for the first time in two days I was again aware of my body, happy to have a dark tan and to be wearing the bathing suit he liked. Now, knowing I wouldn't see him the rest of the day took the meaning out of time, converting it into an indistinguishable flow marked only by waiting.

Before Marta and Eduardo returned from the beach, I got the boys to go to sleep, and I greeted them, happy to have been able to help Marta in some way. The breeze hadn't come in yet, and it was very hot. We decided to leave after sunset to avoid perspiring so much on the way, and after lunch they retired to their room. I knew I wouldn't be able to sleep and stayed in the living room, listening to records. Through the window I could watch the sea, almost devoid of waves, as brilliant as a mirror, apparently also drowsy from the heat. The boats hardly swayed on it. A few seagulls, their wings motionless, glided in the air against a silver, cloudless sky of pure light. The dazzling transparency and the nearly total absence of movement produced the impression of a painting in which each thing contemplated the other, forever held in place. Numbed by the heat, I went out to the porch, unbuttoned the back of my dress, and lay on the cool tile, half asleep, hearing, without listening, the music from the record player. From there I suddenly saw Rafael, walking along the water's edge. Thinking he would come over and talk to me, I sat up to say hello, but when he passed in front of the house and saw me, he hesitated a moment and then just waved and kept on walking, and I couldn't make up my mind to call him either. More than upset, I was disappointed. When he suggested that we go dancing, he was speaking more to me than anybody else and I felt sure he wanted to be with me; now this unwillingness to talk to me when we could be alone took away that security and made me think that if I wanted to have any relationship with him I was going to have to invest a lot more, and my curiosity increased. For a moment I thought again about Mexico City. During that week Marta hadn't written to her father or received a letter from him, and I asked myself if I would like to be so far away from everything that had been my life. Until then, I had only thought of Rafael as someone whom I wanted to like me, without trying to figure out what it would mean for me, or how he really saw me. Maybe I hadn't even considered that we might go to bed. I caught myself thinking about Pedro as a kind of protector whose existence allowed me to return to the familiar, to the life where I already knew everything I wanted and could expect, and I wondered if I wouldn't be better off keeping him more in mind. In the meantime, Rafael's figure had disappeared beyond the pier, a solitary character on the empty beach.

My unbuttoned dress slipped down my shoulders. I took it off and went to sit in the living room, furious with myself. Marta came down much later with the boys and asked me, laughing, what I was doing there undressed.

"Planning to seduce somebody?"

"No, fortunately," I said, laughing also.

"You didn't go up to rest?"

"No, I haven't done anything but sit here and look at the sea."

She left the boys and sat next to me.

"You miss Pedro?"

"If I do," I said, "it's you and your husband's fault."

"I'd like to meet him," she said. "I don't think he's much like Eduardo."

"Not at all. But we all need somebody."

"Yes, true," Marta ended.

She kissed my shoulder lightly and asked me if I didn't want to shower before leaving. I picked up my dress and, as I was going up the stairs, she told me, "I don't want you to get bored."

"I'm not bored," I answered, stopping for a moment. "Don't worry."

And I noticed that the nanny was watching us from the kitchen door, cradling one of the boys in her arms.

We left earlier than we had planned because after the siesta
Eduardo started drinking, and Marta said she didn't want him to
arrive drunk. But on our way through Progreso, Eduardo suggested
that we stop to have some ice cream under the arcades, so by the time
we got back on the highway it was starting to get dark.

The ride seemed shorter than the first time, even though we
hardly talked the whole distance. I was sitting in the back, with both
windows opened. The silhouettes of henequen projecting themselves against the delicate, transparent tones of the sky, in the middle
of the silence of nightfall, produced a marvelous sensation of secret
and eternal stoicism, but the idea of seeing Eduardo's parents again
made me nervous and upset. I couldn't imagine what we could talk
about, and I only hoped the dinner would finish as quickly as
possible so we could return to the house on the beach. Both Eduardo,
who leaned forward and drove at full speed, and Marta, motionless
at his side, never turning toward me, must have been thinking the
same thing.

Upon entering the city, where the street lamps were already lit,
Eduardo decreased his speed; we could feel the heat once again,
much stronger than at the beach, humid and sticky.

"What time is it?" Marta asked.

"Seven-thirty," Eduardo answered. "They must be waiting for us
already."

Marta turned to look at me.

"How do you feel?"

"Fine."

"Ecstatic!" she said, with a sarcastic laugh.

"It's not that bad," Eduardo said, trying to make light of Marta's
bad mood. "After dinner, we can drive around so Elena can get to
know the city a little. Then the trip will be worthwhile."

"Yes. I'd like that very much," I answered.

And in reality, the houses and gardens lining the avenue, with the
skeletonlike silhouettes of their weather vanes projecting above the
trees, had an unquestionable beauty and from the beginning lent the
city a regal aspect, not too provincial, as if each house had been
constructed so that its character assured and represented a form of
concrete life, oblivious to any reality other than its own.

"I've always wondered who lives in such big houses," I told Marta.
"Do you remember our walks in Mexico City?"

"What do you mean, who?" Eduardo responded quickly. "People,
us."

Marta and I laughed.

"Even if they're starving, right?" Marta said.

Instead of answering, Eduardo shrugged his shoulders, but a moment later, he commented, "You'll never understand."

We were on the main avenue. There was a little more traffic, but behind the gardens, most of the houses were dark and the city continued giving the impression of being almost empty. On the other hand, when Eduardo stopped the car in front of his house, all the lights were on, and the brightness made the impression of neglect, of inevitable deterioration of an antiquated splendor, all the more evident.

We crossed the garden among the vibrant and constant murmur of the crickets. All the doors were open, revealing the endless succession of rooms and parlors whose high ceilings and sparse furniture made them seem even larger, but there was no one in sight. Eduardo entered one of the parlors, in which there were only a set of wicker furniture and two rocking chairs, and called toward the interior patio.

"Mother, we're here!"

His voice disappeared into the darkness of the patio, but no one answered, and for a moment I had the sensation that nobody lived there.

"Mother!" Eduardo yelled again.

His mother's voice, sweet and quiet in contrast with Eduardo's shouts, surprised us from behind.

"I'm here, I'm here, don't be so impatient."

As on the day I met her, she was dressed in dark clothes and seemed entirely unaware of the heat. She approached and kissed Marta and Eduardo. Then she offered me her hand.

"Hello, dear, how are you? Was it very hot along the highway?"

"No, not too much," Marta answered for me.

"I'm so glad to hear it. We've had terrible days here," she went on, still addressing me. "If you want, we can sit out on the veranda; it's cooler."

"To be devoured by the mosquitoes?" Eduardo said.

"You know very well there aren't any mosquitoes here," she answered.

She took my arm and while we walked toward the veranda, she commented, "Sometimes it seems Eduardo wants to forget he's lived here all his life. We've never been bitten by a single mosquito."

Eduardo asked about his father.

"He's getting dressed," she explained. "I wanted to help him, but you know how he is . . ."

Marta and Eduardo brought out two more rocking chairs and we sat in a semicircle in front of the living room door. Eduardo's mother pulled her dress down over her knees several times and asked Marta about the children. The four of us began rocking in the chairs in a steady rhythm. The singing of the crickets seemed to come from everywhere, vague, piercing. Later, Eduardo's mother asked me what I thought of the house on the beach and, while I was giving her my impressions, Eduardo stood up and said he was going to get something to drink.

"How is he behaving?" Eduardo's mother asked Marta as soon as he disappeared; she had stopped rocking and was leaning toward Marta.

"Very well, as usual," Marta said, glancing at me for an instant before answering.

"I think his father is a little upset with him, but I don't know what happened. That's why I was asking you," she explained.

"I don't know anything either. You know Eduardo never talks about work," Marta answered.

Eduardo's mother gave a brief sigh and leaned back, setting the rocking chair into motion again.

"Everything is so complicated now!" she said to herself, and then she turned to me. "We were really looking forward to seeing you again. My husband has been worried about whether you'd be happy at the beach. He's going to be very pleased to know you like it so much."

"You can't help but like it," I said.

"No, don't be so sure. Not everybody does," she answered.

Marta glanced at me again as if about to say something, but she didn't. Fortunately, Eduardo returned just then, followed by a maid carrying a tray of drinks.

"I prepared one for you, too, mother," he said happily, handing out the glasses. "We have to get drunk and remember the good old times."

"For God's sake, Eduardo!" she said, with a little laugh.

Eduardo sat down with a glass in his hand and looked at us.

"What's the matter? We have to be happy. Cheer up. I'm in a good mood. Cheers!"

We all raised our glasses and took a few sips. The maid remained at Eduardo's side looking at us and smiling. A soft breeze had started to blow in the garden, shaking the leaves of the trees. Once in a while, the light from a passing car on the avenue illuminated the tops of the shrubbery and plants for a moment.

"Where's father? Isn't he planning to join us?" Eduardo asked, rocking vigorously in his chair. "He's being rude to Elena."

"For God's sake, Eduardo," his mother repeated.

"Go see what's delaying him, nanny," he went on. "And you might as well bring another round of drinks."

"Yes, child," the maid said, smiling at him affectionately before leaving.

"Don't get euphoric too soon," Marta cautioned him.

"I'm not euphoric; I'm happy. Why shouldn't I be?" he answered and emptied his glass. Then he explained to his mother, "We're going to leave early because we want to ride around the city before we go back. Elena has hardly seen it."

"What an excellent idea," his mother answered. "We retire very early; we won't keep you," she finished, addressing me, but I didn't have to answer because Eduardo's father came in.

He was dressed in a white linen suit. He looked better than the day I arrived and it seemed to me he could move with less difficulty, but his right arm, held away from his body in an abnormal position, rigid and immobile, made his illness obvious even before he started talking. He kissed Marta, offered me his left hand, and asked Eduardo to bring him an armchair, talking with difficulty, but completing almost all of the words.

"I can't use a rocking cha . . . ," he explained to me.

Eduardo brought the chair and asked him if he didn't want a drink.

"One . . . now, yes. Very light," he said.

Then he asked me to tell him what I thought about everything I had seen.

"I ca . . . can't ask too many questions . . . You do the talking."

I tried to be as enthusiastic as possible, and he listened, staring at me attentively, nodding his head affirmatively and murmuring "Yes, yes . . ." once in a while.

His look intensified when I started to tell him about the fishing trip and Marta and Eduardo joined in.

"You should go with them someday," Eduardo's mother said when we finished.

Eduardo's father made a brusque, negative gesture with his head and remarked to us, "It was a good fishing trip, yes . . . José knows, knows . . . Now you have to take her to see . . . inland . . ."

"Yes, we're going to," Eduardo said.

He was more at ease but drank continuously, though Marta held his arm several times when he raised the glass to his mouth.

"The ruins are worthwhile," Eduardo's father went on. "They have nothing to do with us, but they're worth . . ."

"I'm anxious to see them," I said and fell silent, unable to say anything else.

A swarm of small insects circled the lamps. The wind had died down again and the stillness of the plants increased the sensation of suffocation. My dress was stuck to my legs and I felt the sweat running down my side. For a moment I felt the enormous size of the house as a living thing, weighing on us. I took my glass and drank almost anxiously.

"If you'd like, we can go to the dining room," Eduardo's mother said at last, breaking the silence from which no one seemed to know how to emerge.

"Yes, very well," Marta said, standing up.

In one gulp, Eduardo finished what was left in his glass and also stood up. As he got up, his father took my arm and we entered the dining room behind Marta, Eduardo, and his mother. I noticed with relief a ceiling fan below the chandelier and, even though the windows were closed, the room was much cooler.

While we took our places, his mother went to the kitchen to tell the maids to serve the dinner. Eduardo started preparing fresh drinks for us. Seated next to Don Manuel, I started unfolding my napkin, trying to find something to tell him, but he asked Marta, "Is he still drinking too much?" pointing at Eduardo with his head, not caring that he heard him.

"No, he has never drunk too much, the same as everyone else," Marta said in a friendly tone, but avoiding Eduardo's father's eyes.

"Fine. You . . . have to . . . that's good," his father answered, with difficulty, making a gesture of impatience.

Eduardo left the drinks in front of each one of us as if he hadn't heard anything and took his place, also avoiding his father's eyes. In the meantime, his mother came back and sat at the other end of the table. It was too large for the five of us and she, separated from us by the empty spaces, seemed to be apart, almost isolated.

"Well, cheers again," Eduardo said, raising his glass.

I also raised mine, but the rest ignored his gesture and his mother started speaking to me very quickly about the dishes we were going to have, as if to keep me from drinking. She finally finished, saying, "I hope all this food isn't too much for you. Here we're used to having a very heavy dinner, not like in Mexico City. But if there's something you don't like, feel free to tell me."

"Yes, ma'am, thank you," I answered.

I realized that I was playing nervously with a piece of silverware and I left it in its place.

"You don't have to make excuses, mother. She's going to like everything," Eduardo went on and looked for a moment at his glass, empty already.

The maid entered with the soup and we started eating. Eduardo's father stopped talking altogether. Marta tried to carry on the conversation, forcing me to talk about Mexico City and telling Eduardo's mother how the boys were, what the maids had done, and what was new among their acquaintances who were now at the beach. She cut Eduardo's father's meat and tried to make him talk, but though he kissed her hand when she put the plate of cut meat in front of him, he didn't speak until the meal was over. They had brought us beer with the food and I had finished mine, trying to overcome the heat that increased as we ate, and my head felt heavy. Eduardo hardly spoke either and left most of his food untouched, in spite of the insistence with which his mother asked him to eat, reminding him how much he used to like each of the dishes. While we were drinking coffee, his father suddenly said to him, "I have to ask you something before you leave. Remind me."

"What?" Eduardo answered. "Ask me now."

Marta and his mother grew tense, as if all they had been waiting for was this moment, which their conversation had tried to avoid, fearing it.

"If you want . . . ," his father said slowly. "Let's go to my study, then."

"Why? Ask me here," Eduardo answered impatiently, irritated, as if knowing what it was about.

As he talked, he unconsciously leaned forward, and I knew he was a little drunk.

"As you wish," his father went on. He waited a moment and added, "Jorge called me."

"What did he want?" Eduardo said, not taking his eyes off his father's, still leaning slightly forward, but motionless in his chair.

"Don't use that tone, Eduardo," his mother interrupted, but he didn't even turn to look at her.

"We'd better go to my study," his father insisted.

"No, what for?" Eduardo repeated, in the same tone.

"Listen, Eduardo," his mother said. "Your father wants to talk to you alone."

"What's the matter?" Marta asked his mother.

"I think Eduardo failed to deliver an important order," she explained.

"No, it's not that I didn't deliver it!" Eduardo yelled. "I couldn't finish it! Which is very different!"

His father looked at him silently.

"Calm down," his mother went on. "That's what your father wanted you to explain to him. Jorge told him that, on the other hand, you had delivered other orders."

Eduardo started to talk very slowly, in an offensive tone, emphasizing each syllable excessively.

"I don't need to explain anything. I know what I'm doing. I give preference to those who pay on time. Nothing else matters. And besides, it's not my fault that the machines produce so little. Father knows it perfectly well."

"Please stop, Eduardo," Marta broke in. But his mother answered at the same time: "You must remember that he owns everything."

"I can give it back to him whenever he wants it," Eduardo answered in the same manner as before.

"That's enough!" his father yelled.

Eduardo stood up, but Marta had already thrown her chair back violently and run out. I had to restrain myself from running after her and sat there staring at my cup of coffee, listening to the low hum of the ceiling fan.

The maid entered and started picking up the cups, looking at us with reserve, making me more aware of the heaviness of the silence, which dragged on until she left again. Then his father told him, "Go after your wife. I want to ta . . . talk to her . . ."

Eduardo stood up and left the dining room without saying a word.

"You have to for . . . give . . . us," his father told me. "When things don't . . . all . . . go . . ."

He spoke with more difficulty than ever, and for a moment I thought he wasn't going to be able to finish. When he did, however, I had to wait a moment before I could answer.

"Of course. I understand perfectly."

And I thought I hated that world and didn't want to know anything about it, or feel anything, not even pity, for any of them. His mother added in a completely casual tone, as if in reality nothing had happened and she just had to fulfill a mere ritual of courtesy, so that

I wouldn't have a bad impression or, even worse, a false one, "They should've considered your presence. It's so embarrassing."

"Don't worry," I answered in the same tone, restraining myself. "The same thing happens at my house."

His mother sighed and adopted a sorrowful tone, which seemed to contain a reproach directed toward no one in particular, but rather at the air, at destiny, because it insisted on punishing them unjustly.

"Children don't understand. It's so sad . . . I beg you not to think badly of us. We love Marta very much. I don't know what would become of Eduardo without her."

Suddenly, I remembered Marta's father and realized that I had felt this same way so many times at her house. The impression that time hadn't passed made me feel worse. While we talked, Eduardo's father avoided looking at me and seemed oblivious to our conversation, but I felt unable to say anything else to Eduardo's mother.

"Do you want me to go after Marta, too?" I said, looking at him.

He just shook his head and with his hand indicated for me to wait. I saw Eduardo's cigarettes in front of his empty place and felt like smoking, but I couldn't make myself stand up to get them or ask his father to pass them. The three of us were silent for an endless moment, and I let my eyes wander throughout the room, not perceiving any of the objects I saw. In the midst of the silence, my body's reality seemed unbearable. Each movement seemed a profanity. I didn't know what to do with my arms, and to increase my discomfort, the sensation of my wet dress against my back kept me from leaning against the chair.

At last, Eduardo returned, a hard expression on his face, controlling himself, and stopped at the doorway.

"Marta doesn't want to come. She's in the car," he said. His father stood up.

"I'll go to her."

As he passed Eduardo, he took him by the arm and they both left. Immediately, his mother rang the bell for the maid and started talking to me, very quickly, not stopping to think about what she was saying, so that the sound of her voice could avoid something worse, which silence might bring.

"I'm going to have them bring the cognac snifters. Everything's going to end well, you'll see. It's always the same, it's really not important: a tempest in a teacup. You're all so young. What we need is for all of you to understand us better, to put yourselves in our place and be tolerant. Don Manuel has been through a lot, too much, and

Eduardo should know it better than anyone. We don't have too many years left. For you, and even for Marta, it's different. She never knew what we were, what we have been. It's so sad, so offensive. Everything seems the same, but in reality it has been eroding little by little, with no explanation. And Don Manuel has endured it all; theft, injustice, bias, everything. I wish I could explain it to you, explain it to myself. But we don't know who's to blame. And he's been the one who has had to endure it, fighting like no one, never giving up, until his illness. You met him in Mexico City. He still had courage to confront anything. They had taken what belonged to us without cause but he went on being himself, when others went under . . ."

The maid was already standing next to her, but she didn't seem to notice until the maid asked if she needed her. She looked up, disconcerted, and finally said, "Yes, yes, bring the cognac snifters, they'd like some cognac."

Then she continued talking to me. Her gaze had lost the transparent capacity of penetration that had surprised me the first day and wandered from one side to another.

"See, at the beginning even the servants and the maids, and the field hands, didn't understand what was happening and they believed we were right. Now we don't even have that, or their trust. All of them rebel. And Eduardo doesn't understand either. Despite everything his father has been. He only wants his own good and Marta's; he loves Marta very much. I didn't meet her until she arrived; I didn't know her, but I love her, too. How could I not love her? It's all we have left, and no one can take it away from us. When they lived here, the boy loved me and I adored him. All of this is theirs, the house, everything. We've saved it for them, with many sacrifices, many. You understand, don't you? Tell Marta. Don Manuel . . ."

Eduardo returned, calmer, almost smiling, embarrassed. He went to his mother and put his arm around her shoulders.

"What's the matter, mother?"

She raised her head to look at him with surprise, as if having to make an effort to recognize him.

"Nothing, son, nothing. We're talking," she said then. "I asked for cognac. You want cognac, don't you? I thought you'd like some."

"Yes, fine, it's fine. Calm down," Eduardo said, drawing her toward him.

But she started to cry. Eduardo hugged her, trying to calm her, repeating over and over again, "Mother, please, please. It's nothing, mother. You know it's not important, please, mother . . ."

She kept crying, making an effort to restrain herself, nodding her head. Then she started talking alternately to Eduardo and me, unable to prevent her sobs, which forced her to continuously interrupt herself.

"It's true, it's nothing . . . You must understand . . . We're all nervous . . . It's not important, right? It's true . . . I'm fine now . . . Go, Eduardo . . . I'm fine now . . . Let's go to the veranda. We'll drink the cognac there, everyone happy again . . . Even I'll have a little . . . Come on, let's go. Where's your father?"

"He's with Marta. They're coming," Eduardo said, still holding her.

She stood up and let go of his arm.

"Come on, let's go to the veranda. I'm fine now," she said, no longer crying, wiping away her tears. "Tell María to take the snifters and the bottle out there."

Before leaving, she turned off the fan and the light.

Outside, she served herself a glass of cognac, forced us to do the same, and started to drink it in small sips. Eduardo looked completely sober, but after the first drink, he served himself another and then a third. The effect of those drinks took him back to his previous state almost immediately. When Marta returned, Eduardo stood up with difficulty from his rocking chair, but she didn't notice. Without looking at us, she told Eduardo's mother that her husband had stayed in his study, and we had better leave.

"Is he feeling ill?" his mother asked.

"No, he's tired, but he doesn't feel sick," Marta answered seriously. Then she turned to me and explained, "He asked me to tell you to forgive him. He's going to go to see you at the house."

"Excellent," Eduardo's mother broke in right away. "It'll be good for him to go to the beach. I've asked him to do it many times."

"Shall we go, Eduardo?" Marta insisted, still standing. "It's already very late."

"Whatever you want," Eduardo said.

His mother tried to convince Marta to at least have a drink, but she refused even to sit down for a moment. From the car, I still saw that his mother, standing on the veranda, made a hesitant farewell gesture, with the natural shyness people feel when they cannot see if their wave is acknowledged, and I waved back, although it was impossible for her to see me.

There were no other cars on the avenue. Eduardo drove at full speed and turned to the right, instead of taking the road home.

"Where are you going?" Marta asked.

"To the square. Didn't you want her to see it? We can stop and have a drink for the road," he answered.

Marta didn't respond. We took a stone-paved street and advanced toward the center of town. People were starting to come out of theaters, giving the streets a little life, but the heat seemed to weigh on all of them; they moved as if through an airless space, empty and pure, that rose up to the star-filled sky. After the dinner it seemed absurd to carry out our plans as if nothing had happened; besides, the heat killed my desire to do anything and made me wish to be back at the beach, but Marta's silence made me assume that she wanted to please Eduardo and I tried to inhale the slight draft of hot air coming in through the window, sitting as close to it as I could.

When we reached the square, Eduardo just circled it once, then took a street that ran parallel to the one that had gotten us there, but in the opposite direction. I barely had time to see the round, dark tops of the laurels and the cathedral's huge light-colored facade; next to its towers the moon could be seen very low, pale, and cool. We passed other parks, crowded with people resting on the benches, and other churches equally huge, resembling forts more than temples; then Eduardo stopped in front of a hotel, got out of the car without saying anything to us, and went toward it, but Marta didn't move from her seat and he had to come back.

"What's the matter? Don't you want to come?"

"Yes, let's go," Marta said, as if suddenly she had changed her mind, turning toward me with a tired expression.

The hotel was actually an old house, with the distinctive turn-of-the-century French architecture, behind which an arbitrary, modern, five-storied building had been constructed, whose facade could only be seen from the interior patio. The ceiling was made of glass and in the center there was an ornate fountain. Around the gardens, decorated in the same style, the rooms on the ground floor had been turned into tourist shops whose cheap appearance contrasted with the old elegance of the construction and made the place look more absurd. The bar was in the modern building, near a swimming pool surrounded by trees. The place was empty, but a pianist played for the waiters and the trees. I followed behind Eduardo, who led Marta by the arm, and we sat at one of the tables. A girl was swimming in the pool under the supervision of a woman, maybe her mother, who waited for her at the edge with a towel over her arm. At that hour, and in front of the huge, deserted bar, they looked strangely out of place.

Marta was still silent and Eduardo hummed to himself the song the pianist was playing. One of the waiters came up to Eduardo and asked what we wanted to drink.

"Scotch and water," Marta said to the waiter.

I ordered the same thing. The waiter warned us that he could only serve us one round because they were getting ready to close, and Eduardo told him to bring six, at once.

"Make mine doubles," he added.

We remained silent once again and Eduardo continued humming the song. Then, as if only saying out loud what he was thinking, he commented, abruptly, "Mother started crying."

"Yes? Poor thing . . . ," Marta said and added for me, "It turned out worse than we expected. It must have been very unpleasant for you."

"Yes, very," I said, knowing it was useless to pretend otherwise.

Marta, trying not to say anything else, turned to look at the pianist. For a moment I had the sensation of having lived that scene before, in that same place, empty and much too big, although I didn't know a place like it.

"Let's leave," Marta said at last, turning toward Eduardo. "This is sordid. I can't stand it any longer."

"At least wait till they bring the drinks," he answered and tried to hold her hand, but she pulled it away with a quick and nervous gesture.

The pianist stopped. In the midst of the silence, the murmur of the fountain proved disturbing. The girl got out of the pool; her mother covered her immediately with the towel and they disappeared down one of the corridors. For a moment the girl's long blonde hair, which she had shaken loose from under the towel with a nervous gesture, made her figure especially grotesque; not knowing why, it reminded me of a girl from grade school whom I hadn't thought of in years, and that memory separated me completely from the reality around us.

When they brought the drinks, Marta took a few sips, then stood up.

"I'll wait for you in the car. I can't stand it anymore."

"Do you want me to go with you?" I asked, also standing up, when she was already walking toward the exit, but she stopped me with a movement of her hand.

"No, stay with Eduardo. I'll wait outside."

Eduardo downed half of his drink and then looked at me, trying to smile.

"What a scene . . . ," he said.

I felt sorry for him, but I didn't know what to say, so I forced myself to smile back.

"I think we'd better leave," I said.

He had finished his first drink, and he put his hand on my arm. "No, stay, please stay. Finish your drink, for me."

It was impossible to refuse. I obeyed, although I knew I would be sick later.

"Marta and I love each other very much," he said to himself suddenly, without looking at me. Then he leaned forward, resting his chest against the table's edge and letting his arms dangle, and looked at me. "You know what I think about when I get drunk? Because I'm drunk now... About my children. Not them exactly, but their things. How I feel when I find their shoes in the bathroom, some foolish thing like that . . . Then they seem more real. They deserve everything, but I don't know what that means. Nevertheless, it exists . . . Marta and I have touched it and she knows it. That's why we're together. You understand? It can't be forgotten. I don't know if you've noticed it."

He had a lot of trouble talking, but he seemed more in control of himself than ever.

"But what's wrong, Eduardo? Why do you drink?" I said and immediately regretted it and noticed I was drunk.

He was quiet for a moment, then he shrugged his shoulders: "Who knows why? Everything, nothing . . ."

The waiter came over and said they had to close. They had started gathering the tablecloths and setting the chairs on top of the tables. Eduardo finished his drink before paying the check; then he picked up Marta's and went out to the street taking small sips. I followed him. When we reached the car, he left the empty glass on the sidewalk. Marta was stretched out almost fully on the front seat, with her head resting on the window and her eyes closed. When we got in the car she opened them for an instant, said, "Let's go, please," and shut them again.

Eduardo drove through the city very slowly, but as soon as we were on the highway, he increased his speed, started singing at the top of his lungs, and didn't stop until we passed the first houses in Progreso. The noise of the wind blowing through the windows and Eduardo's shouting had kept me so dazed that I was surprised we were there already. In spite of the hour, the streets were full of people, but Eduardo didn't reduce his speed.

"Slow down," I said.

Marta sat up at last and looked at the street, surprised.

"Pay attention, Eduardo," she said then. "That's all we need to make it a perfect night, to run somebody over."

"You finally woke up?" Eduardo said, turning his head to look at her. "Don't worry. I'm perfectly sober. And I've managed to cheer up."

Marta laughed, slid over next to him, and kissed him on the neck.

Eduardo put his arm around her shoulders; then he turned to talk to me too.

"No one needs to sleep here, have you noticed? It's the only way to live. We must never sleep again."

"Watch the road," I said.

And he and Marta laughed.

We took the highway toward the house and Eduardo started singing again. The wind blowing through the windows already had the salty flavor of the sea, and I realized I didn't want to get there either and felt an absurd excitement, a desire to have the wind pick us up and take us somewhere else. Suddenly, Eduardo slammed on the brakes, throwing me forward against the front seat, and I had to brace myself with my hands.

"What is it?" Marta said, moving away from Eduardo.

"'Cocoteros.' Maybe Rafael and Lorenzo are still here. Should we see?"

"Yes, let's go," I said immediately.

"There you go," Eduardo said. "That's what I like."

He made a U-turn and at full speed pulled into the hotel, which consisted of some six or seven bungalows scattered under the palm trees and a one-story building in the shape of a ship. On the terrace, around the swimming pool, and near the beach were the tables that made up the nightclub during the summer months. The music reached us as soon as we entered. The place was completely full. Marta and Eduardo got out at the same time and ran toward the tables. When I caught up with them, she was already in Rafael's arms, laughing, and Eduardo, a glass in his hand, was talking loudly with Lorenzo; Celia and another couple were also at the table. Someone put a glass in my hand. I felt a bit dumbfounded by the noise and tried to straighten my windblown hair before sitting next to Celia.

"Cheers," said the young man next to me.

I raised my glass mechanically and took a sip. Marta went to dance with Rafael.

"How was dinner?" Celia asked me.

"Fine, just fine," I said, still trying to straighten my hair.

I saw Lorenzo next to me and his glass hit mine.

"Toast with me, too."

There was a bottle of rum on the table and another of gin, and everyone was drunk. Eduardo, still standing, was shouting more than talking to the couple whose names I couldn't remember, turning once in a while to look at the dance floor. Someone tapped me on the shoulder. It was the young man from the plane.

"Want to dance?"

"Make him happy," Lorenzo said almost simultaneously.

I stood up and let him lead me by the arm, feeling a little ridiculous. Although the dance floor was very large, it was so full you could barely take a step without running into someone. He slipped his arm around my waist. I let him draw me to him but avoided his face, leaning my head slightly to one side. After a moment, he tightened his grip on my back and I felt his knee searching for mine.

"Do you like to dance?" he asked very formally, but bringing his mouth to my ear.

When I answered I pushed away from him a little, but he embraced me even more forcefully and pressed his cheek against mine. My gaze suddenly met Rafael's; he was dancing with Marta but staring at me. Then he disappeared among the other couples.

I danced the next three or four numbers with the young man, not saying anything, letting his knee slip between mine and his right hand rest against my breast so I wouldn't have to fight him, feeling alien and distant; then at last I saw Rafael next to us.

"My turn to dance now," he said.

"I'm dancing," the young man answered very seriously.

But I gave him a smile and told him I had to talk to Rafael. He left us, not deigning to answer.

"Did he give you a hard time?" Rafael asked.

"No, why? He's very nice."

He looked at me but didn't say anything. The orchestra began to play and I let him embrace me. The sensation of his body next to mine for the first time suddenly struck me, and I began to wonder what he felt. His arm barely brushed my back, but I leaned fully against him. I expected to feel something different that would allow me to discover what Rafael meant to me, but I only had the feeling that, in some way, the roles had reversed and now I had the part the young man had played with me. So to keep the game going, I brought my mouth to his ear and, adopting the formal tone the young man had used, I asked him if he liked to dance. Rafael moved back a little, as I had done before.

"I dance badly, don't I?"

I had to laugh.

"What's the matter?" he asked, disconcerted.

"Nothing," I said. "I'm happy."

Rafael embraced me again and I hid my face between his shoulder and neck. The previous sensation disappeared. Now I was alone with him, discovering his smell, a smell different from Pedro's. I tried not to think about anything. We didn't say anything else. The murmur of the sea, so close by, mixing with the music, made everything seem slightly unreal. Much later, I discovered Celia watching us as she danced with Lorenzo. Only then did I notice that there were fewer people on the dance floor, several tables were empty, and Rafael had embraced me completely. At our table, Eduardo sat alone, his head bowed a little, looking at the floor. I asked Rafael if we could sit down.

"Where's Marta?" he asked when we reached Eduardo.

Eduardo shrugged his shoulders.

"She left a minute ago. I think we had a fight."

"Over what?" Rafael asked.

Eduardo looked at us without seeing us and answered by shaking his head, trying to treat it as a joke.

"You know. The same old thing. The family, not the family, the family, not . . . Who the hell knows?"

"How did she go home?" I asked.

"I suppose she drove," Eduardo said. "She took the keys away from me . . . It's her problem. Don't worry. Keep dancing."

"Do you want to leave?" Rafael asked me.

I hesitated a moment, but I said that it would be pointless and I preferred to stay. Celia and the other couple also returned to the table.

"What happened?"

"Nothing," Eduardo explained. "Marta left. As usual."

"Hurray! Cheers," Lorenzo said, laughing and raising a glass.

"Cheers," Eduardo answered, imitating him.

"I think it's time to go," Celia said.

But Lorenzo answered that there was still a lot left in the bottles and besides, they had to keep Eduardo company, and he forced her to sit down. The other couple also sat down, but no one said anything. Now the mood reminded me of Eduardo's house. An absurd, joyless binge. I asked Rafael if we couldn't go and he leaned over to talk to Lorenzo, gave him some money, and stood up.

"We're leaving. Elena's tired," he explained, pulling my chair back so I could stand up.

"Whatever you want," Lorenzo answered for everyone.

The orchestra had stopped playing a moment before and the rustle of the wind in the palms made the almost empty nightclub seem sad and desolate, as if suddenly it too had been abandoned.

"How are you getting home?" Celia asked.

"Walking along the beach. Don't worry," Rafael responded.

He took my arm and we headed toward the shore, not turning to look at the others, but as soon as we left the club behind, he let go of my arm and we walked in silence, on the loose sand. I felt his presence and knew he was going to tell me something, but I liked waiting and almost wished that nothing would happen and we would go on like this, in silence, all the way to the house, perhaps because now everything seemed to have changed, letting me think it was possible to hope for something unexpected and different from him.

The House on the Beach

"Do you know what happened between Marta and Eduardo?" he asked me at last, turning to look back, as if suddenly he needed to make sure we were alone.

I wasn't expecting him to talk about Marta, and the question bothered me.

"No, but I can imagine," I answered. "Marta was upset from before. Dinner was very unpleasant."

"What happened?"

"Eduardo had an argument with his father about something to do with the business, and then his mother started crying . . ."

Rafael remained silent and I felt forced to add, "Does it happen very often?"

"Yes," he said and was quiet again. Then, suddenly, he kicked the sand. "How absurd, everything's so absurd! I don't understand why it always has to be this way. Don't you feel how foreign all of this is to us?" he added, making a gesture to encompass the sea and the beach around us. "We can have it all and yet nothing works out."

He changed his tone abruptly: "I only wanted to be with you."

"You are with me."

He stopped to try to see me in the darkness.

"Tell me about yourself. We've never talked about anything."

"What do you want to know?"

"I don't know. Sometimes everything and sometimes nothing. Whatever can be told."

"You know it already. I live in Mexico City with my mother and my two brothers, I work . . ."

"You're right. We don't have to talk," he said, as if now he wanted to change the subject.

We had walked very slowly, but the nightclub was out of sight and the line of summer houses had not come into view. On the side opposite the sea, beyond the thin fringe of sand, the palm trees could be heard more than seen. Rafael took my arm again and we walked on in silence very close to the sea. I thought that if he had tried to kiss me before, I would have let him, and I wondered why he hadn't done it while we were dancing, because he must have noticed that I desired him. On the other hand, now I felt distant from him. I remembered Héctor and for an instant I was tempted to bring up Pedro, if only to talk about something of my own, but I didn't, and when a moment later he asked me to stop, once again I wished he would try something. Without looking at him, I sat down on the sand, with my arms around my legs and my head resting on my knees. Far away, the long line of lights of the Progreso pier looked like an enormous worm, lost in the darkness. The sea's existence was merely a black rumble and only the sand reflected the light of the stars.

"I don't know what to say," Rafael murmured, at my side.

"You don't have to say anything," I answered, without raising my head from my knees.

I felt his hand on my back and then on my neck, and I turned to let him kiss me. He embraced me, reclined me back on the sand, and lay on top of me, still kissing me. I felt his hands on my body and I wished that we were naked so he could take me, but at the same time I was too aware of him and of myself to really desire him. I slipped away and sat up again.

"I think I love you," he said, still lying on his back, looking at the sky.

"Me too," I answered, but I stood up and offered my hand to help him up.

He tried to pull me down, but I forced him to get up, not knowing exactly why, and when we started walking toward the house again, I began telling him about my childhood, my brothers, and even Pedro, aware of being happy and wanting to be with him, but also knowing that I was talking to keep him from kissing me before he knew more about me, before we reached a point that I was unable to define at that moment.

Nevertheless, in front of the house, he embraced me again and we kissed for a long time, until he stepped back.

"We'll talk tomorrow," he said.

"Yes, tomorrow," I answered, waiting for him already.

When I went inside and turned on the light, I saw Marta in a chair, wearing her nightgown, but awake.

"What are you doing here?" I asked, surprised.

"I was waiting for you. Where's Eduardo?"

"He stayed with Celia and Lorenzo. I walked back along the beach with Rafael."

"Oh," she said without moving. "I found several letters for you in Eduardo's pocket. He must have forgotten to give them to you. I think they're from Pedro. I left them in your room."

"Fine. Do you want me to wait with you?"

"No. You must be tired. I'd rather wait alone," she said.

VII

After Marta's last trip to Mexico City, I was lonelier than ever. With the memory of the months already spent without Marta, her father felt her departure more than anyone, but for the same reason, he refused to accompany her to the airport, claiming that he could not leave his office at that hour. So I went with Marta. After we said good-bye, unable to see her as she moved down the hallway, I ran up to the observation deck and stayed there, staring into the empty space where the plane had disappeared among the clouds, feeling that I hadn't told her any of the things I had wanted to tell her and would never be able to, because the separation was definite and if we saw each other again nothing would be the same, wanting to scream loud enough for her to hear me, asking her to stay, so we could return to the past, to the first day when she talked to me in high school, but in a different way, not repeating any of the unexplainable things that now made those years seem lost, lived without having lived them, preparing for this absence of youth that gave us nothing in exchange, and thinking, also, that even if I could do it, maybe she wouldn't understand and would answer, with her newly found, calm smile, that I was trying to escape the inevitable, inventing a past no better than what we had now.

From the airport I went to the university, trying to recognize the city along the way, looking for the beauty we had found before at every corner. Since Marta had left, I hadn't made new friends at school, only the occasional acquaintances Marta and I secretly used to make fun of, but now I had to choose among them or be alone. I tried to concentrate during the lecture to overcome the feeling of emptiness, but when it ended, I felt the same, and I didn't go to the next class. For a moment I thought about calling Héctor and I went to a phone determined to do it, but I knew it wouldn't help. He would try to take me to his world, and I couldn't tell him what I felt because my tie to the past was, according to him, the real cause of our separation, and he couldn't bear any mention of it. I went home and shut myself in my room, furious with myself and exhausted.

When I wrote Marta, I didn't mention any of this. In her letters, she only told me what she had done and talked about her plans. At the bottom, Eduardo always jotted a hello, and his small addition made me feel, more than anything else, the difference that existed between us. Every time I wrote her, I assumed that Eduardo was going to read my letter and I tried to adopt an appropriate tone for both of them, although I couldn't keep from alluding to our secret jokes. For her part, she was still happy and satisfied, and her tone made me feel how difficult it must have been for her to accept the vague sensation of nostalgia I was trying to communicate to her. I studied more than ever and stayed home most of the time.

With his wife's help, my brother insistently tried to get me back together with Héctor and kept me up-to-date on what he was doing.

During this time, my few childhood memories kept coming back to me. The changes I noticed in my mother and my brother's visits with his son made the passing of time more tangible. When I used to go to the red brick school in front of the park, two blocks from my house, dressed in my uniform, I was as lonely as I was now. Every day, after school, I turned to look at it for a moment, as if fearing that I had forgotten something. The building didn't even exist anymore and, despite my efforts, I could barely remember the name of one of my first teachers or what some of my classmates looked like. None of them had ever visited my house, nor had I ever seen them again after I left the school. On the other hand, when I passed the park, I remembered my father sitting on a bench with my brother while I jumped rope, stirring up those small brick-colored clouds of dust that still form when the wind blows through the park. But as I reminisced, these memories seemed to belong to someone else and I could barely imagine myself in those circumstances.

In the meantime, Marta's son was born. I didn't find out from her but from her father, who called, happy, to tell me that Marta and Eduardo wanted him to be the godfather and he was leaving for Mérida. From then on, Marta stopped writing almost completely, and I felt my few letters had to seem more distant to her each time. One night, at her father's house, I saw a picture of her son and, sitting with him in the living room where Marta and I had spent so many afternoons together, I found out, before she wrote to tell me, that she was pregnant again. It was my next-to-the-last year at the university and I was starting to think about my thesis. Whenever I saw him, Marta's father talked about her in the only way I could understand, forever held in the time she had lived in that house, but I saw very little of him, because in spite of the affection and even the pity I often felt for him, he was her father and between us there still existed the distance I had sensed between him and Marta, which I never felt when I talked to my mother or brothers. Besides, to avoid being alone, and forced by the need to study with someone, I had made a new friend. Marta and I had met her at the university and talked to her a few times because she seemed the only one among our classmates worth the effort, but with our natural aversion to mixing with people, we'd never become friends. Her sister, two years older, used to pick her up at school; one night they offered me a ride home and I began to see more of them, first mostly Lucía, because we could study together at her house or mine; but later, when the three of us started going out, I got to know the other one, Cristina. She had finished secretarial school and was working already and, from her different experience, she looked at us sometimes with a certain envious nostalgia and at other times with an amiable superiority because we were still in school.

When we started talking more openly, Lucía told me she had always liked me but thought I was utterly dominated by Marta, and only now did she understand that it had been the other way around. I thought this was very funny and immediately wrote to Marta, telling her many other things about them as well that in the beginning amused and surprised me, especially in their relationship as sisters, and about what Cristina's life-style revealed to me. The whole world of offices, with the bosses making passes at Cristina and the employees grouping into a ridiculous community, seemed terrifying and made me wish my university years would never end. Cristina felt the same way and wanted to get out of it, but her plans were very different; it fascinated me to listen to her talk about them. When Lucía and I would finish studying, the three of us would go for coffee, or sometimes out to dinner, if Cristina invited us. Then she would start to talk, in a manner somewhere between cold and desperate, about her plans. More than anything, she wanted to stop working, have money, and live comfortably, and to attain all this the only logical thing to do was to marry the right man. She had been in love with a guy who worked in the same office, but though she still missed him and remembered their relationship as something exciting and marvelous, she had refused to go to bed with him and had managed to end it because she knew that wasn't what she wanted. But in spite of the apparent coldness with which she talked about them, her goals imposed something painful on her, and I could never help feeling that she was paying too high a price for them, especially when she would pick us up at school and I'd notice her well-intentioned envy because we were still studying and had greater independence, though in exchange we couldn't buy clothes like hers and had to let her pay for dinner.

Lucía loved her as much as she respected and admired her, but in reality there was a strange lack of intimacy between them. Both of them told me about their adventures separately and in that respect they seemed to live in two different worlds, voluntarily ignoring what they were really capable of, although it was never much because even Lucía didn't have any interest beyond winning a scholarship to go anywhere outside of Mexico. Although I never became as close to them as to Marta, I was comfortable with them. Lucía was a magnificent student and helped me a lot. Her parents— naive, rather than unpretentious—treated me with enormous consideration, and my mother liked her right away. Besides, my youngest brother, who was also at the university, very nearly fell in love with her. Lucía confessed it to me, laughing, which upset me a little, but when I saw her clumsy shyness around men and her inability to play any kind of seductive games with them, I couldn't understand it. We studied, and in the meantime the only thing we accumulated was time. My plans for the future were limited to getting my degree and, vaguely, finding a job, while their goals were completely foreign to me; I didn't want to get married or continue studying indefinitely no matter where. I was happy at home; I liked going to the movies with Cristina and Lucía; once in a while I went out alone, or in a group with some man, without being particularly interested in any of them; I didn't lack anything. Cristina finally found the boyfriend she wanted and through him I met an engineer whom I started dating. I liked him a little and one night very nearly went to bed with him, but then the idea of going to bed with everyone merely because I liked them annoyed me, so I stopped seeing him. That's how the year ended, and in the following one I had to start preparing my thesis. I chose my adviser and after a few meetings with him, I realized I liked him and he also liked me.

The House on the Beach

In his courses he had been very friendly, which was probably why I chose him as an adviser for my thesis, but I never thought it could be anything else. When I realized he was interested in me, I decided to go ahead with it, out of curiosity more than anything else. He was married. My male classmates claimed he fooled around with the female students and many of them teased me when they started seeing me leave the university with him. He knew it and treated the male students with a kind of condescending superiority that made me admire him in the classroom, but now, when we were alone, the superiority disappeared and, in the middle of the guidance and suggestions for my thesis—which only thanks to him started to interest me—I had to wait several weeks before he decided, in his office one afternoon, to hold my hand, with a gesture somewhere between casual and intentional, which, nevertheless, disturbed me a great deal. Up until then he mentioned his wife and children normally, but from that afternoon on he stopped, and we started meeting at out-of-the-way coffeehouses instead of in his office. At the beginning, the contrast between his self-confidence in public and his shyness with me increased my fascination. For several days all he did was hold my hand once in a while and look at me affectionately, without our conversation going beyond the impersonal level except for brief comments about my clothes and hair, even though he no longer respected the distance that was natural between professor and student and the kinds of places where we met brought us closer together. One night he invited me to dinner and when we were leaving, he tried to kiss me in his car. I didn't let him, but afterward he confessed he loved me and for more than half an hour he explained what I meant to him, joking about himself once in a while, but never asking me how I felt. When I got out of the car I kissed him on the cheek, and he promised to call me the next day "to see how I was doing." My mother and brother had gone out and the empty house bothered me, but it was too late to call Cristina or Lucía. I sat on the living room couch, unable to shut myself in my room as usual. Whenever he talked to me, the professor had constantly used words like "freshness" and "youth"; now that aspect of the conversation disturbed me the most. I didn't feel young, but without a doubt, independently of my state of mind, my youth was an irrefutable fact in relation to him, who must have been around forty-five. And all of a sudden I liked my youth; it made me feel strong and happy, revealed to me as a kind of quality from which I could still expect many things.

The following day I told Lucía everything. She had heard a few comments and had seen me leave with the professor, but now she got very scared. She told me I had to prevent anything from happening, for my sake and his, but above all for mine, because while I had nothing to gain, on the other hand I would experience a lot of grief. That night, at her house, lying on the beds in her room, smoking and drinking coffee, with the books and notebooks still open on her small desk, while her parents watched television in the living room and voices from the set reached us, we told Cristina. She, too, advised me, very seriously, to be careful. She was getting ready to go out to dinner with her boyfriend; she had definitely separated from us by then, but still, once in a while, when he had a business appointment, she'd pick us up at school, and though we didn't do more than go for a cup of coffee or to a movie, she assured us that those were her only moments of fun. The fact that they felt I was going through a special and very delicate situation made me feel good and increased my interest in the professor. I wrote to Marta telling her what was happening, trying to adopt the same humorous tone as always, and she answered more quickly than usual, saying she remembered the professor perfectly well and advising me to "go for it." Her answer made me feel the difference between the life I had shared with her and the one I led at present. Even by letter, it was much easier to talk to her than to Cristina and Lucía, and her advice had the residue of a loyalty to our old dreams. When I showed the letter to Lucía, she assured me that Marta didn't believe anything she told me and was only trying to play my game. It bothered me for a moment; then I preferred to think that maybe she was right, but I liked the fact that Marta had answered me the way I had expected. Nevertheless, nothing ever happened with the professor. He didn't call and the next time I saw him, he treated me as if he had forgotten everything he had said, although once in a while I caught him looking at me, and both of us were very nervous. His silence offended me at first and I even thought I was in love and wanted to go to bed with him, but this state of mind only helped make the time I had to spend on my thesis more interesting. I would go to see him with expectation and always came away with the feeling that we were prolonging some sort of waiting period. He behaved with the same pleasant formality as before, avoiding my eyes and making me regret not having taken advantage of the opportunity the day he talked to me; now his attitude made me feel my youth as a disadvantage. I talked endlessly about him with Lucía and wondered why I'd never noticed before that I liked him. Meanwhile, I killed time with other men, not really being with anyone, feeling a desperate uselessness.

The day I turned in my thesis, he again invited me to dinner. It was early and we went to a restaurant in Las Lomas, which at that hour looked enormous and deserted. Along the way, while I watched the light filtering through the trees, I wished it would get dark all at once, arbitrarily. The professor ordered two martinis, without asking me, and it hit me that he was going to try to seduce me like a whore. I felt an absolute hatred, more than anything, for all the time he had made me lose, leading me on to think of him as something better, so I didn't respond to any of his moves, reacting with cold disgust each time he tried to insinuate something. When he dropped me off, I shut myself in my room to cry, furious with myself; later I didn't even want to tell Lucía what had happened, not for his sake, but for mine.

At the beginning of the next term, I took my professional examination. My older brother and my mother, with Lucía's help, insisted so much that I had to let them put together a graduation party for me, although I didn't feel like inviting anybody; since the dinner with the professor I hadn't gone out with anyone. Knowing he would be among the examiners, instead of calming me, made me more nervous, increasing my fear, but I was sure that in spite of everything he would help me. That morning Marta sent a telegram of congratulations, and her father came to the university for the examination. As nervous as I was, his presence moved me more than anyone else's. I had asked my mother not to attend, but when I saw him, I wished she were there, sitting next to him. He kissed me, moved as well, and said something about Marta. I told him about her telegram.

"It would have been nice if she had been here," he commented. "I can still see you perfectly, studying with her in the house. And I miss you both. You should visit me more often. We don't know anything about you anymore."

"I'm the same," I said, sincerely.

Then I entered the room and passed the exam enveloped in a kind of fog, feeling my friends and the interested spectators behind me like a heavy weight, trying to avoid the professor's gaze, and listening to my own answers, surprised by the false security I was progressively revealing and hearing my own voice as if someone were speaking for me. When it ended, I didn't realize it was over. People were hugging and kissing me, though I didn't know who. At the end, Marta's father came up to say good-bye, apologizing for not attending the party. In the car, while my sister-in-law and Lucía explained to me how well I had done, and my brother turned every other moment to look at me proudly, I began to feel an enormous sadness, as if everything had abruptly ended forever, without leaving me anything in its place.

On the other hand, at the party, everyone around me was overjoyed. Cristina came with her fiancé. We got drunk right away and started making fun of him, but she soon regretted it and quickly left. Feeling out of place in the midst of the noise, I saw Héctor enter. He came straight over and embraced me. It had been more than two years since I had last seen him and I was happy he had come. He was very excited.

"I had to come to congratulate you. I hope my presence doesn't bother you," he said after hugging me with that rugged and clumsy tenderness I knew so well.

"Of course not, on the contrary," I answered sincerely. "Come on, let's dance."

I introduced him to Lucía, who looked at him surprised, making me laugh, and I danced with him the whole time. When the guests started to leave, my sister-in-law suggested that we go to a nightclub, and I asked Héctor to accompany us, under my brother's approving eye. There, Héctor told me he still loved me. As before, his seriousness, timid and intense, which always gave me the impression that his feelings had to fight their way through something, bothered me again, but I let him kiss me, pretending to be more drunk than I actually was, and then asked him if he wanted to go to bed with me.

"No," he said. "What I want is to get back together in a different way. What happened before was all my fault."

I was moved, but instead of answering in the same tone, I insisted, "And if I asked you?"

"Not even then," he said. "But do you really want to ask me?"

"No," I answered, about to cry, full of an absurd self-pity. "Please take me home. I'm tired."

My brother's jokes when we said good-bye depressed me even more. In the car, Héctor put his arm around my shoulders and asked me what was wrong. I started to cry like a little girl, unable to restrain myself or to understand why I wasn't happy. His presence saddened me, but at the same time I wanted to hold on to it, as if it represented a reality I didn't want to go back to, but that was, nevertheless, better. When I said good night, I asked him to please not come back again. He accepted with the same exasperating, touching seriousness, and then, alone in my bed, I regretted having done it, but I knew I wouldn't call him either. Before going to bed, I had sat for a long while in the living room with the lights off, among the half-empty glasses, the ashtrays full of smelly butts, and the furniture in disarray, trying to figure out what Héctor had meant to me—he had been the first one—forcing myself to believe that now that I was through with school forever, I had to start something different, remembering myself, still a child, doing my homework in that same living room while my mother listened to the radio, unable to imagine any scene in the future, disconcerted because I wasn't happy about my success.

Lucía graduated a little later and left Mexico; before that, Cristina finally got married, exactly as she had planned, to her rich, stupid boyfriend. I attended both the wedding and Lucía's examination with the feeling that, in spite of everything, they had never been my friends, thinking about the letter I would write Marta to make fun of all the details.

Six months before graduation, I had started working in a law firm. But though the job was easy and it kept me busy, it gave me no satisfaction. Now, with the degree, nothing changed. Some class-mates got in touch with me and we talked endlessly about setting up our own law firm, but since no one had a penny, the project seemed too risky and we finally abandoned it. I started to look for another job, simply to earn more money, and thanks to a professor's recom-mendation, I found one; nevertheless, the idea of being a "lawyer" still seemed strange to me. When Marta and I were in high school, the years at the university looked endless, and they were the only future we could imagine. Now, just like that, in an absurd and unexpected way, everything had ended, and I hadn't found anything to take its place; time opened before me without any deadlines that could at least fix my mind on a firm goal. I wrote Marta about it and she sent me a long, nostalgic, and moving letter, advising me in one paragraph to get married, then contradicting herself in the next, assuring me that in spite of everything I was closer to our dreams and shouldn't stop until I knew for sure how far I could go. She was already living at the house on the beach and described her days in a tone that, though too unreal, nevertheless revealed her happiness.

The atmosphere at Cristina's house was unbearable, above all because her husband never left us alone, and I stopped seeing her almost entirely. Lucía wrote me some enthusiastic letters from Europe. Once in a while I thought about Héctor and, in the meantime, I attended some weddings, went out with different friends, saw how most of them were starting to live the way their university years had predicted and how others dropped out of sight and then reappeared, sometimes turned into different persons, with political appointments or unbelievable jobs, to invite me to dinner at some elegant restaurant and proposition me, more out of habit than desire, showing me at the same time pictures of their wives and children with much more enthusiasm. I earned plenty of money and for a while I thought I should live alone or visit Lucía in Europe, but my mother begged me not to leave her and I realized she was right. At home I had the freedom I needed and was much more comfortable than anywhere else, and I didn't go to Europe mainly because Pedro started working at the firm.

I vaguely remembered having seen him at the university, although he must have graduated several years before me. His first weeks at the office he hardly spoke to anyone, though he always said hello to me, and several times I caught him staring. He always wore the same style of sport coat, and his tall, slender figure had something fluid about it that made his movements very pleasant. We got used to smiling every time our eyes met and at last, one afternoon, we ran into each other as we were leaving work and he invited me for coffee. He had a beat-up old car that somehow went well with his figure. He told me he was divorced and had a son. Then he changed the subject, but a moment later he was talking about his son again and showed me a picture of him, as if that was something he didn't want me to forget. I felt like asking him why he had gotten a divorce, but I realized he didn't like talking about himself. We both felt at ease and talked for hours. When we left, it was already dark. He asked me if I wouldn't like to go to a movie.

"I must confess that I don't like being alone," he added with a smile that was intended to lessen the seriousness of the statement.

I accepted, and later we had dinner. I told him I had to call home and only then he asked me with whom I lived. The subject of the university came up and, without giving it much importance, he said he remembered me and had recognized me right away. To prove it, he said I was always with the same friend and asked me about her. Unconsciously, I started talking nonstop about Marta and those days. For a long while he listened to me with a slight smile without interrupting, one elbow on the table and his chin resting on his hand, and suddenly he commented, happily, "You're very young."

"And you're not?" I said defensively.

"Yes, me too," he said, laughing. "Don't think I'm offering to protect you."

And it struck me that I had reacted the same way I used to when Marta and I started dating. When he dropped me off, I realized that it had been a while since I had felt comfortable with anyone, and knowing I would see him the next day at the office made me feel secretly happy.

Very soon, we got used to leaving together, ignoring the stupid rumors about us that started to drift around the office. Some weekends he would come to my house and we would just stay there. He had a true passion for music and could spend hours listening to records, not minding if I talked in the meantime. He would arrive with new records under his arm and calmly settle on the living room couch to listen to them, hardly talking, once in a while glancing at me, and drinking coffee the whole time. Then he would stay for dinner and talk to my mother about his son or discuss politics with my youngest brother, adopting a totally skeptical attitude. My opinions made him laugh and he always sided with my brother against me. I knew I didn't love him, but sometimes the naturalness with which he accepted everything exasperated me. Although whenever something I said made him laugh he would caress my hair with a quick, affectionate gesture, and he always made kind remarks about the way I was dressed and said he liked my mouth or my neck, he never even tried to hold my hand. One day, I had had enough; while we were having dinner at a restaurant, I asked him why he went out with me.

"Because I like you very much," he responded without hesitation, looking at me very seriously.

After a moment of silence, he added, "You know what? I don't know if you've noticed, but before I met you I was very lonely. You've been marvelous. You are marvelous."

Embarrassed and without thinking, I asked him why he had gotten a divorce.

"For no reason and for every reason you can think of," he answered. "We were no longer in love. I was her boyfriend for several years and I think I married her because I thought I had to."

"But why did you get a divorce?" I insisted.

"It's not easy to live with somebody you no longer love. And maybe I'm a difficult person. We fought a lot. It wasn't good for our son, or for us. Now my wife is better off; we're even good friends. Civilization . . . ," he ended ironically.

I kept quiet and he added, after hesitating for a moment, "Do you want me to tell you I love you?"

"I don't know," I said, suddenly frightened. "Is it true?"

"Of course," he answered.

I laughed, not knowing why, feeling a great happiness, as if knowing I had achieved something difficult and I liked it, but at the same time I felt scared again.

"I don't understand you," I said.

"What don't you understand?"

"Everything. I don't understand anything. Your way of saying it. I don't think it's true you love me. The problem is that you're alone, as you just said."

"No. It is true. And I'd like you to love me."

"Do you want me to tell you?"

"Yes."

"I love you."

Now it was his turn to laugh; he moved toward me but held back to stare at me, as if wanting to verify its truth.

"What are we going to do?" he said then.

"Nothing. Continue as we are," I answered.

"No. There are so many things I want to explain to you and I'd like you to tell me everything I don't know about you. But I'd rather start."

He began telling me about his marriage, trying to explain why it had failed, taking all of the blame and insisting on his indifference and on what, according to him, his wife called his "selfishness."

"Deep inside," he ended gravely, "I think she was right. It's true, I was unfaithful once, but it wasn't important. I liked her more than anyone else, but not enough. It's hard to live with someone, and the bad part about me is that I have no ambition. Nevertheless, I love my son. And now I love you. It hurts. Although I knew it was going to happen."

"Why does it hurt you?" I broke in. "I like it."

"I don't know what I can give you, or what you expect. And I'd like to make you happy," he answered. "Deep inside, I respect your kind of beauty. I've admired it always, since we were at the university . . . It was strange to run into you again."

Except for us, the restaurant was empty, and one of the waiters patiently waited a few steps away from the table. Pedro looked at him for an instant, then asked me, "Shall we go?" with the tone I already knew he used every time he wanted to change the subject, creating something like a pause.

Outside, we walked to his car in silence. The sky was clear, full of stars, and it was cold. I felt like taking his arm to get closer to him, but all the natural intimacy of our relationship seemed to have disappeared. Before we got in the car, he turned to me.

"Do you want to come to my house?" He paused and added, "To see it, really. And to tell me about yourself."

We laughed and I kissed him on the cheek.

I already knew where he lived, but I thought, as we climbed the stairs to the sixth floor, that the building revealed new things about him. The stairs were poorly lit, with that yellow light that seems to stain everything, and the wall had a sad, old appearance, neglected rather than dirty, but when I told Pedro, he confessed that he had never noticed. Before opening the door, he stopped to warn me, "The place is a mess. The cleaning lady hasn't been here in three days."

The apartment had a living room and a bedroom, plus a huge kitchen and a tiny bathroom, without a tub and without a shower curtain to keep the water from splashing on the floor. In the living room there was a studio couch with several pillows on it, three wicker chairs, a low, long, and narrow table covered with unwashed dishes, magazines, record jackets, and dirty ashtrays, the record player, and an unfinished piece of furniture for storing records, with a few books on it. The other room had a bed with a small end table and more magazines on the floor. None of the light bulbs had lamp shades, there were no curtains on the windows, and the raised venetian blinds gave the impression of not having been lowered in a long time. The kitchen, which had an old stove, was an absolute mess.

"What do you think?" Pedro asked, after leading me by the hand through the whole apartment.

"It's very much you. This is the way I imagined it. But lower the blinds. I feel like I'm being watched," I answered.

"It's not necessary," he went on, taking me to the window. "Look, there's no building in front. During the day you can see the mountains. It's very beautiful."

Then he put on a record and asked me if I wanted some coffee.

We prepared it together and, to drink it, we had to wash two cups in which old coffee had dried and stuck to the bottom. Then we sat in the living room and he kissed me for the first time. I started telling him about Héctor, but he moved closer and, very slowly, began to unbutton my blouse; then he stopped, kissed me again, kissed me once more, picked me up, and carried me to the bed. There he finished undressing me very slowly and we made love with the same patience, searching for each other with affection, with him pausing at every moment to look at me and find me again, until I could only think about being there with him in a way at the same time both absolute and calm.

We spent the next few weeks making changes in the apartment. I bought curtains, although Pedro assured me that they were unnecessary because he would always want to be able to look outside, shades for the light bulbs, and finally a table. Pedro accompanied me to the stores and once in a while disagreed with some of my suggestions, but in the end he always laughed and gave in. I felt as if I was really with somebody. One night, in bed, after making love, I said I would like to spend the night with him.

"You can," he answered right away, with a happy expression, leaning on one elbow and resting his face on his hand to look at me.

"No," I said. "Mother likes you very much. I don't want to let her down."

I kept quiet for a moment and then added, "Would you marry me?"

"Yes," he said. "If you want."

"It's better not to talk about it. We're perfectly okay this way," I answered, regretting having asked the question, although I knew we would have to face it someday . . .

He hugged me and that same night we decided we would continue this way until one of us felt it was really necessary to make a change. I got home very late and found my mother waiting up for me; she spoke to me from her room as soon as I turned on the light in mine, but neither she nor my brother said anything, because they liked and trusted Pedro.

From then on, Pedro tried to make me see that he respected my independence, but I didn't feel any need to exercise it. I was with him most of the time, and little by little we got used to going out with my brother and his wife and other friends, as a couple. One Sunday he wanted me to meet his son, and we spent the afternoon with him. He was two years old and it wasn't hard to win him over, but I didn't feel as if he was related to Pedro or close to me, and we repeated the experience very few times. This detail helped to establish even more the tone of our relationship. Pedro made a few jokes about my lack of motherly instinct, but our love didn't change. I knew I loved him and could always be with him in an absolute way, because we both accepted each other completely. Nevertheless, when Marta wrote inviting me, I suddenly became aware of how long I had been seeing Pedro; I accepted the invitation thinking, in part, that I would like to find out if I would miss him. On my last night in Mexico City we went to his house, and he said that when I returned I'd find it as messy as the first time. He was a little sad, talked about the countless times we had planned to take a trip together, and asked me several times to think about him. But even though we were together, and I knew I loved him the same as always, I realized that I liked going away alone.

VIII

Among the letters I found in my room that night, in addition to the three from Pedro, which I barely read, there was one from my mother with a few lines from my oldest brother at the end teasing me that Héctor had gotten married and I had lost my chance. It didn't affect me at all. None of that seemed to have happened to me, but to another person I hardly recognized. Undressed and with the light off, looking through the window toward the darkness of the sea from which I could only hear its rhythmic pounding, suddenly I remembered that I had forgotten to ask Rafael why he hadn't stopped to talk when he passed by the house that afternoon and, more than anything, the absurd need to ask him increased my impatience for the next day to come so I could see him again, as if the whole relationship depended on a question that I now understood to be unimportant. I slept, sure it would be the first thing I would ask him, but contrary to what I expected, he didn't show up until after midday, and by then the urgency of the night before had disappeared and I had so much to tell him I forgot about the question.

That morning, when I went downstairs, I was surprised not to find Marta with the boys, although it was already very late. While the nanny served me breakfast, she told me Marta had stayed up all night waiting for Eduardo and only went to sleep when she herself brought the boys down. Eduardo still hadn't arrived.

"That's too bad. I don't know why Don Eduardo does it, do you?" the nanny commented, shaking her head. "Where can he be at this hour after staying up all night?"

It was even harder for me to imagine where he could be. I told her I would ask Rafael as soon as I saw him, just to mention his name, and I returned to my room to put on my bathing suit. Before going downstairs I stopped for a moment in front of Marta's door, trying to listen for a noise that would indicate she was awake and pondering whether I should go in and talk to her, but in the end I decided it was better to wait. I sat in the living room to rub on some suntan lotion, and the boys came up to me. The nanny appeared right behind them and asked me if I wasn't going to take them to the beach. I said yes and, when she went up to get them dressed, I opened the curtains expecting to see Rafael arrive any minute.

Umbrellas covered the beach, and there seemed to be more people than ever. Motorboats pulling water skiers crisscrossed everywhere, children played along the shore, and farther out the sea was full of heads bobbing on the smooth waves. The morning's bright and happy appearance brought back to mind what had happened the night before. In some way, Eduardo's parents no longer belonged here. Even though the peacefulness and the silence of the house were those of any Sunday morning, something oppressive shattered the usual order. Upset, I went to the refrigerator to look for cigarettes. The cook, cleaning fish on the table, smiled when she saw me enter but didn't talk to me. Back in the living room, the nanny had already come down with the boys. I picked up my towel and a book, although I knew I would not be able to read, and went out with them, wondering what could have happened to Rafael.

The nanny followed the boys, who ran straight toward the sea, while I stayed near the terrace, lying on the sand, unable to divert my eyes from Celia and Lorenzo's house. Acquaintances said hello from afar, but no one came over, giving me the absurd sensation that they didn't want to ask about Marta and Eduardo. I lay on my stomach and opened my book, but a moment later, tired of flipping pages on which the sun glared and of not understanding anything, I went to play with the boys. Eduardito began to ask where his mother was and started to cry when I tried to take him into the water. I left him with the nanny and swam away. The water was warm, but there were too many people around me. When I got out, I saw Lorenzo walking toward me.

"How's the hangover?" he said.

He was wearing a shirt that covered his trunks.

"Just fine," I said, brushing the hair from my forehead to avoid looking at him. "Where's Celia?"

"She went to get the children dressed. She'll be right back," he answered. "How's the water?"

"Fabulous. As always," I said, bothered by his stare.

When I walked back to my towel, he followed me and sat down

silently. I could feel he wanted to tell me something but didn't know how to start.

"Eduardo's not back yet?" he finally asked.

"No. Do you know where he went?" I said, finishing drying off and covering my legs with the towel.

"To Progreso, I suppose. Or maybe all the way to Mérida. Rafael came back after he left you and they took off together."

The surprise kept me from saying anything for a moment.

"And Rafael hasn't returned either?" I asked then, trying to sound casual.

"No, he hasn't," Lorenzo said.

"Do you think something might have happened to them?"

He laughed.

"Oh, no! They do it all the time. Eduardo was very drunk, but Rafael wasn't. If something had happened, we'd know by now. How's Marta? Really upset?"

"She's sleeping. I think she waited up for Eduardo until dawn."

Lorenzo remained silent. I looked at his legs, too thin for the rest of his body, and I wondered what kind of life he had with Celia and what made Rafael and Eduardo seem to exist in a world different from theirs. Then I saw Marta's children, sitting on the sand with their nanny, oblivious to everything, and I realized that Rafael's absence bothered me less now that I knew he was with Eduardo.

The long white line of the beach, in which the color of the umbrellas and the movements of the swimmers looked like colorful ornaments, faded in both directions under the sun's brilliance high above and in front of us, over the peaceful immensity of a sea broken by the silver wakes of boats and the billowing whiteness of the sails. Lorenzo yawned and leaned back, propping his hands on the sand and turning his face to the sun.

"It's too bright to think about those things," he said. Then he sat forward, bringing his legs up to his chest and wrapping his arms around them. "Have you and Marta been friends long?" he asked, turning to look at me.

"Yes, I feel we've always been friends, but actually, if I think of all of you growing up together, it's not so long. I met Marta when we started high school. We must have been around fifteen. Why?"

"I don't know. You remind me of Eduardo and Rafael. They've always been inseparable. You and Marta look the same."

For the first time Lorenzo was talking to me naturally, but I didn't know how to react, because I no longer considered myself that close to Marta. The nanny brought the boys and told me it was late and she was going to get them dressed. I approved, adding that I would go in soon; then, just to say something, when the nanny left, I asked Lorenzo if he didn't want to get in the water.

"We'd better wait for Celia. She should be here any minute," he answered.

I wanted to keep talking to him, so to continue the conversation I asked him if he thought Eduardo and Rafael would be back sometime that day.

"Of course," he said. "They have to sleep. They can't take as much as they used to."

"You don't drink as much, do you?" I asked, regretting it right away. Lorenzo seemed to withdraw.

"We all drink," he answered.

We fell silent, with a feeling of uneasiness that we both tried to break without success. Celia came over a moment later, stopped in front of us, covering her eyes with her hand to protect them from the sun's glare, and asked Lorenzo if he wanted a beer. When he said yes, she turned to me.

"What about you, do you want one too?"

"Yes, I think so. It's hot," I said.

"I'll go get them. Where's Marta?"

"Sleeping," Lorenzo answered.

I realized that Celia was thinking of going to the house for the beers and I stood up, saying I would go for them, upset at not having offered Lorenzo one before.

"By no means," Celia said, putting a hand on my shoulder. "I'm also like part of the family. It's not important. You stay here. The sun bothers me."

"Forgive me for not offering you a beer before. I'm not good at these things," I told Lorenzo as soon as Celia left.

"Don't worry," he answered. "That's what she's here for." He made a gesture imitating Celia, and we both laughed. Then he added, "All of this must seem crazy to you."

"No. I like it very much. Honestly."

He smiled again.

"I don't doubt it," he said with no aggression.

"And all of you, what do you think of me?" I asked.

For a moment Lorenzo didn't answer.

"I can't speak for the others; I like you. I love Marta very much," he said then. "You shouldn't feel uncomfortable among us."

"I don't."

"In spite of everything, the people around here are nice," he went on. "You've probably noticed. Nothing's done maliciously. They're just traditions."

"And all of you defend them."

"Yes," he answered simply. "I don't know why. Maybe because they're worthwhile. Wouldn't you do the same?"

"I actually do," I said.

He laughed: "We're acting so serious!"

Celia came back with the beer. Marta appeared behind her and shouted from the terrace.

"Wait for me. I'm going to put on my bathing suit. I'll be right out."

Celia sat next to me on the other end of the towel, while Lorenzo and I drank our beer. She put her hand over her eyes again and commented, "Eduardo and Rafael aren't back yet. It's too much."

"Don't act so surprised. It happens all the time," Lorenzo answered.

"That doesn't make it right," she went on. "The bad part about it is that you men think it's so funny, but I'm sure Marta doesn't, and she's right."

In front of Marta, however, when Lorenzo started joking with her about Eduardo's absence, Celia joined in, and Marta went along with the joke, blaming Celia because Rafael was her brother, as if all three had to follow this ritual simply out of habit. I had stopped being conscious of waiting and it seemed better that way, but the anticipated encounter with Rafael was losing its charm.

We stayed on the beach much longer than usual, while Lorenzo drank one beer after another; Celia protested every once in a while because we refused to seek protection from the sun under the umbrella of some friend or another, although their friends were starting to leave little by little. Lorenzo had to give her his shirt, and then Marta went inside and brought her a hat. Finally, we were practically the only ones left on the beach, as if something prevented us from leaving. Without the swimmers, it now really felt like late afternoon, and although the sun was beginning to descend, its brilliance was just as intense; the solitary beach regained the wild appearance I had liked so much the first day. With Marta beside me, I felt exempted from having to pay attention to Celia and Lorenzo and I lay on my stomach, eyes closed, hearing the words they exchanged as a faraway murmur fading into the sound of the rising breeze. When I sat up again, I saw that Marta had gone swimming without telling me, but before I could get up to follow her, the nanny came out to tell us that Eduardo had just arrived and had gone up to his room.

"I can imagine the condition he's in," Celia commented, and Lorenzo laughed.

The three of us went to tell Marta; when she came out of the water, Celia said that they were leaving because Rafael must also have arrived. Lorenzo still made a last joke about the affection with which Celia cared for her brother, and I walked with Marta to the terrace, but then I told her I wanted to swim again and let her go in by herself.

From the water I couldn't avoid looking toward Rafael's house hoping to see him, but there was nobody on the terrace and only the glaring sun reflected on the first-floor windows, erasing the lines of the construction. I swam for a moment, feeling the pleasure of the warm water on my tanned body, wanting to take off my suit and have somebody touch me underwater, waiting again for Rafael as impatiently as that morning; then I went back to the house, crossing the beach slowly, tired and happy, with a foolish excitement.

Marta was in her room, and I got into the shower without seeing her. Trying to retain the shower's freshness, all I put on was a backless dress, and I went downstairs. Marta was sitting alone at the table.

"How's Eduardo?" I asked her.

"He's sleeping, of course. He couldn't even talk to me."

I sat down and asked her if she was angry.

"No, on the contrary. Sometimes I understand him perfectly. I wish I could do the same. What about you, how are you?"

"Me? I'm fine. Why?"

"You have to tell me what happened last night."

"What do you mean?"

"With Rafael. I've been wanting to ask you all day, but with Celia there it was impossible."

"Nothing. We walked along the beach. That's all."

She looked at me for an instant and started playing with a fork. I felt the silence between us. I don't know why I lied, but I told myself it was because I wanted to keep it to myself until there was something more concrete to tell.

The maid brought the first course, and we started eating.

"At least I'm terribly hungry," Marta said, and then added, "Do you like Rafael?"

"I don't know. I think so. He's very nice."

"And do you think he likes you?" Marta went on, still eating.

"I hope so!" I said, laughing.

She tried to smile.

Then we started talking about the dinner the night before. In spite of everything, Marta made excuses for Eduardo's father and attempted to combine her affection for him with her love for Eduardo, but on the other hand, she didn't try to hide her resentment of his mother.

"It's not all that great for her either," I said, trying to defend her.

"True," Marta answered. "But people who can only see one side of things exasperate me. You'd have to know everything they've gone through to understand it. The important thing is that nobody's guilty. Eduardo least of all. They educated him for one thing and now they have nothing to give him. That's it. His father understands it clearly. That's why he loses his patience. He never really gets angry at Eduardo, but at everything else."

In spite of the breeze, it was very hot. The food made me sweat. I wasn't hungry and everything bored me. Marta noticed and asked me what was wrong.

"Nothing. Why?" I lied.

"You're uneasy," she answered. "I still know you."

I smiled, defending myself.

"Sometimes I think I'm an idiot. I don't understand anything, and it exasperates me. You truly must explain it all to me."

"It's not so easy," Marta said. "Do you realize, for example, that this is the first time we've eaten alone?"

"Yes, I know, but . . ."

"But what?" she said, when I interrupted myself.

"I think you've changed a lot. For the better," I answered.

"No. I'm still the same," she insisted. "For better or worse. To the extent that I haven't dared to talk to you the way I would've liked. Simply because I can't, because I'm such a fool. I feel that once things are said they lose their meaning or they change, they become different, making you think it's not worth saying them."

I was very tense and felt frightened, without knowing why.

"Maybe that's where you've changed," I said, evading the issue and feeling guilty for it.

"Maybe," she went on, pensive. "Anyway, it's too late now."

"For what?" I asked timidly.

"For everything. Now I think we were always different."

"But that has always joined us."

"I feel close to you. And I like seeing you."

The nanny came down with the boys, who had just gotten up from their nap, and they sat at the table and started talking. The nanny stood next to them, looking at us with the open curiosity that she never considered it necessary to hide; Marta, exasperated, told her to take the boys for a walk along the beach, but we didn't continue our conversation anyway. As soon as we finished eating, she went up to see Eduardo, and Rafael arrived a moment later.

I was still at the table, smoking and looking at the ocean without seeing it, stupefied by the heat, and I didn't notice him until he said "hello" behind me. He was barefoot and shirtless, and you could tell he had just showered.

"Hi," I said, also, trying to smile in spite of my surprise. He sat across the table and stared at me, without talking.

"How are you?" he said then, as if before asking he had tried to find out for himself.

"How are you?" I answered.

"Exhausted."

He reached for the cigarette in my hand, took a puff, and put it out.

"I waited for you all morning," I said, getting up from the table and walking toward the terrace to keep the remark from sounding like a reproach.

The sun was shining on the terrace and the tiles were hot, but a strong breeze rustling through the palm trees produced a sensation of coolness. Rafael came up behind me, grasped my shoulders, turned me around gently, and very lightly kissed me on the mouth without embracing me.

"Eduardo was very drunk and couldn't come back," he said then. "I was pretty drunk myself."

"Where did you go?"

He was still holding my hands, but then he moved away and walked toward the terrace railing and leaned on it.

"To Progreso. And then to Mérida."

"I thought you weren't going back to the nightclub."

Rafael shrugged his shoulders.

"I'm like everyone else. I was curious. I don't know why, but you never know when something might happen." He paused and added, "We shouldn't talk about it. Come here."

I sat next to him and put one of my feet on top of his.

"Have you thought about me?" he asked.

"I don't know. More than anything else, I wanted to see you. It's too unreal. Two weeks ago I didn't know you. These things aren't suppose to happen."

"And the man you told me about last night?"

"I got a letter from him, several. But I could hardly read them. And I haven't written to him."

He kept quiet for a moment.

"I've thought about him; I've tried to imagine what he's like," he said then. "Do you love me?"

"I think so."

"Here?" he asked, making a gesture that encompassed the house, the beach.

"Does it matter so much?" I asked, upset.

"I don't know," Rafael said.

He put his arm around my shoulders and hugged me again. I felt his chest and legs against me. I caressed his back, recognizing his skin and breathing his smell, so different from all the others. He kept kissing me, moving his hand toward my breast, but never reaching it, although I was waiting for him; then he hid his head between my neck and shoulders, still embracing me. I thought it shouldn't matter to me if I loved him; it should be enough just to like him.

"I'd like to discover you," Rafael whispered just then in my ear.

Then he moved away again and took my hand.

"Come on, let's go inside. I don't want anyone to see us. Where's Marta?"

"Upstairs, with Eduardo. Why?"

"It was strange not seeing her with you."

Inside, we sat on the wicker sofa. Rafael ran his hand lightly through my hair, stood up, and took a few steps.

"I just thought of something. Would you like it if we went to Campeche?" he said then, turning to look at me.

"Who is 'we'?" I asked, surprised.

"The four of us. It'd be interesting, don't you think? There are too many people here now. You can't even take a step. And I'd love to have you to myself for a few days. Besides, the trip can be very beautiful. Campeche is worth seeing and we would stop at Uxmal, too. You must see the ruins. It'd be a change. You'd get to know the sea and the jungle, which is another sea, but in a different sense. Eduardo and I were talking about it last night. He's willing to take a few days off, and right now I can, too. How much longer are you planning to stay?"

As he talked he moved from one side to another, with a sudden enthusiasm, as if he was also convincing himself and the happiness created by the prospect of a trip had something to do with us.

"I'd like to go," I said, still surprised. "And I have the time. I was thinking about staying five or six more days. But I can't decide . . ."

He sat next to me again.

"Only five days?" he asked childishly.

I laughed.

"Rafael, don't be silly."

"Why?" he asked seriously. "Because I want you to stay?"

"Because it's absurd. Rafael . . . Your name still sounds strange to me. But I like saying it. It's a way of having you. Rafael. Can it be true?" I said sincerely, aware of his presence, trying to understand him and to find what I liked about him.

"Yes," he said. "I love you."

"Are you sure? Why?"

"Because I've seen you or because of what I imagine you are. You have to stay longer. As long as necessary."

"I can't."

"You have to. It's important," he said.

I didn't know what to answer, disturbed and unsure, and I kissed him on the cheek affectionately.

"Shall we go to Campeche, then?" he said.

"Yes, of course. But we still have to talk to Marta. We have to think about the boys."

"It's true," he answered somberly. "If only you and I could go alone . . ."

For an instant I thought that was what he had had in mind all along, but he added right away, "It can be arranged. The four of us have to go." Once again he seemed too young.

"When are you a doctor?" I asked him.

"All the time. Right now. Why?" he answered.

"Because I still can't imagine you anywhere else. I'd like to see you in Mérida, working. More than going to Campeche."

"If we go tomorrow, you can stop by my office. That would be perfect, don't you think?"

"And I'd also like to see your house there."

"It's not worth it," he answered. "It's a huge empty house. Celia and Lorenzo should live there. I get lost in it. But when they got married, they went somewhere else and I haven't been able to convince them. The house looks like Eduardo's, without parents. That makes it different."

"I thought you lived with Celia and Lorenzo."

"No. I live alone with my aunt. As a child I used to spend a lot of time at her house. She lived in Campeche. I thought Marta might've told you."

"No. We've talked very little about you," I said and realized that I didn't even know when his parents had died or remembered who told me they were dead. Rafael was only his own presence, and I actually knew nothing more about him, but it didn't bother me, at least not yet.

He had become serious and silent.

"What are you thinking?" I asked him.

"About what brought you here and us together."

"It's very simple: Marta," I answered.

"Yes. I know," he said, still serious.

At that moment Marta started coming down the stairs and stopped, surprised.

"I didn't know you were here," she told Rafael. "How can it be you're not sleeping? Eduardo's out like a light."

"See for yourself . . . ," Rafael said, getting up and going toward her.

Marta came down the rest of the way and asked him what we were talking about.

"A sensational plan," Rafael explained. "We're going to Campeche, Eduardo, you, she, and I."

"We can't," Marta answered. "You know I don't have anyone to take care of the boys."

She sat in front of me and said she thought I would have been in my room resting.

"Leave them with Eduardo's mother," Rafael insisted in the meantime.

"Impossible," Marta said, turning toward him. "It's too hot in Mérida, and they're not used to it. I couldn't do that to them."

"Then leave them with Celia and Lorenzo. I'll arrange it," he replied.

Marta looked at him, hesitating, but he kept insisting with the same enthusiasm as before, assuring her that he would take care of everything, and he managed to convince her. The three of us kept on talking about the trip, but the fact that Marta already knew the places and helped Rafael explain things about them to me seemed to unite them, leaving me apart. Nevertheless, we were all happy and tried to keep the excitement by returning to the topic over and over again.

Eduardo woke up close to nightfall. He came down in a bad mood, but with Marta's help Rafael also convinced him; the four of us went to talk to Celia and Lorenzo, because Rafael insisted that we should leave the following afternoon, spend the night in Uxmal, see the ruins in the morning, and go on to arrive at noon. Without a second thought, Celia agreed to take the boys. Eduardo and Rafael decided they would take Rafael's car to Mérida in the morning and we could pick them up in the afternoon. Afterward, both of them started talking to Lorenzo about the details of their binge; Celia and Marta laughed along with them, no longer giving it any importance. We stayed over for supper, and I was never alone again with Rafael. In front of everyone else, although he looked at me continuously and as he talked he addressed me specifically on several occasions, he didn't even try to hold my hand or do anything that might reveal that there was something between us. At the time I liked his discretion, but again it made me feel like a stranger. Around eleven Marta said that he must be tired and we had better go, and Rafael agreed with her. Lorenzo offered to take us in his car, but we decided that we preferred to walk back along the beach. Then, Rafael accompanied us to the terrace and took my hand for a moment, pressing it lightly.

"We'll talk tomorrow," he said very quickly, in a low voice.

"Yes, tomorrow," I said, as I had the night before.

Then he spoke to Eduardo for a moment, while Marta and I went down to the beach. When he joined us, Eduardo walked between the two of us and took me by the arm.

"It's tragic, but I'm not sleepy at all," he said.

Marta and I laughed. I thought that I was with them as Rafael was with Celia and Lorenzo and I felt happy.

"Shall we go to Progreso?" Eduardo whispered in my ear, without any real intention of keeping it a secret.

"No, we have to get ready for tomorrow, remember," I said, thinking Marta might want to be alone with him.

Nevertheless, it was true that it seemed impossible to go to bed. A soft breeze rustled through the palms and the moon traced a line of light over the sea; as they broke on the pale sand, with the same smooth, delicate rhythm as the breeze, the waves covered it for a moment with undulating shapes in continuous transformation. Eduardo kissed Marta's hair and took her in his arms, lifting her up. She let out a happy scream; for an instant I felt alone again, but not bothered by the sensation, experiencing it like a vague nostalgia, like the need for a presence that belonged to me, whatever it might be.

As if she'd noticed this, Marta came over to me when Eduardo put her down again.

"It's good to be happy, isn't it?" she said.

And she took me by the arm to continue walking.

When we got to the house, I went up to my room right away and from there heard Marta and Eduardo coming up the stairs, laughing and running; then the door to their room slammed. It wasn't hot at all. I threw myself on the bed still dressed and almost instinctively picked up Pedro's letters, which were still stacked on the nightstand. Even though I recognized each one of his words and could almost imagine his face as he wrote them, they talked to me about a world I could recall affectionately, but which I didn't want to return to at the moment. Nevertheless, in the last letter, Pedro complained about the lack of news from me and talked of listening to records all night, thinking about me; for a moment I saw myself in his apartment, secure and happy, and I reproached myself for not having discovered the touch of loneliness, so much a part of him, the night before. I decided to write to him, without feeling I would be betraying Rafael, because it simply didn't touch him, but before I started, I caught myself thinking what Rafael's letters would be like if he ever wrote me, and then there was a knock on the door.

I recognized Marta's voice asking me if I was still awake. I told her to come in and she opened the door. She was in her robe. She and Eduardo were having a drink in their room, and she invited me to join them. She had the ice bucket in her hand. I followed her out of my room and into theirs. Though there was a hammock, Eduardo was half sitting up in bed, probably naked, and pulling the crumpled sheet up to his waist. I had never been in Marta's room when they were both there and at first I was disturbed by the air of intimacy. Eduardo had a glass in his hand and a bottle of rum at his side. Marta put some ice cubes in his glass, served me and herself a drink, and lay on the hammock, her nude legs dangling toward the floor, swaying softly. I took a sip of my drink, still feeling uncomfortable, and sat on the edge of the bed.

"What are you doing still dressed?" Eduardo asked me. "You can't sleep either?"

"I was reading some letters," I answered.

"Oh!" Marta exclaimed, teasingly.

"Don't be stupid," I said. "I have to answer my mother. She's worried. From your descriptions, she thinks this is a primitive place."

"She's right," Marta said.

"Don't start," Eduardo warned her affectionately. He took a long sip of his drink and turned toward me. "You've found things, haven't you?"

Marta's attitude reminded me of one she used to adopt sometimes in high school when some guy came to her house. She had the same expression, a mixture of complicity and mockery. But now there was no tension. It was only a game the three of us enjoyed. My uneasiness disappeared, and I made myself more comfortable on the bed. Eduardo gave me a pillow so I could lie back; we all drank without talking for a moment.

"It seems as if you've always been here. It'd be perfect if you stayed," Marta said then and, almost without a pause, added, ". . . with us."

"Yes, maybe it'd be good," I said.

"Stay. I'm sure you're really bored in Mexico City," Eduardo went on.

"A little, yes," I admitted.

Eduardo sat up straight in the bed and pulled the sheet to cover himself.

"Mexico City is fine, but I remember when I met you I told Marta you weren't happy, didn't I, Marta?" Eduardo said with a somewhat naive but pleasant security.

Marta confirmed it with a nod and went on: "The boyfriend you had then was repulsive. Whatever happened to him?"

I told her that in one of the letters my brother mentioned that he had recently gotten married, and Marta asserted, "You're going to become a spinster. It's horrible when your boyfriends start getting married."

But Eduardo commented seriously, "You didn't lose anything."

Marta and I laughed, and she got up from the hammock and went to sit by him, leaning against him.

"What happened was that he made you self-conscious," she said, caressing him. Then she turned toward me. "Do you remember how shy he was? Poor thing . . ."

But then she continued, serious all of a sudden: "Those times weren't bad, and we used to have fun. At least now, I think we used to have fun. I don't know why the past always seems better when you reminisce. I don't know why I can't recall things when I try to imagine Mexico City; I always think about high school or maybe a little further back, before I met you. I must not have had a childhood, that's why I envy him and Rafael," she said, pointing to Eduardo. She smiled slightly and asked me: "Do you remember that when I met him I thought he was a tycoon?"

"Well, you see, you were wrong," Eduardo said.

Marta jumped up.

"Let's have another drink."

Maybe at that moment I could've really talked to her. We were never able to be so close again. It seemed to me that she understood everything I thought and felt. Nevertheless, the only thing I could do was ask her, in a false tone, if she really planned to stay up all night again.

"Maybe," she said.

But the magic had been broken somehow. I felt distant again and wanted to be alone or maybe very far away, with Rafael, with whom I still didn't share mutual memories. Marta served us the drinks and went to stand in front of the window, turning her back to us. I looked at Eduardo. He seemed very young, sitting on the bed, his hair in disarray. He took a sip, mechanically, and stretched out, yawning.

"I'm tired," he said then. "If you want, go and talk in Elena's room. I can't keep my eyes open."

Marta turned immediately and said, very quickly, "No, I'll stay with you."

I got up and she walked me to the door. There she kissed me on the cheek, putting her hand on my shoulder.

"Good night."

"Sleep well," Eduardo said from the bed, lying back down.

Marta closed the door. The house was totally dark, submerged in silence, but listening closely, you could hear the murmur of the sea. Without turning the light on, I went out through the hallway to the second-floor balcony to look at the sky. The breeze had died down and everything was still, wrapped in itself, in the middle of the night, a great distance from the cold and pale light of the moon that seemed to float in the emptiness of a cloudless sky. Suddenly the murmur of the sea frightened me, and I went back to my room, on tiptoe, though not knowing why. The crack of light under Marta and Eduardo's door had disappeared.

IX

We left for Campeche around five in the afternoon. That morning Rafael picked up Eduardo. It must have been very early. Still half asleep, I thought I heard his voice and then the sound of the car, but I couldn't manage to wake up. Marta and I spent the day moving the children over to Celia's, deciding what we would take on the trip, and closing up the house. We were able to spend only a moment at the beach. Amid all the work, she looked happy and excited. She laughed at everything and locked the house with the meticulous care and serenity of someone leaving for a long trip. We left for Mérida before the breeze started, around four, in a piercing, overwhelming heat. All the way in I had to fight to stay awake, though we had the windows open and the hot wind hit my face, messing up my hair. The sky looked silvery, almost nonexistent, and the sun formed mirages over the asphalt, creating the impression that we were constantly heading toward pools of water we never reached. Even the few dark green trees in the distance, surrounding the spiked tower of some motionless weather vane, looked unreal under the light. Amid the drowsiness, I felt a happy sensation of independence, sitting next to Marta, who drove very fast, not talking, but with a slight smile on her lips.

When we entered the quiet, empty city, suspended in the afternoon heat as if time had stopped for it, we went to Eduardo's office, but they told us he had gone to see his parents. Marta then suggested that we pick up Rafael first. She drove down an avenue—bordered by some trees with white trunks and wide, flat tops, full of red flowers instead of leaves—and sped up. In Mexico City I had never seen her drive and looking at her, I thought she looked very attractive, recognizing each one of her expressions and gestures. I told her I couldn't get used to the idea that the life I had been sharing with her those last few days was actually her life.

"You're right," she said. "Your presence makes me watch myself, too. You've made me feel as if I've changed without realizing it. But at the same time, I think you're so removed from all this that you can't understand it; I don't know how to explain it to you, either. It doesn't bother you, does it?"

"Of course not. On the contrary. I like to see you this way," I said.

She glanced over at me, and I had the feeling that she was going to touch me, but she didn't carry out the gesture.

A moment later she pointed to a large, one-story modern building on the other side of the street, painted white, with a small, fresh, and well-kept garden in front, and told me it was Rafael's clinic.

"He owns it?" I asked, surprised.

"Not alone. There's a group of six or seven partners. I told you he was a very good doctor," she said.

At the corner she made a U-turn around the median and we parked in front of the clinic.

"Come on."

I followed her. In the reception room the nurse got up to greet her, asking about the children, while I stood next to her in silence, foolishly looking around, as if I had never been in a clinic. After Marta asked the nurse to tell Rafael we were here, we sat down to wait, along with five or six other people with that tired appearance and empty expression people always get in clinics. The room was air-conditioned, and the contrast with the heat outside made me feel cold. The familiarity and naturalness with which Marta could come in and ask for Rafael, like someone who carried out an unimportant task, made me uncomfortable. To me the place had nothing to do with the Rafael I knew, and I felt I was going to meet a stranger. I lit a cigarette and mechanically picked up one of the magazines from the table in front of me. Rafael appeared right away, dressed in white, and came over to us. The white outfit accentuated the bronze color of his skin. He didn't ask about Eduardo. He explained that he still had to see a patient, not talking to either one of us in particular, and after greeting someone else, he left again, promising to return as soon as he could. I felt relieved and silly; he was the same as always. Then I opened the magazine again. Marta laughed.

"You look scared."

"No. Why?" I lied.

"That's what I'd like to know," she answered, still smiling, but using the tone of certainty I knew so well.

Then the nurse called us into Rafael's office. I followed Marta again and we entered a large, well-furnished room. I saw Rafael in the next room saying good-bye to his last patient, a fat woman with a small boy, who left through an outer door. Rafael came toward us.

"I thought you'd like to see this," he told me. "But, as you can tell, there's not much to it."

"No. It's a beautiful clinic. I didn't think it'd be this big," I said, looking around, not knowing what I should notice.

"It isn't. But it is pretty," he said. "My suitcase is in the next room. I'll change and then show you around. If you don't mind, Marta."

"No, of course not," Marta said. "I know you're dying to show it off."

He smiled at her, a little embarrassed, and went back to the other room. Then the three of us walked through the clinic. Rafael introduced me to two doctors who worked with him and though he showed me the equipment, explaining its use jokingly, as if he wanted to make it clear that he didn't expect me to be enthusiastic about it, I felt I shared his pride and understood that he also felt close to me, in spite of Marta's teasing. But somehow the visit was a test, a way of introducing me to his everyday life, and the idea of being so close to it frightened me a little; it seemed to anticipate a style of life very different from the one in which I had met and come to know him. Even if Rafael was the same one I liked, he certainly wasn't that person to his partners, for example, or to the patients we ran into in the halls, or to Marta, who, seeing everything as natural and familiar, suddenly seemed much closer to him.

When we left I felt relieved. Rafael said he would follow us so that we could all go in his car from Eduardo's house. As soon as we were alone, Marta allowed an expression of disgust to show on her face.

"What's the matter?" I asked her.

"I hate going to my in-laws'," she confessed. "I hope they don't think of some way to ruin our trip. Eduardo should have waited for us at the office."

"We would have had to say good-bye anyway," I said.

"That bothers me, too. I can never do anything on my own," she answered. "But it's not worth talking about it. Don't listen to me," she added, and glanced in the rearview mirror to see if Rafael was behind us.

I turned and he raised his hand from the wheel to wave. When we reached the house, Marta decided it was better to leave the car inside, so we drove it in, the aged maid following behind as we moved slowly between the rosebushes, which almost crept in through the car windows. Rafael parked on the street and walked in behind us. Eduardo's mother met us on the veranda. Rafael kissed her on the cheek and Marta asked for Eduardo.

"He's with his father, who's in bed," she explained.

"Is something wrong?" Rafael asked.

"The same thing. He's not well. Go see him. He's waiting for you," she answered.

As we walked along the veranda, she caressed Rafael's hair.

"You never come around anymore. Have you forgotten us?"

"I've been very busy," Rafael explained affectionately.

"I can imagine. But you must come once in a while. Manuel is always asking about you, and for you to tell him he's better does him more good than anything else. You know it."

Rafael put his arm around her shoulders and Marta turned slightly to look at him.

It was very hot in Don Manuel's room even though the three windows were open, allowing the trees in the patio to be seen, their low branches crossing in front of them like a curtain. Although the room was large, the bed seemed to take up most of the space. Lying down with his wrinkled pajamas open at the neck, exposing the gray hair on his chest and accentuating his thinness, Don Manuel looked very sick, or at least totally exhausted. Eduardo was sitting next to the bed in a small wicker chair. Marta and Rafael went up to them, while I stayed at the door, with Eduardo's mother.

"What's the matter with you? Are you giving up?" Rafael said, after he leaned over the bed to kiss Eduardo's father.

"Nothing of the sort," he said, trying to smile. "It's just that I can't . . . I can't . . . sleep," he ended with difficulty.

"It's understandable, with this heat . . . ," Rafael went on. "You should be at the beach."

Don Manuel moved his hand to say no.

"It's not that . . . It's worry . . . I don't know."

"I can't see anything wrong with you. And Dr. Henríquez doesn't either. I just thought I'd tell you," Rafael answered.

"That man . . . ," Don Manuel said. "What does he know?"

Marta moved away from Eduardo to lean over the bed and kiss Don Manuel. From where I stood, watching their reflection in a big dresser mirror, the scene had something theatrical about it. Don Manuel signaled me to come closer.

"You look very well . . . I'm glad they're taking you to Campeche . . . You'll like . . . it . . . Although the heat . . ."

"Heat is just what you like. Don't you want to come with us?" Rafael said.

"No," he answered, smiling again with only one side of his mouth. "And I don't wa . . . to waste your time either . . . Go on . . . What are you waiting for?"

Eduardo stood up, but no one else moved.

"We're in no hurry, Don Manuel," Marta said.

"It doesn't matter. I'm tired," he answered. "Go on . . ."

He gestured toward the door and sank into the bed. Eduardo's mother went to him and automatically arranged the sheets, almost without looking at him.

"Go on," he insisted. "And . . . see Peniche, Eduardo, don't forget . . . He can help you."

Everyone kissed him again; not knowing what to do, I imitated them. In spite of the heat, his face was cold and his skin exuded a sweet odor.

Once outside, Rafael asked Eduardo's mother when the doctor had seen him last.

"Yesterday," she answered. "He said he's not worse. What's bad are the cigarettes and the food."

"I know," Rafael said. "Make sure he doesn't stay in bed. It depresses him."

"You know him," Eduardo's mother answered and then, turning to me, as if wanting to change the subject, she said, "I hope you like Campeche. Have a good time."

Followed by the nanny, she accompanied us to Rafael's car and stood there until we pulled away. From the back seat Eduardo commented, "She's shocked because we're two couples. She told me to take very good care of you, Elena."

Rafael and I laughed, but I avoided looking at him, a little embarrassed; Marta, who hadn't even smiled, asked Eduardo who was the Peniche his father had mentioned.

"A man I should see about getting credit," he explained. "More than anything, I made him up to justify the trip. You know how father is about the factory." He paused, then added, "How did you find him, Rafael?"

"He's not well," Rafael said. "But I don't think it's serious. He has to take better care of himself. And not worry about anything."

"True," Eduardo said.

As we crossed the city, he remained silent, staring out the window, not getting close to Marta, who sat at the other end of the seat. But as soon as we reached the highway, Rafael started asking me to light one cigarette after another and commented about the view, the henequen, and the haciendas, little by little communicating his happiness to Eduardo. On both sides of the highway, the henequen extended to the horizon, with nothing, not even a tree, breaking its harsh and extremely austere uniformity. Rafael was driving so fast that the wind kept us from noticing the heat, but it also forced us to shout, which seemed to increase the trip's excitement. We came to the first town almost immediately. On the outskirts, the round, red-earth, thatched-roofed huts, encircled by whitewashed rock walls, soon gave way to a long row of colonial homes, with barred windows and high roofs, until we reached a huge plaza with low, luxuriant trees of an incredible dark green color, in one of whose corners stood a colossal, towerless church built out of pink rock, which, like some I had seen in Mérida, looked more like a fortress. From there, the town followed the same pattern but in reverse, from the colonial houses to the thatched huts to an abrupt end. In front of almost all the huts there were people dressed in white with a clean appearance. Rafael didn't slow down through the town, but back on the highway, he turned to me for a moment and commented, "It's different, isn't it?" with the same enthusiasm in his voice that Eduardo had when he was showing me everything the day I arrived, as if he were oblivious to the sad air of boredom and poverty the town gave off, revealing something forever dead.

In the meantime, between the two of them they had explained to me the whole process of cultivating and marketing henequen, lamenting the catastrophe of land expropriation; Marta teased them, insisting that we were socialists and that she had heard the story a thousand times. But now the henequen disappeared and the highway was flanked by a miserable thicket of low, dry bushes, so tangled that they formed a kind of light green wall, solid and continuous. We passed three more towns, with the same huts, the brilliant red-earth side streets, the plazas with trees, the dead air, and the inevitable church of faded rock; after the last one, for the first time, the highway's straight track curved to surmount a short string of rugged hills, covered with rocks and a thirsty earth, from whose peak one could see the endless, arid, and wild jungle. Back on the plain, the smell was much more penetrating, as if all at once the weeds and bushes had acquired new life.

"It rained here and it must be raining up ahead," Eduardo said, pointing at the black clouds running along the sky across the opposite end of the horizon.

Rafael checked his watch and pressed down on the accelerator. "If we hurry, we'll still get there in time to see the ruins," he explained.

Marta had moved over to be close to Eduardo and he had his arm around her shoulders. Both he and Rafael seemed enthusiastic, anticipating the pleasure I was going to experience seeing the ruins; though I didn't feel the expectation they thought I did, their excitement made me feel close to and distanced from them at the same time, as if on the one hand I was already part of their lives and on the other, something made me feel distant and forced me to observe them with the curiosity and attraction the unfamiliar provokes. Nevertheless, I was comfortable and, above all, I felt we were united by the trip's rhythm. The smell of wet earth was becoming more and more intense, and suddenly we caught up with the rain, which began to strike the car with terrible force, as if unexpectedly we had driven under a waterfall. We had to roll up the windows quickly, and Rafael decreased the speed. In an instant the windshield and windows fogged up completely. The inside of the car seemed to close within itself and acquired a warm intimacy, although the penetrating smell of the vegetation never lessened and, through the curtain of rain, the rays of a pale and faded sun blotched a well-defined silver and yellow zone into the endless gray sky. After a moment, as abruptly as we had entered it, we left the rain behind, but the puddles on the highway indicated it had rained there, too. We had all grown quiet. Crossing the puddles, the car raised a curtain of water. I wondered what Rafael was thinking, unconsciously saying it out loud, surprising myself when I heard my voice. Instead of answering, he turned, took his right hand off the steering wheel, and holding it at a height where the seat hid it from Marta and Eduardo, pointed at me. I didn't know how to react and immediately turned to ask Marta if she had brought her bathing suit.

"Of course," she said. "Didn't you?"

"Yes, me too," I had to answer, feeling like an idiot. "I don't know why I asked, it just popped into my head."

And I saw that Rafael was listening, without taking his eyes off the road. A moment later, he pumped the brakes and took a side road.

"We're here," he announced. "Let's see if they'll let us in. It's not six yet."

Marta leaned forward and rested her arms on the top of our seat. We drove a few more miles and stopped in front of a wooden fence. From there a pyramid was already visible, tall, slender, and melancholy, much more deteriorated than I had imagined from the pictures I had seen, but also with much more charm than I had expected, a sad and mysterious enchantment, accentuated by the afternoon's pale light and the appearance of the wet earth and bushes. I stayed in the car, but Marta, Eduardo, and Rafael got out.

"Hurry up. We only have ten minutes. They close at six," Rafael said.

In the gate house, the guard, who sold us the tickets and forced us to waste time signing a book, also warned us about the closing time, but Rafael didn't pay attention.

"Come on, come on," he said, taking me by the hand, "you have to see the nunnery!"

And he dragged me along, running.

"Wait, don't be so impatient," Eduardo said behind us.

The wet ground was very slippery. I had to ask Rafael to slow down and I stopped for a moment to look around. Once we were past the pyramid that obstructed the view, the rest of the buildings appeared scattered on an open esplanade in the middle of the jungle, which sealed it off on all sides. The setting gave an astonishing impression of perfect equilibrium in the spacing between one building and another.

"You have to see the nunnery. It's a wonder. Come on," Rafael insisted, impatiently.

It seemed as if he wasn't really letting me see anything and it upset me, but as soon as we reached the next courtyard, he lost all signs of impatience. He looked from each detail of the construction to me and back, as if wanting to discover my reaction, but without saying anything. Marta and Eduardo caught up and stood beside us, not speaking either. A flock of swallows fluttered in all directions through the courtyard, shrieking, and disappeared into the alien and desolate building; the pure beauty of the construction, more impressive than any attempt to define it, sprang not only from its heavy delicacy, but also from its present state of abandonment in the middle of solitude and time, its incredible and unavoidable closeness and its inevitable distance, which forced us to contemplate it as something that doesn't belong to us and never will, but whose mystery lives forever. Rafael spoke of it in these terms, and I had to agree. The shrieks of the swallows—black stains more than birds amid the orange brightness of the afternoon, which, on top of the memory of the rain, stained the friezes with an even darker color—increased the melancholy.

"There's something very sad about it," I said then.

"Yes, exactly," Rafael answered. "That's why I like it."

"You're very lucky," Marta added, next to us. "At this hour they look much more beautiful than when I first saw them."

"You're seeing them now, too," Rafael said, suddenly putting his arm around her.

Then he began to tell us a legend about the founding of the city, but he didn't remember it well and in the end he admitted that none of it mattered.

"It reminds me of when we used to come here as kids, doesn't it, Eduardo?" he finished. And he suggested that we go to see the Governor's Palace before they made us leave.

Eduardo suggested that it would be better to climb the pyramid.

"Is it worth it?" I asked, looking at its height and the steep stairs.

"There's nothing to see inside, but the view is wonderful," Rafael explained. "The jungle looks like a green sea, but with a different meaning. It's not like the sea, as you've noticed. There's something destructive about it. It's neither cheerful nor clean, it only looks that way."

"There you go again," Eduardo said. And he commented to me, "I've heard him say that a thousand times."

"It's true," Marta said. "I've heard him too. It'd be better to go to the Governor's Palace. Tomorrow we can climb up to the castle before we leave for Campeche."

"That's what I suggested first," Rafael answered, a little embarrassed.

Nevertheless, from the low mound on which the other palace stood, the jungle looked as he had said it would, with an absurd beauty, too secretive, under a sky full of drifting, dark clouds, through which the sun's rays filtered to form an enormous rainbow. We circled the building, amazed by the facade's inexhaustible arabesques, and at last Eduardo commented, "So much for tourism. It's time for a drink. Let's go to the hotel."

"Yes, let's go," Marta said.

She walked ahead with Rafael. I stayed behind talking to Eduardo, and when we got to the car, Rafael asked him to drive and sat in front with him.

The hotel was a two-story modern construction imitating the colonial style. The rooms took up two sides of a square, the dining room and reception rooms another; in the center was a patio with well-kept tropical vegetation and a swimming pool. With the exception of a few old Americans, it was empty. When we arrived, the sun had disappeared, but there was still light. Murmurs from the forest reached us faintly, making the place more intimate. As we entered, Marta took my arm and rested her head on my shoulder.

"Are you sad?" I asked her.

"No, on the contrary. Are you?"

"No. But I feel out of place," I confessed sincerely.

"Don't be foolish."

Rafael and Eduardo went to the desk, and then the bellboy, who had gone for our luggage, took us to our rooms on the second floor of the central wing. He opened the door to the first room, left Marta and Eduardo's bag, and they went in. The bellboy hesitated in front of the next room.

"Do you want to be next to Marta or do you prefer the other room?" Rafael asked me.

"It doesn't matter. This is fine," I said.

The bellboy left my bag inside. I went in and closed the door. The room had two beds and the furnishings repeated the colonial motif too, with a few reproductions of idols on the dresser. The window looking out toward the forest had a screen. I sat on the edge of the bed, unable to decide whether to open my suitcase. Someone knocked and I heard Marta's voice: "Are you there, Elena?"

I opened the door. She had changed from slacks and a blouse into a dress. Eduardo was with her, but he stayed at the door and said he was going to the bar with Rafael.

"Okay," Marta said. "We'll join you shortly."

She lay back on one of the beds and commented, "You're not going to change? My feet were soaked."

"Yes, I think so," I said, wondering what I should wear.

I went to the bathroom to wash up, then got a dress out of my bag, while Marta talked to me from the bed.

"You know, I miss the boys? It's too much, but I'm worried about having left them. Celia's so different. At least the nannies already know how to take care of them. What slavery, don't you think? You can never do anything. Sometimes I envy you. You don't have any problems."

I didn't answer, so she insisted: "What are you thinking?"

"Nothing. I'm washing up."

She kept quiet for a moment, then, "Did you like the ruins?"

"Yes, very much," I said, coming out, with the towel in my hand.

I started to put on my makeup in front of the mirror and Marta commented, "Rafael gets all excited about them, as if they were his."

I saw her in the mirror. She was lying on her stomach, with her elbows on the bed and her face resting on her hands.

"You look very attractive," I said, finding her eyes in the mirror.

"We are very attractive," she answered, getting up to zip my dress.

Then, at the bar, while Rafael lit my cigarette, I caught Marta staring at me, and she repeated quickly, "We are very attractive."

We both laughed. Rafael asked what was the matter, making us laugh even more. Though the few Americans around us looked quiet and bored, we were happy. The night, full of murmurs, the illuminated garden, and the pool, like a changing stain of light in the center, created a magical atmosphere. In the dining room, while we ate, we laughed about every foolish thing that popped up, from the squeak of one of the waiters' sandals to the appearance of the rest of the guests and the horrible taste of the coffee; but when we left, we discovered that it was barely nine o'clock and although no one wanted to go to bed, there was nothing to do, and the solitude of the hotel was too oppressive. Eduardo suggested that we go to the bar and get really drunk, but not even he seemed to feel like drinking, and after one cognac he forgot the second and started talking about the visits he and Rafael had made to Uxmal before the hotel was built. Both of them got lost in their memories, excluding Marta and me, but suddenly Rafael asked me if I was getting bored. I said no, but Marta broke in: "Frankly, I am. It's exasperating how you two always leave us out of the conversation."

"Which conversation?" Eduardo asked, surprised.

"It's always the same one," Marta answered. "You don't realize it, but you're in love with everything you've done together in your life."

Rafael agreed.

"You're right. The best thing to do is go to bed, don't you think so? That way we can get up early tomorrow."

The bored waiter watched us from the bar. Rafael signed the check. With the exception of two bellboys dozing on a couch, the dining room, hallways, and lobby were completely empty. As we walked through them, the waiter turned off the record player, which had been on the whole time, and the silence made me feel the solitude of the hotel. Marta yawned.

"That was a good idea. I'm tired," she told Rafael.

But I didn't feel tired and was nervous. Eduardo put his arm around Marta's waist and kissed her on the neck. I felt Rafael's hand brush mine. We passed Marta's room, but she kept walking, and the four of us stopped in front of my door.

"Well, good night. Sleep well," she said, kissing me on the cheek. Rafael's eyes met mine, but all he did was wish me a good night, and I had to go into my room. When I was alone, I instinctively looked in the mirror, not really seeing myself. Then I sat on the bed, hesitating about going to sleep, listening for a noise in Rafael's room, but the shrieks coming from the jungle were too loud. I wanted him to come to my room and at the same time I realized that I preferred it if he didn't. Although I had felt close to him all day, I thought too much time had gone by since we had had the chance to talk alone, and I would feel uncomfortable next to him. Besides, in some way, I wouldn't have liked him to think he had the right to come. I started to undress mechanically and put on a nightgown, thinking it would be better to be dressed like that in case he called. I waited about half an hour and finally understood that he wasn't coming. Then I felt much better and began to really desire him. The room had a ceiling fan and it wasn't hot, but I took off my nightgown before getting under the covers. Amid the silence, the slight hum of the fan proved soothing. I turned off the light but kept my eyes open for a long time, trying to identify the different shrieks coming from the forest, feeling my body and, now, wanting Rafael to come, at least to feel him beside me, wondering why he hadn't, and reproaching him.

The following morning his voice woke me up, asking me if I was awake yet and knocking softly on the door. It took me a moment to react, but as soon as I was aware that it was daylight, I got up and ran to the door.

"What's the matter?" I said, leaning against it, still half asleep.

"Nothing," he said. "It's almost nine. Did I wake you up?"

"Yes, but it doesn't matter."

"I'm sorry," he said. "I've been up for hours. I thought that . . ."

"Wait a minute."

I checked my face in the mirror and straightened my hair, opened the door a little, and stuck my head out. He was wearing a bathing suit and his hair wasn't combed.

"Good morning," he said, looking at me.

"I can't open it any further. I'm undressed," I explained. "What is it?"

"I thought you might like to swim before breakfast," he said. "And I wanted to see you."

"I wanted to see you, too," I said. "But don't look at me. I'm still asleep. I'll be right down."

"Okay. I'll wait for you by the pool."

He got close and kissed my hand, which was resting on the door, but I closed it immediately.

When I went down, he was sitting at the edge of the pool, his feet in the water. His gaze embarrassed me a little.

"I got you some coffee," he said, pointing to a cup on the arm of one of the canvas chairs.

"That's nice. Thank you. Where are Marta and Eduardo?"

"They must still be asleep. I didn't want to wake them up," he said.

I sat on the chair to drink my coffee. Rafael took his feet out of the water and turned around to look at me. I had the absurd sensation of having spent the night with him and avoided his eyes, but when I finished my coffee I went and sat next to him. He took my hand.

"I couldn't sleep thinking you were in the next room," he said.

"I thought about you, too, before I went to sleep," I said, and wondered if he had thought about the possibility of coming to my room.

Rafael kissed me lightly on the shoulder, stood up, and moved away a few steps.

"Shall we swim?" he asked.

I told him I preferred to take in a little more sun, so he sat back down next to me but remained silent, with a distant gaze.

"What's wrong?" I asked him.

"I don't know. Sometimes I don't know what to do when I'm next to you," he answered.

"Why?"

"Because I'm not sure I know what I'm looking for. Do you know?"

"I can speak for myself, but not for you," I said, realizing that it was a lie and I didn't know either.

At that moment, Marta yelled at us from her balcony, "Traitors! Why didn't you call us?"

She was wearing the same pants she had worn the day before. Rafael stood up immediately.

"Hi! Don't you want to swim?" he said, shading his eyes from the sun with his hand to see her.

"We still haven't had breakfast," Marta said.

"Neither have we. We're waiting for you. Come down," Rafael answered.

"I'll go ask Eduardo," Marta said. "But we'll come right down anyhow."

And she disappeared again.

Rafael said he was going to get coffee for them, too, and left me alone. Not knowing why, I felt upset, and in revenge I decided to get into the water without waiting for him, but when he returned, it didn't seem to surprise him. Instead of joining me, he waited for Marta and Eduardo. As soon as he came down, Eduardo jumped into the pool and from the edge told Marta and Rafael to join us.

After breakfast, Rafael and Eduardo decided it would be better to leave the hotel and stop by the ruins with the luggage in the car in order to continue the trip without losing any more time.

Though it was only ten, the heat was so intense that it seemed to spring out of the earth and rise toward us, enveloping us along with the persistent and monotonous strident song of the cicadas coming from the forest. Under that penetrating light the ruins looked different. Their beauty withdrew, separating itself from the land-scape, instead of joining it as on the previous afternoon; life moved away from them, as if amid the heat it was impossible to think of them as the result of a human effort. I thought I would have preferred to keep the first impression. Rafael didn't have the same enthusiasm, either; we all agreed that it was better to leave without trying to climb the pyramid, in order to get to Campeche as soon as possible.

Although we had parked the car under a tree, it felt like an oven inside. Rafael asked Eduardo to drive and sat with me in the back. Before we got on the main highway again, Marta said she couldn't stand wearing pants and asked Eduardo to stop for a moment so she could change into shorts. I did the same.

Sitting next to Rafael, perspiring in spite of the wind coming through the windows, numb and drowsy from the heat, I felt as if I were floating outside of myself in a thick unconsciousness, and I started to feel an almost painful need for Rafael to touch me, to touch him in order to disappear at his side. It wasn't just arousal or simple desire, but something else, a kind of nostalgia for him to make my body real, to take me beyond the heat, which now seemed its sole owner. He was at the other end of the seat, but if he extended his legs, they could almost touch mine. I raised my foot and caressed him with it. He didn't turn to look at me, but he stretched out his legs even more, searching for me. The four of us were quiet and Marta, completely stretched out, with her head resting on the top of the seat, seemed to be falling asleep. Little by little Rafael and I got closer, and he started caressing my leg and then my thigh with his hand. But Marta moved and both of us separated automatically, only to get close again a moment later, without looking at each other or talking, but each one aware of the other's movements and searching carefully for every possible secret contact. Then Rafael took my hand and put it between his legs. I closed my eyes, also pressing his hand between my legs, not caring about him, but only his presence, trying to doze off in order to feel him beyond myself, with a strange and distant pleasure.

Throughout the entire trip we played the same game, without really responding, like two robots moving mechanically, obeying orders given long before. When we passed through towns or when Eduardo said something without turning around to look at us, we separated for a moment, and I was able to maintain that state of drowsiness with my eyes open to watch Marta, looking at the monotonous landscape parading by me without really seeing it. Once she turned and I thought she noticed how we separated, but she looked away immediately and only after a moment turned again to ask why we were so quiet.

"For the same reason you are," I said, clearing my throat. "It's too hot to make the effort."

"It's not that bad," she answered, but she didn't continue either.

It took us longer to get close again, but we eventually found each other.

Toward the end of the trip, another series of almost white hills broke the monotony of the plains, and while Eduardo decreased the speed on the curves, he announced, "We're almost there."

Rafael and I separated for good, as if suddenly the spell had been broken, leaving in its place only a heavy fatigue through which I began to recognize him little by little. The four of us started talking again; as we pulled out of a curve the ocean reappeared, intense and peacefully blue like a lake, no whitecaps breaking its apparent stillness. Beside it, the white city—flat roofs dotted with church towers and the green stains of trees—was shining under the sun, with an oppressive and sad appearance. Leaving the last hill behind, we started to advance between the first huts, which later gave way to one-story houses, like the ones in Mérida. Eduardo went down an avenue lined with palm trees, running parallel to the walls surrounding the center of the city. We crossed through the walls and continued to drive next to them along the seashore. The trip had passed like a dream, but now it was harder to be next to Rafael. Though we had already been talking to Marta and Eduardo, I felt embarrassed. On the road everything had been natural, but now the awareness that I had only searched for the sensation and not for him, made me feel degraded, as if upon arriving I had returned to reality and we had to start all over again without taking into account the previous experience, which belonged to us separately.

When we got to the hotel, I got out of the car without looking at him, talking to Marta about how dirty and poor the city looked. Eduardo and he went to the desk, and we stayed in the lobby. The hotel was a modern building, situated outside the walls, on the narrow strip of land between them and the sea. When we were alone, Marta told me I looked tired; I didn't know what to answer. Then Rafael called me to register.

"They don't have rooms available on the same floor," he explained. "Where would you rather be, on the third or fifth?"

"It doesn't matter," I said. "The fifth is fine."

He turned to Eduardo.

"Then I'll go to the third, with you and Marta."

"Okay," Eduardo said, handing the cards back to the desk clerk.

He suggested we have a drink, but Marta said she wanted to shower before anything else. Marta and Eduardo got out on their floor and Rafael accompanied me upstairs. After tipping the bellboy, he stayed inside. Disturbed, I went to the window, opened it, and went out onto the balcony. The cathedral was almost in front, and the line of the walls could be seen encircling the center of the city.

"It's such a pretty view," I said, turning to Rafael, who hadn't moved.

He came close, took my hand, and pulled me inside. He kissed me, caressing my back and pressing me against him, but I didn't feel anything, and when he started unbuttoning my blouse, I pushed him away, almost with fear.

"No, please," I begged.

He looked at me, surprised.

"What's wrong?"

"I don't know. I'm embarrassed."

He drew me to him again, but now gently, making me rest my head on his shoulder and caressing my hair.

"You're right. Forgive me. I love you."

I smiled, not daring to answer, regretful, but knowing the moment had passed. Rafael lightly brushed my lips with his mouth.

"I'll wait for you downstairs. Don't take too long, please."

I followed him to the door and kissed him on the cheek before he left.

I undressed and got in the shower. The water washed away

Rafael's smell; while I dried off, I realized it with a sensation of emptiness. Before I finished, Marta called to say they were waiting for me at the bar. I dressed slowly, standing in the flow of the air coming from the fan and trying to make the least possible number of movements so I wouldn't start perspiring. When I looked at myself in the mirror to put on my makeup, I felt that I belonged to Pedro and the whole situation with Rafael was nothing but an attempt to test my faithfulness, but I also knew I wouldn't hold back because now to the initial curiosity was added a dark hope impossible to define, but absolutely real.

Although there were fans in every corner, it was very hot in the bar, a dense, heavy heat, crushing us to the chair and forcing us to avoid any unnecessary movement.

"It's worse here than in Mérida," Eduardo commented. "What are we going to do?"

"You, before anything else, are going to look for the so-called Peniche," Marta answered.

"Yes, I know. On top of everything else," Eduardo said. "But later? This trip was your idea, Rafael. What do you suggest?"

"Wait for it to get dark and go to see the city," Rafael answered.

But we all seemed to be out of place, as if the hidden meaning of the trip had been lost, leaving only the need to complete a series of pointless actions. Eduardo stood up, saying he was going to call Peniche to get it out of the way; he returned smiling.

"Saved! He's out of town. Now we can get drunk in peace."

Rafael glanced affectionately at him for an instant, the way you look at a younger brother, then looked away when he noticed I was watching. Eduardo finished his second beer and ordered rum all around, but when he was about to ask for another round, Marta insisted that we go to lunch. From the dining room, we could see the ocean, bluer and smoother than the one I was used to looking at from the dining room at the house on the beach, as if it were dead, devouring instead of reflecting the light. Its own too penetrating odor insinuated an element of decay. There were a lot of people eating, and the service was exasperatingly slow. When we finally left, Eduardo and Marta said they were going to rest for a while. Rafael responded that he wasn't tired and would wait in the lounge or go for a walk, but he didn't ask me to accompany him, so I also went up to my room. Although I didn't feel tired either, I threw myself on the bed and fell asleep right away.

I woke up around six, dazed. The afternoon sun penetrated

through the open window to the middle of the room, and I had to make an effort to recognize the place and remember where I was. I went out to the balcony and, seeing the city, white and dry, flattened by the light, I felt an urgent need to stop everything and return to myself, but as I stood in front of the mirror it returned an equally strange image. I picked up the phone and called Marta to hear her voice. Eduardo answered. Marta had gone down a moment before; I could find her in the lobby; he was also on his way down. I left the room immediately, barely fixing myself up; after vainly looking for her in the lobby and the bar, I found her sitting at a table on one of the terraces facing the sea, with Rafael. Both of them looked happy and rested, and I felt better. Rafael gave me his chair and went to look for another.

"Did you sleep?" he asked me then.

"Yes, like a rock. But I don't think I like Campeche, I didn't feel well when I woke up."

"Why?" Marta broke in.

"I don't know," I said.

"What a sad voice!" Marta commented, and she and Rafael laughed.

"Take a drink of this, it'll do you good," he said, offering me his glass. "We have to take good care of you."

He leaned forward, put his hand on mine for a moment, and then sat back. Marta took a drink from her glass.

The sea was beginning to retreat into itself as sunset drew closer. From the terrace, with our backs to the hotel and the rest of the city, only it seemed real in front of us. I felt how little by little the heat was retreating, devoured by the peacefulness of that almost motionless sea. As they broke against the terrace, the weak waves made a hollow sound; the afternoon stretched out holding on to itself, with a lazy insistence. Rafael ordered another drink for me, bitter and cold, very pleasant. When Eduardo arrived the three of us were submerged in a languid drowsiness, almost speechless. He too ordered a drink and forced Marta to sit on his lap, in spite of the waiter's stare. I felt distant from everything, but once in a while I turned to look at Rafael and his presence gave the evening a different meaning, filling it with expectation. Before the sun disappeared completely, the tolling of the cathedral bells reached us, rhythmic and monotonous, with every new ring erasing the one before when its sound had not yet ended, but as if all of them were coming from far away. Marta left her glass on the table and stood up.

"I think we can walk around the city as we planned," she told Rafael. "It's not so hot anymore."

"Would you like to?" Rafael asked me.

"Yes, fine," I said, but I felt that after sitting peacefully for an hour, it was hard to move again.

While we were waiting for the check, Rafael stood up and walked to the end of the terrace. I followed him and he put his hand on my shoulder. Behind us I heard Eduardo telling Marta that he didn't feel like walking and would rather wait for us in the hotel with her.

"What did you do all afternoon?" I asked Rafael.

He looked at me and removed his hand from my shoulder.

"Think about you," he said.

"That's a lie," I answered.

"Okay," he agreed. "Talk to Marta about you. It's almost the same thing, isn't it?"

"What did you tell her?"

"Everything and nothing." He shrugged his shoulders.

"Come here, Eduardo's beginning to complain," Marta informed us.

"And I have reason to," Eduardo said, as he signed the check.

Before leaving the terrace, I saw the last orange fragment of the sun disappear into the sea. The silhouette of a ship divided the horizon in two. At the hotel door Eduardo insisted that we at least take the car, but all of us convinced him that it was better to walk. The street was full of people, talking in loud voices or sitting silently in front of the open doors of the houses. The endless string of all kinds of stores along the seawall reminded me of what I imagined an Arab city must be like. The whole setting had something exotic about it, but at the same time it was very closed. At my side, Rafael insisted that we cross the street to walk along the walls, but they could be seen better from the opposite side, graceful and heavy, under the shadowless light of the disappeared sun. In front of the central plaza, the walls had been cut absurdly to make room for a small garden behind which stood a museum, but instead of going in, we went and sat on one of the benches in the plaza, to one side of the cathedral. Although the plaza didn't have trees, there was a continuous murmur of the flight and singing of birds.

"It's very different from Mérida," I told Eduardo, who sat next to me.

"But which one do you like best?" he asked.

Rafael suggested that we enter the cathedral and inside he told me he had made his first communion there because, as a boy, he spent a lot of time in Campeche with his aunt.

"It was a sacrilegious first communion. I ate a cookie before we left for church, and during the mass I waited for the ceiling to fall on my head," he explained to me and then went on, "Now it looks pretty firm, doesn't it?"

But he became pensive, only laughing again when Marta came up to ask us what we were talking about, and he repeated the story for her.

Then, while we walked through the streets to the other side of the walls, he continued telling us anecdotes of when he lived there with his aunt and uncle. It was completely dark now and the people disappeared from the streets. It was starting to get very hot again, and it felt more humid than in the afternoon. When we got to the avenue parallel to the walls, after walking through innumerable empty streets, past the same white houses, Marta let herself fall on one of the benches and—in a childish bad mood that made me nervous, as if something bothered her that she couldn't or wouldn't define—said she was exhausted and would not take one more step. While we waited in vain for a taxi to pass, Eduardo and Rafael's attempts to cheer her up only upset her even more. I felt that if I intervened we would end up fighting, so I went to wait on a bench under an enormous tree. From one of the dark patios, the sound of a guitar could be heard, pausing once in a while to begin the same tune again. A group of drunks emerged from the darkness and stood almost in front of me until Rafael came and sat down. Finally, we decided to walk to the restaurant in front of the hotel, where Eduardo and Rafael wanted to have dinner. Marta held Rafael's arm with both hands and little by little recovered her good mood. In the last two blocks, Rafael and Eduardo crossed their arms so she could be carried; we entered the restaurant laughing, but Marta was a little embarrassed with me and, as dinner began, she talked to me as though more than anything she wanted me to forget her previous behavior; then we really forgot everything. The food was delicious. Eduardo ordered a bottle of chilled white wine and when it was barely half empty, he asked for another one. The restaurant was crowded and several people came over to say hello. The couples looked more provincial than in Mérida, and everyone spoke loudly, talking from one table to another but the atmosphere was pleasant, with a kind of open and happy familiarity. Unconsciously, the tone of our voices rose until we were almost shouting, and after we finished the wine, we started drinking cognac. Eduardo repeated over and over again that Rafael was really from Campeche and that was why he was so happy, and suddenly I realized that Marta and I were talking about Mexico City by ourselves. Eduardo had disappeared and Rafael was listening to us attentively. The waiter came to tell us that they were getting ready to close. Rafael paid, then went to the bathroom to look for Eduardo. The place was empty except for us, and from the other side of the dining room the smiling waiters were watching us. Marta stared at me in silence.

"I'm trying to look at you the way Rafael does," she said then, trying to joke, but obviously irritated.

"Does it bother you?" I said, also irritated.

But she didn't answer, and Rafael and Eduardo returned before I could decide to ask her if there was actually something between her and Rafael.

We were all perspiring, so when we went outside it felt cold, but then the hot air engulfed us. The dirty, empty street looked depressing. Marta hugged Eduardo and kissed him on the neck, with a phony gesture that annoyed me. The sea's strong and penetrating odor reached us. We stood in front of the restaurant not knowing what to do. Eduardo and Rafael staggered a little, but no one was really drunk. Eduardo asked what time it was.

"Barely midnight," Rafael answered.

And we instinctively started walking toward the hotel. I took Rafael's arm, forcing us to lag a little behind.

"I'd like to be alone with you," he said.

"Me too," I answered.

He put his arm around my waist.

"It's been the same since the first day. It's useless. I love you," he said, looking into my eyes.

"Me too. And I want you to show me everything that's yours. I love it," I said. And then I added without thinking, "Come to my room later."

"Yes," he said and drew me close, but then he kept quiet and quickened the pace. "Let's join them," he said, not looking at me anymore.

Marta took his arm as soon as we caught up with them, making me feel jealous for a moment, but I forced myself to think it was foolish. We walked along the shore; garbage scattered everywhere gave it a dirty appearance, entirely different from the one in front of the house on the beach. The lights of the seawall reflected on it. Rafael asked Marta if she was tired, and she laughed.

"Of course not."

"We can still have another drink at the hotel. Maybe the bar's still open," Eduardo commented.

We spent almost another hour there, until they closed, although there was only an American couple besides us and it was very hot. I couldn't concentrate on the conversation and just tried not to get too drunk. I wanted to be with Rafael, but I regretted a little having asked him to come to my room. Nevertheless, he seemed to have completely forgotten it and drank as much as Eduardo. When we left, the lobby was deserted. Eduardo, who now really was drunk, put his arm around my shoulders and walked ahead with me.

"Leave those two behind."

I laughed, but he rested his head on my shoulder and started talking very seriously, in a sad, affectionate tone, leading me toward one of the terraces.

"I'm very happy you're with us . . . And you're happy, too, right? . . . It's been a nice change . . . This may not be like Mexico City, but it's obvious you like it, and we like you, too . . . Do you remember what I told you the first day? Life isn't easy, no, not at all, but I like it, and Marta and I love each other, in spite of everything . . ."

"Of course, you're right," I said.

He kissed me on the cheek and dropped into one of the canvas chairs. I stood in front of him, smiling, a little disturbed.

"No," he went on, "don't agree with me as you would with a drunk. I know I'm serious."

"I know," I answered.

He took my hand.

"Marta and I have to go to Mexico City sometime, don't you think? She needs it. It'd be good, very good, very good . . . ," he finished, almost to himself, his voice fading out.

Marta and Rafael came up to us.

"What are you whispering?" she asked.

"Secrets," Eduardo answered, standing up and hugging her. "Terrible secrets . . . Against you. Right, Elena? Come on, let's go to bed. I'm tired . . ."

Marta also hugged him and kissed him on the mouth.

The clerk, who was dozing off behind the desk, hardly looked at us when he gave us the keys, and we also had to wake up the bellboy at the elevator. Marta called out my floor; when we got there, Rafael, who had my key in his hand, walked me to the door.

"I'll be back," he said, as he was opening the door, and he walked to the elevator without turning back to look at me.

"Sleep well," Marta yelled.

I went in and threw myself on the bed, my head empty, but

nervous and excited, not wanting to move or do anything that required thought. Then I turned on the fan and undressed in front of the mirror, trying to see in my body what Rafael would see, with the anticipated sensation that I was his, which somehow made me better, but not desiring him yet, as if only his presence could awaken me and in the meantime all I could feel was an emptiness. I went back to the bed and stayed there waiting, without getting under the covers, isolated from the rest of the room, unable to feel myself completely in it for an endless time; when I heard a knock on the door, my first reaction was to refuse to open it. Rafael was already an absence felt like a presence, and the need to confront him seemed unbearable. But when he knocked again, I got up, went to the door, and asked who it was, without opening it.

"It's me," Rafael whispered.

"Wait a moment," I said.

I unlocked the door, went back to bed, and got under the sheet. Rafael came in, sat on the edge of the bed at the height of my shoulders, put an arm over my body to support himself, and stared at me, without saying anything. I took my arm from under the sheet and caressed his shoulder.

"Are you sorry you invited me?" he asked in a low voice.

"No, I wanted you to come."

He started caressing me through the sheet, without looking at my body, his eyes on mine.

"We have to talk about a lot of things," I still added.

"Yes," he answered. "Yes, later . . ."

He drew the sheet back and bent down to kiss me.

"Get undressed," I said.

His body wasn't the same as it was in swimming trunks; it was a different revelation that made me forget myself and want to serve him, kiss him. And he used me like that, not letting me think about myself, making me do everything, obliging me to thank him for what I felt, uniting me to that body that wasn't his, but mine, more than anything else.

"It's you, it's you," I murmured, convinced, when he was inside of me, more to hear myself than for him to hear it.

"Are you going to stay with me?" he said after the long silence, still on top of me, but almost coldly, as if he knew the answer.

"Yes, if you want," I said, nevertheless, and pushed him off so I could kiss his chest and legs.

"Yes, I do," he insisted. "Are you going to stay?"

"You'd have to come for me," I said, almost frightened.

"I would," he answered.

He turned onto his back, one leg over mine, and stared at the ceiling. I lay on top of him and kissed him again. He lowered his head and kissed my breasts, but I moved away.

"What are you thinking?" I asked him.

"About the first time I saw you," he answered. "And about the times Marta talked to me about you. Now they have a different meaning. And I don't know when they started to change, when I first really saw you. But now it's impossible. You'll always be the one you are now."

"You're different, too. Your body's different. It's not like when you're in trunks. I only know it now. And I know it's you. I'm not going to forget you."

He smiled and drew me to him.

"Marta never talked to me about you," I said.

"Stupid," he said, and started kissing me as he had before, making me discover my body.

Then, I couldn't let him go when he wanted to return to his room; before switching the light off, he went to the window to draw the curtains. From the bed I saw his thin body far from me. I thought I was going to marry him and it scared me.

$$X$$

Marta woke us up before dawn. Eduardo's father had had another attack and died that same night. Rafael was still with me. When Marta knocked on the door, Rafael sat up instinctively, but I managed to stop him before he said anything. Wrapping the sheet around me, I went to the door.

"Open up," Marta insisted, "open up . . . Something's happened . . ."

"Wait a moment," I said, frightened by the tone of her voice.

I put on a robe without looking at Rafael and went out to the hallway, closing the door behind me. Marta looked at the closed door for an instant, then told me about Eduardo's father. The doctor had just called. He and Eduardo's mother were alone in the house.

"Where's Eduardo?" I asked.

"He's getting dressed," she said. "We have to get back right away." She paused and added without any intonation, in a neutral voice, "Is Rafael in there?"

"Yes," I answered.

She didn't look at me. She said it was good that Eduardo hadn't come up and with the same dead, dull tone asked me to tell Rafael what had happened. I put my hand on her shoulder and she hugged me for an instant.

"I don't understand anything," she said, then moved back and added, "Hurry up and get dressed. We have to leave right away."

I just stood there while she went toward the stairs and only when she started going down could I call her, but she didn't turn. I went back in and told Rafael what had happened. He listened to me with an empty look, then hugged me, not saying anything, although his lips moved against my ear. Then he started dressing very slowly,

146

while I watched him from the bed, my arms around my legs, not knowing what to do. Before leaving he came and kissed me on the lips.

"I'm with you. Don't worry. Get dressed," he said from the open door.

When I went down, all three of them were waiting for me. Eduardo looked very calm. I hugged him. He smiled timidly, and after we separated, he continued to pat me lightly on the back. Marta stood at his side, avoiding my gaze. The sky was growing brighter, and a timid, silent light was filtering through the windows, but the lights in the lobby were still on. From behind the desk, the clerk looked at us sleepy-eyed, not daring to ask what was wrong. Rafael picked up the luggage and said he would take it to the car. Marta suggested that we eat a little something before leaving, but the clerk, happy to be of help, said that the dining room was still closed.

Outside, the sunlight now shone clearly over the sea and reflected off the fronts of the houses. In spite of the buzzards hovering in circles over the shore and the market and the city's dirty appearance, everything seemed magical and unreal, separated from us, with a moving and intimate indifference that in some way brought Eduardo's grief to mind. When Rafael started the car, I thought about the long ride ahead of us and felt we would never get there. The sea's intense odor was like something rotten, and only the movement now beginning in the streets forced the sensation of time's flow on us.

We were driving along the seawall when Eduardo commented, "It's unbelievable, unbelievable. What are we going to do?"

But it was almost all I heard until we got to Mérida. Marta sat next to him in the back seat, holding his hand. They hardly moved throughout the trip; they looked lost in thought, numb, and I barely dared to look at them while I desperately searched for something to say, unable to avoid the feeling that as soon as I opened my mouth everything I said would seem stupid. Rafael also drove in silence, at full speed, constantly glancing down at the speedometer. Among us there seemed to be an inevitable union that, nevertheless, separated us even more. The sun rose very quickly above the hills, erasing any trace of the night's humidity with the same intensity that made every morning at the house on the beach appear to rush to a center of hard and relentless heat, a heat that now seemed to spring from the jungle instead of the sky, related to the cicada's shriek, in the same way that at the beach it had something to do with the sea's murmur. I felt my dress sticking to my legs and I closed my eyes, not sleepy, just trying to recover a sense of reality that would let me think. Marta talked softly to Eduardo the whole time: a monotonous and uninterrupted murmur impossible to penetrate. Once in a while I would open my eyes to see a miserable town, with dry trees and the same clean, skinny people, then the jungle, solid and burning, with the car, more than the highway, apparently slicing it in two. I felt that if I looked over my shoulder I would see it close again, but I didn't want to turn.

We reached the ruins much faster than I had expected. Rafael slowed down at the other line of the hills, and when we passed the ruins he turned to look at me and smiled for the first time. Then we had to stop to get gas. I got out of the car and Rafael came close to me.

"Are you tired?" he asked, taking my hand.

"No," I said. "But I don't know what to say to them. It makes me nervous."

"I don't either. Don't worry about it," he answered in the same tone he'd used in the room in Campeche.

Eduardo also got out and suggested we get some coffee. We went to a stand and he started talking about the heat, but suddenly he interrupted himself to ask Rafael, "How could it have happened? Can you explain it? He was the same as always, wasn't he?"

I realized that throughout the trip he must have been thinking the same thing without asking the question; I felt that, in spite of Marta's hand, right then he was only close to Rafael. The two of them looked exactly alike. On the other hand, Marta and I accompanied them as though the news was not yet real. Back at the car, Eduardo wanted to drive, but Rafael didn't let him. He sat in the back again and sank into silence. A little before we entered the city, Rafael asked him if we were going directly to his house.

"Yes, I think so," he said. "What else can we do?"

"Maybe we should change," Rafael suggested.

"What for?" Eduardo answered.

I turned around and saw him sitting with his arms crossed, his head leaning against the window.

Several cars were parked in front of the house, among them Celia and Lorenzo's. Nevertheless, no one came out to greet us as we crossed the garden; only in the dining room a gray-haired woman came out from one of the rooms and hugged Eduardo.

"Where's mother?" he asked.

"There, in the bedroom. She's waiting for you," the woman answered.

She also hugged Marta, kissed Rafael, and, after hesitating a little, offered me her hand.

"She's Lorenzo's mother," Rafael explained, although I had already recognized her.

We had to go through the living room, where several people were gathered, but no one approached us. Rafael and I followed a few steps behind Marta and Eduardo, and he held me by the arm. In the room, Eduardo's mother was sitting on a chair, next to the bed, separated from everyone; she wasn't crying, just staring at the body. Celia stood a few steps behind her with two women and a man, all of them dressed in black. When his mother saw Eduardo, she stood up and ran to embrace him. Then she started crying very slowly and caressing his hair and face.

"Good," Celia said, in a low voice. "She hasn't been able to cry until now."

Though the windows were open, there was the sweet, sticky odor of a closed room. Flowers stood at the foot of the bed; at each corner, tall candlesticks held lit candles. From one of them rose a long, straight line of black smoke. I tried not to look at the body, but it was unavoidable. He looked younger now, as if suddenly he had returned to a previous time. His face reminded me of how he looked when I met him in Mexico City, in spite of the paleness and his closed eyes. His head rested heavily on the pillow, creating a hollow in the white cloth and making everything else seem abnormally stiff. Through the window, the tree's greenness, motionless under the morning light, had something offensive about it. Eduardo left his mother in Marta's arms, went over to the bed, and looked at the body for a long time. Then he leaned over it, resting both hands on the edge of the bed, kissed the forehead, and, as he straightened up, instinctively wiped his mouth with his hand. Eduardo's mother went to embrace him again. He led her gently back to her chair. Rafael went over to kiss her and I followed him.

We remained there an endless time. Little by little, people started coming in to offer their condolences to Marta and Eduardo. I drifted toward a corner, and Celia stayed by my side, but she didn't talk to me. Then one of the women knelt and started praying the rosary. The rest of them joined in. Eduardo stood next to his mother, but Rafael, Marta, and Celia also knelt; I suddenly found myself alone, standing between the two windows, feeling it was too late to kneel with them. The murmuring of the voices rose and faded in a mechanical rhythm, unreal, alien to the dead body, which filled the room from where it lay. When the rosary ended, Celia came over to say that she had brought clothes for Marta and me and we could change at her house, but she explained that she hadn't wanted to touch my things, so she had brought me one of Marta's dresses. Then she went to talk to Marta. I had a real need to get out of the room, but I didn't move until Marta came and told me we should go to change.

Eduardo stayed with his mother. On the way, Celia told us that because of the heat the burial would be that same day at five in the afternoon. Rafael, who was driving, muttered that, nevertheless, it was too soon and it could have been delayed if the necessary precautions had been taken. His eyes were red and he was actually talking to himself, in an obstinate, almost childish tone. When we got to Celia's, he said that he was also going to change and would pick us up later; he didn't even get out of the car. In the meantime, Marta had been talking to Celia about the boys, trying to repress her anger toward her for not having brought them. She also looked tired, but she seemed oblivious to everything, as if she still hadn't been touched by the event, which remained outside of her. But while we changed, she suddenly commented that she would have to tell her father and started writing a telegram before she finished getting dressed.

Celia lived in a new part of town that had modern houses with low ceilings and lawns in front, totally different from Eduardo's. When we entered, Celia asked me to remember that she had been living at the beach for over a month and not to mind the mess, but the house looked spotless, everything in its place. We went straight to her room. The dark dresses and lingerie were laid out on her bed. Celia told me that if Marta's dress didn't fit me, she would lend me one of hers.

"There's no problem," Marta answered for me. "We've always worn each other's clothes, haven't we?"

While we changed, Celia sat on the bed, watching us. It bothered me a little to have to undress in front of her. When Marta started writing the telegram, kneeling on the floor and leaning on the bed, Celia commented, "It must have been very unpleasant to have your trip cut off this way. Deep inside we all knew he was worse, but no one expected this."

"I didn't know he was worse. He was the same as always," Marta said, leaving the pad of paper and picking up her dress.

"Of course," Celia said. "It was impossible to foresee it. I'm not reproaching you. It would be ridiculous. It was such bad luck. It could have happened while you were at the beach. The real problem is what you're going to do now. I can never accept it when someone dies. I don't even want to think how Eduardo must feel. I always remember Rafael. For him, father's death was much worse than for me. And now he feels terrible, too. You must have noticed already."

"Yes. It's true," Marta answered in a friendly tone, as if a tie had just been established between them.

"He loved him a lot, didn't he?" I interposed, unable to keep the words from sounding false and empty.

"Very much," Celia said. "And Don Manuel loved him, too. Since we were children. Rafael spent much more time with them than at home. I can't believe it. I remember him perfectly, always sitting on the veranda, before his first attack, when he stopped going out almost entirely. And at my wedding. He escorted me to the church and gave me away. And most of all at the beach, going fishing with Eduardo and Rafael. And he can't even cry. I can't either, how strange . . ."

Marta put an arm around her shoulders but moved away almost immediately to come and zip up my dress.

"Let's go," she said.

Then she turned to Celia.

"I must confess that sometimes I didn't love him."

"It's not true," Celia responded very quickly.

We sat in the living room waiting for Rafael. The heat was unbearable. I had the feeling that I was dressed for a performance whose meaning I didn't understand. Marta asked Celia for some lemonade, and as soon as we were alone I told her how I felt.

"Yes. It's totally absurd," she answered. "Everything jumped a thousand years away. I can't believe we were in Campeche last night. Were you very drunk? I don't remember what happened at the end. But suddenly again it seems to me that you've always been here."

"I feel exactly the opposite. I don't belong here."

Marta kept quiet.

"What are you going to do about Rafael?" she said then.

More than anything else, it bothered me to be wearing a black dress just then.

"I don't know," I answered; as I looked at her, the sensation that we were again at her house in Mexico City made me feel divorced from reality.

"Are you in love with him?" Marta insisted, in a sharp tone, perhaps trying to be ironic.

"I think so."

I thought she was going to ask me if he was also in love with me and I didn't want to answer her because that was up to Rafael.

"I don't want to talk about it. It bothers me," I added.

"Yes, you're right," Marta said.

But the conversation hadn't ended. I stood up and walked over to one of the windows. Marta followed me and put her arm on my shoulder.

"Nevertheless, you're still not a part of this," she said.

"No, I don't think so," I confessed and went back to the couch.

Celia came in with three glasses of lemonade and sat next to me. She handed me one of the glasses and commented that it was going to get terribly hot. Marta came to get the other glass, but before taking it she started laughing between her teeth, trying to control herself, but to no avail.

"What's the matter?" Celia said, frightened, and both of us went to her, not knowing what to do or daring to touch her, with the feeling that at any moment she would burst out laughing and we wouldn't be able to stop her, but she just kept laughing like that, inwardly, not getting any louder but not stopping either, and finally she started murmuring to herself between laughs: "I don't know, I don't know what's wrong with me . . . I'll be okay . . . don't get scared, it's nothing . . . I don't know what's wrong . . . it's as though I weren't here . . . everything's a lie . . . wait, wait, leave me alone, I'm getting over it, don't touch me, don't touch me . . ."

In the meantime her laughter rose and fell, making it hard for her to talk, but gradually it faded until she became quiet, her eyes staring at the floor, holding her breath.

"Do you want something?" I said, not daring to get close yet. Marta shook her head.

Celia took her by the arms and led her to a large armchair. Marta sat there, eyes to the floor, motionless, for a long time, while we looked on, waiting for her to talk. Then she raised her head and looked at me, smiling shyly.

"Don't worry. And forgive me. I'm fine now. I don't know what came over me. I couldn't control it."

I sat next to her and took her hand.

"I'm so glad you're here," she said. "You did what I expected. Exactly what I expected. Exactly."

Celia watched us without saying anything. Then she also sat next to Marta on the arm of the chair.

"You're exhausted. You should take a sedative," she said.

When Rafael arrived she told him what had happened and asked him to stop at a drugstore for a sedative. He was wearing a dark gray, slightly shiny suit; though he must have showered, he still looked very tired. In the car Marta sat in the back, holding Eduardo's black suit in her arms; it covered her legs. I sat next to her. As he drove, every once in a while Rafael turned slightly to look at her and smiled, without receiving a single gesture of response.

There was already an impressive line of cars in front of the house, and the wreaths were starting to pile up on one side of the veranda. We had to start greeting people from the moment we entered, but Marta kept moving, with the excuse that she had to take the suit to Eduardo, leaving me alone with Celia and Rafael. Lorenzo emerged from somewhere and, after talking to us for a moment, took Celia with him to say hello to someone. I took Rafael's arm and asked him not to leave me alone.

"Of course not," he said, talking almost in my ear.

Then he immediately introduced me to a very old man who came up to say hello to him, explaining that I was Marta's friend who had come to spend my vacation with her.

"Poor Manuel," was the old man's only response.

Marta's dress was a little tight on me, making the heat even more noticeable. Rafael tried to take me where there would be fewer people, but every room was full, and the small groups waiting in the corridor made it hard to get through. The muffled murmur of the conversations blended with the monotonous voices praying one rosary after another. I completely lost any sense of time. And though Rafael never left me, I still felt alone and out of place. People seemed to be there to carry out a communal ritual that involved more than the death of a friend or relative. To me, though, everything was new, secretive, and difficult to comprehend. The wake lacked the certain abstract character of distance you get at a funeral home. Here, the whole house seemed to have died with its owner. Nevertheless, for a long time I forgot or stopped feeling that it was Don Manuel who had died and that I would never again see him move with difficulty or hear him talk. Only when Rafael suggested that we go and keep Marta and Eduardo company did the event become real again. The tall candles next to the bed had burned down almost halfway, covering the top of the heavy candlesticks with wax. On the bed, Don Manuel looked much smaller now; only his hands, crossed over his chest and holding the crucifix, maintained their normal size. Nevertheless, the paleness of his face seemed an artificial effect caused by the candles' distortion of the light coming in through the open windows, hard and indifferent, accentuating each one of the drops of perspiration that ran down the faces of the people in the room. Eduardo's mother was still in the chair next to the bed, staring at her husband's body, indifferent to the heat and the suffocating odor of flowers and wax. Behind her, standing, with his two hands resting on the back of the chair, Eduardo was also looking at the bed, without noticing anything else either, as if only his gaze could keep the body from suddenly disappearing. Marta was farther back, among a group of women; when I saw her, I realized that there were almost no men in the room. More than heat, what I felt now was a lack of air that made it hard to breathe. The murmur of the prayers, the sticky smell of the flowers and the bodies, the faint hiss of the candles, absurd amid the dazzling light, devoured the air, creating a type of emptiness. I tugged on Rafael's arm so he would take me over to one of the windows. From there I saw that they had put ice under the bed, and as it melted, water began to spread. My eyes started to burn, and not knowing exactly why, against my will, I started crying, not for Don Manuel, but because of the total effect of the scene, the tears flowing more strongly when I tried to hold them back.

"Get me out of here, please," I asked Rafael.

My heels made too much noise, but I thought that if I tried to avoid it, I would lose my balance, so I held onto Rafael's arm. He went over to Marta and told her we would return in a moment.

"Where are you going?" she asked.

"Just outside, to the veranda," Rafael explained. "Elena doesn't feel well."

We passed the closed door to Don Manuel's study, where I had seen him the day I arrived, and went out to the rear patio through the kitchen, in which the maids were sitting. When she saw Rafael come in, the oldest one stood up and went to him, wiping her tears on her apron, while the others looked at us from their chairs.

"You've seen him, Rafael, you've seen him; what are we going to do?" she asked.

Her gaze seemed to expect everything from Rafael's response. He put his arm around her shoulders and kissed her hair lightly, but said nothing.

In the patio, the trees, so close to one another that their branches blended together to create absurd combinations of leaves, were completely still, as if suddenly they had become petrified, but the sun creeping through the branches created an impression of false movement produced by the lights and shadows, a movement too silent and secretive to be real.

"Do you feel better?" Rafael said.

"Yes," I answered.

My heels sank into the thick layer of fallen leaves, some of which stuck to them, dry, but full of whispers, with a different life now that they were dead. I leaned against one of the trees, my eyes burning, feeling somewhat ridiculous. Rafael stood in front of me, a few steps away, looking at me; then he leaned against me, his arms dangling, without embracing me, but enclosing me between his body and the tree. First I felt the roughness of the trunk on my back, then only Rafael's body, alive.

"I have to rescue you for myself," he said, his face touching mine. "Everything changes when we're alone."

For an instant I felt as if we would never really be alone. I kissed his neck and desire came like an emptiness in my stomach, an absence. But then I put my hands on his shoulders and pushed him away a little.

"What's going on with Marta?" I said without thinking, against my will, as if the words had been dictated to me.

"Everything and nothing. We'll have to talk about it," Rafael said, surprised. I felt he was withdrawing once more, and, as if humoring me, he added without embracing me again, "Do you feel better? We can't stay here too long. I'll explain everything to you. I'm with you," he insisted.

The house, which seemed to have been left behind, revived again.

"Tell me one thing," I asked Rafael, "why do they leave the body in the bed instead of putting it in . . . somewhere else? It's horrible. He's out of place all this time, as if he didn't belong to one thing or another."

"I don't know," he answered. "It's a custom."

"But it doesn't serve any purpose. And the ice under the bed is horrendous," I added, a little exasperated.

"Yes, it's true," he said pensively, "but it has to be done, because of the heat."

"It'd be better to forget the custom."

"Maybe," he answered, without looking at me. "Shall we go back inside?"

I didn't want to upset him, but I didn't know what else to say, so I only asked him if the patio in his house was as big as this one.

"Identical," he answered coldly.

Then he left me with Celia and Lorenzo to go back to Don Manuel's room. A continuous movement of people went in and out, from one side to another, approaching and moving away. Once in a while, someone spoke in too loud a voice, but quickly lowered it again. Sitting in the living room, I surrendered to the wait, not thinking about anything. At my side Celia looked equally distant, but she had a rosary in her hands. Twice Marta came to talk to me briefly; Eduardo went by several times without seeing anyone, looking lost. Suddenly, amid the stillness, a general movement started. Celia got up and I followed her to the veranda; Eduardo emerged, holding his mother, followed by Marta, Rafael, and the others who had been with them in the room. Rafael told me the people from the funeral home had arrived. The undertakers took the coffin into the room; Eduardo followed them, leaving his mother with Marta. For a long moment everyone seemed to wait in emptiness, motionless, holding their breath, as if every sign of life had something offensive about it and had to be concealed. Then Eduardo reappeared, followed by a priest, and the people started back into the room. Rafael was again next to me, while at the same time holding Marta's arm. A white lace spread covered the bed, which seemed like a useless and absurd object in a room entirely filled by the coffin's presence. I started wondering over and over, mechanically, if I cared about Don Manuel's death, if it meant something to me, if I could see it as something personal. The candlesticks had now been placed beside the coffin, and the flowers at the foot of the bed looked out of place. The priest, flanked by altar boys, muttered some prayers quickly, in a scratchy and unpleasant voice, and the people kneeling around him made him seem too tall. Then, he took the aspergillum from one of the altar boys and with an almost violent movement sprinkled holy water on the coffin, around the room, and on us. Some drops hit my face, and I felt revulsion. The undertakers went to the coffin, which now seemed totally impersonal, a mere object unrelated to Don Manuel. And he was alive again, exactly as I had met him in Mexico City, with Marta's father, talking to me in his study, even as Eduardo or Rafael remembered him and I had never seen him. Then I felt sorry that he had never been to the house on the beach while I was there. There was another general movement, confused and uncertain, awkward, and we all advanced in no special order along the veranda, toward the garden and the street. I lost sight of Rafael, Marta, and Eduardo. The sun sizzled on top of the endless line of cars parked in front of the house. I stayed close to the gate, not knowing what to do, looking at the garden behind me, neglected and beautiful, vibrating under the light, full of whispers and songs, until Rafael appeared and indicated that we should go to his car. Two men and a girl, whom I had met at the beach, were with him.

The funeral procession began in confusion, like the one in the house. Rafael honked impatiently. Then we were left isolated inside the car, far from the hearse at the head of the procession. No one talked at first, but gradually the two men and the girl sitting in the back started exchanging comments, leaving Rafael and me even more isolated, although once in a while he had to answer one of their questions in a monosyllable. At that hour the streets were empty. We advanced through a deserted city, a city in which the heat, unbearable inside the car moving at a minimum speed, had made all its inhabitants flee. Rafael stared steadily at the back of the car in front of us. Only for a brief moment, he extended his hand and took one of mine, without turning to look at me.

Before we got to the cemetery, the procession stopped in front of a small church, built on a hill in the center of an arid plaza. A bell was ringing with a broken, uneven sound. Rafael explained to me that all the processions stopped at "La Ermita" for the prayer of the dead; but the ceremony seemed to me a useless, exasperating delay, which only increased our exhaustion, making the funeral end in indifference. I'm not Catholic, I told myself, astonished, thinking that perhaps for the first time I truly understood the difference. Although the music, the prayers, the monotonous bell, and the presence of the coffin—elevated, enormous under the black shroud, with a golden cross in the center covering it—were impressive, the mixed smells of incense and flowers increased the stupor produced by the trapped heat of the church's dark space. Don Manuel's death was part of a ritual. Only Eduardo's mother's pain, as she leaned against Eduardo, at the door of the church while we were leaving, was real. Later, outside the cemetery, when we went back to the car, I told Rafael what I thought.

"Yes, you're right in a way," he answered. "But it means something and it's necessary. I've had the feeling all this time that he left us something greater than himself, something he stood for and we have to maintain so things can have a meaning. You would have to understand it. I love him very much; he's a part of me. He has existed for me as long as I can remember. And won't stop existing. I can't explain it to you. Though I should be able to. At best, it's just a kind of . . . what, sentimentalism, perhaps? Because I loved him very much; I loved him very much."

Eduardo came up to us then. During the burial I had observed him. He hadn't cried, but his presence was more of an absence, as if he were only there for his mother to lean on; while at the same time he needed Marta's support. I had stayed behind, not knowing why or at what moment Rafael had left my side. Under the sunlight the group surrounding the grave became a series of shiny silhouettes, blurred by their paleness. The monotonous tolling of the bell at La Ermita weighed on the silence, as if it had accompanied us all the way to the cemetery. When the grave diggers began shoveling the hard, dry, almost white dirt onto the concrete slabs, Eduardo's mother hid her face in Eduardo's chest and moved away from the grave. Marta and several other people followed them; others stayed there, faces shiny with perspiration, engrossed in watching the grave diggers' work, their shovels breaking with difficulty the hard clods of dirt. But little by little the people started to leave, and when they began to place flowers on the grave, only Rafael, Lorenzo, three or four others, and I remained. The rest were gathered around the cars, talking, delaying their departure. Now everything had ended. Rafael and Lorenzo took me by the arms, gently, as if they suddenly realized that I felt apart from the whole thing.

"Your being here is going to be good for Marta and Eduardo," Lorenzo said, naturally and sincerely.

While we walked toward the car, nobody talked, until I commented about Eduardo's mother, and Eduardo came to tell me that he and Marta would wait for me at his mother's house.

"We're going also, for the rosary," Celia said.

She and Lorenzo stopped to say good-bye to someone, and Rafael and I got in the car.

"Aren't you going to wait for those people who came with us?" I asked, when he started the car.

"It doesn't matter. They'll get a ride with someone else. I'd rather be alone with you," he said.

But instead of driving, he just sat behind the wheel, staring straight ahead, as if unable to leave the cemetery, which now, with the light beginning to fade, took on a sad and solitary appearance.

"It's painful for you," I said, caressing his hand.

"I think so," he answered. "I was expecting it, but now I realize that something else died with him. I feel he left without telling us something indispensable, as I told you," he insisted with ill-humored desperation.

On the way back, he commented that he was going to take me to his house so I could see how similar it was to Eduardo's; but when we got there he only stopped for a minute and started the car again before I could try to get out.

"What's the use?" he said. "I'll show it to you some other day. But they look the same from the outside, don't you think?"

"Yes," I admitted.

In truth, they didn't look much alike at all. What the houses had in common was the style created by the same form of life; but Rafael's loyalty bothered me—a loyalty directed against himself and me.

"Is your aunt home?" I asked him.

"She should be," he answered. "She hardly ever goes out; she has difficulty walking."

It sounded like a lie, but I didn't say anything.

At Eduardo's there were fewer people than before the funeral, but the line of cars in front was still impressive; inside you couldn't enter any room without running into somebody. Eduardo's mother had lain down to rest, so Marta and Eduardo had to tend to everyone. As soon as she was able to give me a minute, Marta took me aside and told me she would have to stay overnight with Eduardo and his mother.

"There's going to be a rosary and it's impossible to leave my mother-in-law alone. What do you want to do?"

I answered that I didn't care.

"If you'd like, you could go with Celia and Lorenzo to look after the children. I'm worried about them," she told me.

Then she smiled for an instant and asked me if I was capable of taking care of them.

"I hope so," I said.

Rafael came up and asked what was going on.

"Or I can take you," he said, after Marta explained that I was leaving with Celia.

"Perfect," Marta said, without looking at him. "Arrange it among yourselves, then. I'm going to Eduardo."

When we were alone, Rafael searched for my hand and squeezed it. Then, casually, he said that we could leave as soon as Eduardo's mother got up, because he wanted to say good-bye to her. Celia came up to us.

"You're going to look after the children?" she said.

"Yes," I answered. "That's what she wants."

"She told me," she continued. "Lorenzo and I are also leaving in a little while. If you want, you can follow us. That way we will arrive together and I can give you the children. Are you thinking about staying or are you coming back later?" she asked, turning to Rafael.

"I don't know. Right now, I think we should be with Eduardo, don't you?" he suggested.

Eduardo and Marta were in the main living room, with several other people. We sat next to them and Eduardo leaned toward me.

"How do you feel?" he asked.

"A little tired," I said. "And you?"

Eduardo shrugged his shoulders. He looked younger than ever, much younger than any of us, with the same moving, pleasant, clumsy air as when I met him in Mexico City. Rafael patted him on the back and he attempted a smile, but then we all fell quiet for an endless time. Seated in the living room, we seemed to be expecting something that would never arrive. It wasn't as hot as before. A soft, light wind, which a little earlier had started stirring the plants in the garden, was coming through the doors and windows, barely puffing up the sheer curtains, but the room retained the sticky smell of dead flowers that weighed on the entire house and made it hard to breathe. Suddenly I wanted to be in Mexico City, far from everyone, not at home, but at the office, in the daily routine, so familiar as to be pleasant. But the possibility of returning seemed lost forever, as though it lacked reality, like a dream from which I had definitively awakened to enter, for the first time, my inevitable reality.

Once in a while someone came in to say good-bye to Marta and Eduardo, producing a series of movements that pulled us out of a stupor within which the only reality was the knowledge that we had to be there to keep them company. On top of everything else, we were all wrapped up in ourselves, oblivious to the others, but supporting each other in some way. However, when Eduardo's mother came in again, I realized that it was just seven o'clock and only now shadows were forming in the room. Outside, the garden was still filled with light.

Eduardo got up to greet his mother and Rafael told me we could leave.

"Yes, you should go see the boys," Marta commented.

I had completely forgotten the previous conversation and it took me a while to believe that I was returning to the house on the beach. We went to say good-bye. Eduardo's mother kissed me on the cheek and looked at me with the same clear, shiny eyes that had stared fixedly at me the day I arrived.

"Thank you for everything. I knew we could count on you. Don Manuel was very fond of you."

Then she hugged everyone, without allowing the tears that were beginning to glisten in her eyes to flow. I had to say good-bye to all the people we encountered on our way out; I couldn't remember anyone's name, and all they cared about was Rafael's presence next to me. Marta accompanied us to the door and made a series of recommendations concerning the boys.

"Don't worry," Celia said. "I'll help her."

I would have liked to have changed before leaving.

"Don't drive too fast," Celia warned Rafael when they left us at the car. "We're all tired."

The city streets had recovered their activity. A faint light enveloped the houses and the trees, softening their profiles and accentuating the sheer heaviness of their volume, although the wind swayed the treetops. I rested my head on the back of the seat, free now of the weight I had felt before, becoming myself again. Rafael turned to look at me. Even though I knew Celia and Lorenzo were behind us and would be watching, I slid over next to him and kissed his neck.

"I couldn't wait any longer," I confessed.

"Yes, it hasn't been easy."

Then he pointed at the clouds gathering in the distance, far from the city—dark gray at the very top and silver where the sun's rays still touched them, somewhat menacing, being pushed along by the wind.

"Look," he said. "The summer's over."

"Do you think it'll rain?" I asked, surprised.

"Not yet. It's too soon. The breeze will take them inland. But perhaps in a few days."

"Maybe I won't be here by then," I said.

"Don't say that. I don't want you to go," Rafael answered, taking my hand.

I moved closer to him and he put his arm around my shoulders.

"We have to be together; I love you," he said.

"Me too," I answered, sure of myself. But what made it easier for me to be with him was knowing that one of these days, not too far from now, I would have to leave, although right then I felt that I wanted to return as soon as possible.

"Do you realize you'll have to go to Mexico City to get me?" I asked him, without moving away from him.

He kissed my hair and removed his arm from my shoulders to hold the wheel with both hands. We were already on the highway and, in spite of Celia's recommendation, Rafael drove extremely fast. Through the rear window I saw the outlines of trees and weather vanes fading behind us and realized that I felt the hard, dry landscape on both sides of the highway as something known, familiar.

The wind blowing in through the open windows made an unbearable noise. I had to ask Rafael to repeat what he had said. He rolled up his window and repeated his question: "Is there someone waiting for you in Mexico City?"

"There was," I told him. "I told you about him the night we left the nightclub together."

Rafael kept silent, so I added, "I haven't written to him."

"Is he your fiancé?" he asked.

"He was my lover," I said. "He's divorced and has a son. He's a very good person. I thought I loved him, but now I know I don't."

"Why?" he said, distant.

"Because I love you. Are you angry? I had to tell you."

"No, I don't think I'm angry," he said. "You're right."

I observed his profile in the darkness starting to surround us and—recalling the first day I saw him and then the last night in Campeche, the care with which he had taken me, the fact that he was young and I liked him more than I had ever liked anyone before, and the solid, strange feel of his body next to me when I was falling asleep, knowing it was he, and on the other hand, since I had never spent the night with Pedro or anyone else—I felt I must love him. I put my hand on his arm, desiring his touch, but he kept driving with both hands on the wheel until he turned on the headlights.

"I'm happy being with you," I told him.

He touched my face.

"Yes, it's wonderful," he said. "I didn't expect to have you, though I wanted you from the first day."

"I didn't realize it."

"I did," he said, laughing. Then he added, "Can you smell the marsh?"

Eduardo had asked me the same thing the day I arrived. Far away, the lighthouse beacon could be seen, reappearing periodically in a steady rhythm amid the starless sky.

The wind was shaking the palms more than ever when we reached the port. Celia and Lorenzo caught up with us when we turned into the plaza and she stuck her body halfway out the window to yell, "I told you not to speed!"

Rafael turned to look at them, smiling. I instinctively separated a little from him. There were fewer people than usual on the streets, but still, the commotion was greater than in Mérida. Rafael stopped at a store to buy cigarettes, and Celia and Lorenzo parked behind us. I stayed in the car while he went to talk to them before entering the store. The sand from the street rose in the wind, whirling around in the beam of the headlights, and the salt in the air stuck to my body. The day's events seemed far away now that I was close to the beach again, although Marta's black dress and the strange feeling of wearing stockings for the first time in so many days brought them back to mind constantly. I took off my shoes and stockings. When Rafael got back, he noticed immediately and caressed my legs.

"I like you that way," he said, before starting the car again.

I put my feet up on the seat and circled my legs with my arms, resting my head on my knees, happy and a little embarrassed.

We took the highway again, with Lorenzo's headlights behind us. The palm trees swaying from side to side made a terrible noise; in the darkness the idea of having to sleep alone in the house with the children and the maids frightened me, and I asked Rafael if he thought there was going to be a storm.

"No, it's only the wind," he explained. "But the sea must be rough already. What a shame."

"It scares me," I confessed.

"Don't be silly. Nothing's wrong," he said, very seriously.

He grasped one of my feet and didn't let go of it until we got to their house. The lights were off in the back and it looked as if no one was there. Rafael stopped the car in front of the kitchen door.

"Should we wait for them?" he asked.

"Yes, I think it's better," I said.

Rafael kissed me and I hugged him, feeling a need for his protection, but he withdrew quickly when Lorenzo pulled in behind us and his car's headlights lit up the patio, tracing a half-circle in the darkness that reminded me of the lighthouse beacon. Celia came over to us.

"It's strange the lights are off. I hope they haven't put the children to bed already. Let's go and see."

We entered through the kitchen. Celia turned the light on and called the maid.

"There's going to be a norther," I heard Lorenzo say as he came in.

"I don't think so. It's just a strong wind," Rafael repeated.

Nevertheless, the beach felt different, although we had encountered several cars on the highway and there was as much general movement as before. When the maid came in, I noticed that Celia was staring at my bare feet with a puzzled look. She asked what was wrong with the children, and the maid said that they hadn't wanted to go to sleep and were playing in their room.

"That's good," Celia said. "She's going to take Marta's children home to sleep."

"Poor Doña Marta," the maid commented, but Celia ignored her. We went into the room. The boys were in pajamas, playing under the hammocks, which hung in different directions and at different heights, like an absurd circus net. Eduardito came to Celia when he saw us.

"Where's my mom?" he asked, hugging her legs.

"She stayed in Mérida with your grandmother. But you're going home with her," Celia said, pointing at me.

The boy looked at me for a moment.

"When is mom coming?" he asked again.

"Tomorrow," I said, bending down next to him, disturbed. "Don't you want to go home?"

"I want to stay with them," the boy said, very seriously, returning to the other boys.

Celia and the nannies laughed.

"They've had a lot of fun," Marta's young maid said.

Then she asked me about Eduardo and if I had seen her mother.

"Don't talk about that. The boys might understand," Celia said, and added, "It would be better to take them now. It's time for them to go to bed."

Eduardito started crying when I tried to pick him up, and I had to let the nanny carry him; however, he went with Rafael without complaining when we went back to the living room. Celia accompanied us to the car and asked Rafael if he was coming back to spend the night.

"Yes, I think so," he said. "But you don't have to wait up for me."

"It doesn't matter. We're not going to bed yet," Celia answered. She stuck her head in the window and said, in the same formal tone she still used with me: "Excuse me for not accompanying you. I also have to see to my children. I'll stop by for you tomorrow morning."

Then Rafael told her not to be ridiculous and to quit talking to me like a stranger, but she never did. Before Rafael started the car, Lorenzo came out to ask him for some cigarettes.

"Your wife is a snob," Rafael said, handing them to him.

During the entire ride, the nanny talked about her mother and how she must have felt about Don Manuel's death; I couldn't muster enough courage to ask her to be quiet. But the boys began to doze off as soon as they got in the car.

The house was completely closed; as we went in, after struggling for a long while with the rusty lock, its loneliness depressed me. I turned on the lights, and Rafael helped me open the curtains. The rumble of the sea reached us with more force, confused and agitated, blending with the uninterrupted lament of the palm trees; beyond the windows it was impossible to see anything, not even the moon, as if the house were isolated in the middle of darkness, surrounded only by vague murmurs.

Thanks to Rafael, I managed to put the children to sleep without too many problems, although I had to let them fill their beds with toys. The nanny stayed with them, and Rafael and I went downstairs, without touching each other. He lit a cigarette and looked at me without talking, as if waiting for me to speak.

"Do you have to leave?" I asked him.

"No. I'll stay and keep you company," he answered, smiling through the cigarette smoke.

"What's so funny?" I asked.

"The way you act around children," he said, laughing this time. "I've never seen such ineptitude."

"I know. It's terrible," I said, smiling also, but a little embarrassed.

"I love it," he answered and started kissing me.

I kissed him back and embraced him; but then I pushed him away, disturbed, and told him that, if he didn't mind, I was going to change.

"Good idea," he answered. "I'll wait here."

While I undressed, I realized that what bothered me was being alone with him in the house. Deep inside I would have preferred for him to go so Celia wouldn't have the right to assume anything, but I was scared to stay there by myself, too. I kept staring at my reflection in the mirror, trying to convince myself that above all I wanted to be with him. Then I put on shorts but changed my mind and put on a skirt. One of the palm trees was pounding monotonously against the wall of my room; I thought the noise wasn't going to let me sleep, trying to imagine myself alone already, in bed.

When I got downstairs, Rafael wasn't in the living room. I thought he had left and ran to the door.

"I'm in here," he said, then, from the kitchen.

He was fixing something to eat. I sat on one of the maids' chairs to watch him work. He was as nervous as I was, and while he prepared things, all he did was smile at me once in a while, not knowing what to say. When he put the plate in front of me, I discovered I couldn't eat, and he didn't seem to be hungry either. Nevertheless, both of us tried to take a few bites before pushing the plates aside.

"What's wrong with us?" I asked then.

"We're trying to get to know each other," Rafael said.

"No, it's not that. What bothers me is to think of your sister waiting for you."

"I know. Me too. But there's something else I can't even explain to myself. Maybe it's everything that's happened. And we're tired, too. I don't know what to tell you. I miss those first days. Come on, let's go outside. Maybe we'll feel better out there."

He put his arm around my shoulders and led me toward the door. As soon as we opened it, the wind hit us in the face; the sea's roar, wild and undefined in the darkness, enveloped us totally. Rafael held me to him and led me outside.

"Everything's changed," I said. "The wind bothers me."

"Yes, you're right," he answered. "There's no purpose in being out here. Let's go back inside."

His tone revealed that something had upset him. We went back in like two strangers unable to touch each other in spite of their desire, and suddenly I thought that this had never happened to me with Pedro. Nevertheless, Rafael sat in one of the armchairs and asked me, in a delicate and gentle manner, to sit on his lap. I obeyed and he began to caress my hair with obsessive intensity. Once again I felt the emptiness in my stomach that made me want to lose myself in him.

"I have to take good care of you and respect your distance," he said in a hoarse voice. "I'll always remember you on the beach, your legs next to mine in the boat when we went fishing, and your face last night when I removed the sheet . . ."

He started kissing me and then unbuttoned my blouse, with his eyes closed, but suddenly moved away.

"Celia and Lorenzo might come looking for me. I think I'd better leave," he said, buttoning my blouse again with affectionate concentration, as if he had to protect me from something.

"I don't care!" I said. "I want you to stay."

"It's impossible."

"Why?"

"Because that's the way things are. And we can't change them. Or maybe I don't want to change them."

"But do you love me?"

"Yes, of course."

"Then stay."

"No, I shouldn't."

He stood up, but didn't leave. We stayed in the living room, kissing until my lips hurt, partially undressing and dressing again, suddenly talking about Eduardo and Marta and the funeral, and what I had felt the first days or whatever came to his mind to forget our kisses, but returning to them right away, like someone who performs a useless act but forgets its uselessness in the action itself, never going upstairs to my room as we both wanted but unable to separate, until only our bodies existed and I had his hands and his kisses like a living trace on my body, when we heard the sound of Lorenzo's car in the yard.

"We should have gone to bed," Rafael said, in a tone of exasperation, and I hugged him for an instant longer.

Celia and Lorenzo entered, claiming they were worried that we wouldn't know what to do with the boys, trying to discover in each of our answers and attitudes what had happened; they stayed, talking about Don Manuel's death and of many other people who had died, until I confessed I could no longer stay awake. They left together with Rafael, without giving us a chance to be alone for a moment.

I left all the lights on and, before going to my room, I went in to see the boys. Their nanny had fallen asleep on the bed next to the youngest boy. Her hammock hung empty, dividing the room. I didn't want to wake her. Eduardito was sleeping on the other bed with his face among his toys, breathing in a slow, peaceful rhythm. When I returned to my room, I discovered that I felt like an old aunt, close to them and inevitably far away at the same time. While I was trying to fall asleep, the sound of the palm tree against the wall reminded me of the rhythmic sound of the bells during the burial. I was alone.

XI

At dusk the next day, Marta returned to the beach without Eduardo, still in the same black dress she had worn to the funeral. Rafael had just left, and I was trying to help the nanny feed the boys.

I had gotten up very late and when I came down the boys had already eaten breakfast and were dressed to go to the beach, waiting, with the maid, for Celia to pick them up. The nanny explained that Celia had come very early and taken care of everything, without letting them wake me up. The news bothered me a little, but in reality it was a relief. I couldn't make them obey me and, even now, I didn't know how to answer their questions, still groggy from too much sleep and feeling more tired than the day before. I told the other maid to fix my breakfast and I went to the living room with the nanny to try to play with them. With shovels and pails in hand, they insisted that I take them out to the beach and asked when their Aunt Celia was going to pick them up. Through the window the sea looked the same as always, as if the sun, which was already glaring high in the center of a cloudless sky, had erased the traces of the previous night's gale, but outside I noticed that it had lost some of its clearness and the waves dragged heavy clumps of algae onto the shore.

Celia arrived, wearing the same old hat to protect her face from the sun and a blouse over her bathing suit. The boys immediately went to her and hugged her legs. After kissing them, she pushed them aside, called the nanny to take care of them, and sat next to me at the table. She wanted to know if I had slept well and then asked me for a cigarette, explaining that she wanted to take advantage of Lorenzo's absence to enjoy one. Although I knew it wasn't true, I asked if he didn't let her smoke.

"It's foolish. He doesn't ask me not to smoke, but I know he doesn't like it and I prefer not to do it when he's around."

"How considerate of you. I would never have thought of doing anything like that," I said.

She looked at me for an instant, trying to decide how to take my words. Then she adopted a friendly tone and asked me if I planned to go to Mérida to Don Manuel's rosary. She and Lorenzo could take me, she added, without mentioning Rafael. I told her I thought I should stay and take care of the boys, and she got up from the table.

"Yes, you're right. Maybe it is better. Besides, Marta may come back today. Not having a phone at a time like this is a real problem. I'll take the boys, then. Mine are already in the water with Lorenzo."

She called the nanny but, before leaving, turned back.

"Rafael asked me to tell you he'll be right over. He said to wait for him here or at the beach. If you want, we could all have lunch together."

"No, thank you. I already asked the maid to prepare something for lunch," I lied.

I stayed in the dining room, without deciding to go up to get dressed, looking through the window at the happy, lighthearted people on the beach, who seemed to contradict everything that had happened the day before. Nevertheless, to me, the beach looked different. Something I couldn't define separated me from it, making the glass in the window very important, as if that distance had to be maintained so I could feel comfortable; I caught myself remembering Mexico City again with nostalgia, but thinking of Rafael and knowing he would arrive at any moment made me see that leaving wouldn't be so easy. Then I realized that without Marta the house seemed strange and I didn't know what to do. Someone had set up a huge red beach umbrella almost directly in front of the window. I went to talk to the maid, worried because I really didn't know if the children had something to eat; then I went up to my room, threw myself on the still-unmade bed, and started reading one of my mother's letters, distractedly, trying to recognize her in those cold and distant lines relating trivial events, knowing I wasn't really interested in them—until Rafael appeared at the door.

"What are you reading?" he said, without entering the room, one hand resting on the door frame.

He was in trunks and had a towel around his neck.

"A letter from my mother," I said, still surprised, dropping the letter next to me on the bed, but not moving either.

"Did you sleep well?" he asked.

"I think so. I woke up very late," I answered. "And you?"

"Badly. I wanted to be with you."

I started to get up, but he came toward the bed, sat on the edge, and put his hand on my shoulder, gently pushing me back down.

"Stay like that. I like to see you lying down."

I obeyed and raised my hand to my shoulder, on top of his. He stared at me without moving. Then he leaned forward and kissed me for a long time. I caressed his bare back, wanting to scratch him and for him to bite me, wishing the kiss would never end, without knowing if I cared for him or if his presence just came to fill an emptiness; when I felt him sliding my nightgown off, I raised my body to make it easier, helping him with my movements. Rafael leaned back and looked at me again, no longer touching me or talking; I knew he was the one I needed, definitely. I closed my eyes, feeling first his gaze, then his hands, on me. I brought him to me, took off his trunks, and guided him with my hand.

Afterward, I took my mother's letter out from under me and threw it on the floor. Rafael—lying face down next to me, still breathing hard, his leg between mine—kissed my shoulder.

"Don't treat my mother-in-law's letter like that."

"Don't say that," I said quickly.

Rafael moved on top of me, propped his elbows on the bed, close to my shoulders, and rested his face on his hands, looking at me.

"Why not?"

"I don't know. I don't like it. We're fine this way. I love you," I said and forced him to lower his face to kiss me.

He sat up and looked at me again, resting one hand on the bed and caressing me absentmindedly with the other.

"I like to look at you. I've never been like this with anybody, not like this. Did you know that? I could look at you forever. We should never have to speak. People should simply exist, be, and discover each other without talking. But people always want to know everything."

"What do you want to know?" I said, taking hold of the hand he had on my breast.

"What you are."

"What you've seen."

"It's never enough. What am I to you?"

"You are Rafael, and you're wonderful."

I kissed his hand and he withdrew it.

"No, seriously."

"Seriously? Then, you're a friend of Marta's," I said, but added right away, "and a doctor who has a clinic. What else? You're a fisherman, but you like to think. And I love you for all those reasons. How foolish!" I ended, laughing.

Nevertheless, Rafael insisted, "Is it enough?"

"For me it is. What are you trying to find out?" I asked, seriously.

"I don't know. Don't pay any attention to me," he answered and kissed me again. "I can't believe I'm with you."

Suddenly I felt ill at ease.

"Rafael, do you think it's been too easy?" I asked and right away regretted having said it, but he broke out laughing, stood up, and took me in his arms, lifting me off the bed. I felt as if I had always known him and laughed, too.

When he set me on the crumpled sheets again, I had the sensation that the room had changed and we were alone in a strange place. His trunks looked like a stain on the floor. He picked them up and put them on.

"Let's go to the beach, okay? Celia and Lorenzo are waiting for us," he said, jumping on the bed beside me.

"Okay?" I said, imitating him. "I want to stay here."

"Me too," he said. He kissed my shoulder, stood up, looked for my bathing suit in the closet, and tossed it to me. "But it's impossible."

I put on my suit and stood in front of the mirror to comb my hair. Rafael embraced me from behind, resting his chin on my shoulder. I saw his face next to mine in the mirror and I felt proud and happy that he liked me.

"Tell me one thing," he said, not letting go, looking for my gaze in the mirror. "Aren't you afraid of getting pregnant?"

"I'm taking precautions, silly. I'm on the pill," I answered, looking at him through the mirror, too.

For an instant I saw a look of surprise on his face, but he recovered immediately.

"Oh, good," he said then, with a difficult smile.

I chose not to say anything. He moved away to pick up his towel and sat on the bed to wait for me to finish, pensive, unaware that I was watching him in the mirror. When I finished, I went and sat on his lap.

"Stop thinking nonsense. I love you," I said, with a true need for him to believe me.

"Me too," he said, almost to himself.

"It sure took you a long time!" Celia commented when we got to the beach.

Lorenzo and a group of friends were drinking beer under the umbrella, but she was somewhat apart with the children. Rafael was holding my hand and didn't let go. Marta's boys came up to us and the youngest one let me carry him without putting up a fuss, asking me in his baby talk to take him into the water.

"They just got out," Celia warned me, but I told her I would only take him to the water's edge.

Rafael carried the other boy, putting his free arm around my shoulders as we walked toward the sea.

"Like husband and wife," he insisted.

Later, when we joined Lorenzo and his friends, several of them asked me about Marta and Eduardo and commented about Don Manuel's death. I felt Marta's absence again and thought it absurd that, after the burial, the beach would go on looking the same as before. But actually the sea and the sun closed over it, erasing it, as if it had no place among them. Someone offered me a beer. Rafael sat on the sand, and I lay next to him, face down. Then suddenly I felt uncomfortable listening to them return to their usual conversations about people I didn't know or couldn't recall, so I went to sit next to Celia and the children. The sun shone fully on my back, and the beer was cold. Together they made me feel an inner pleasure, and I wanted to be alone, enjoying my own sensations, without sharing them with anybody, not even Rafael. For a long time I stared with my eyes half closed at the brilliant, almost colorless sea, turned into a pure reflection of light; then I felt the youngest boy's arm on my shoulder and the contact of his skin excited me. I hugged him and fell backward, with him on top of me.

"Let's go to the water," he said, and I took him back to the shore, a little ashamed of myself.

Rafael came and suggested we swim out to a friend's launch, which was anchored a few yards out. We left the boy with the nanny and ran into the sea. Rafael got there before I did and waited for me with one arm on the gunwale and his wet hair covering his forehead, with the same smile and very young appearance as the day I met him. He helped me climb aboard holding me by the waist, and we fell onto the covered part of the bow with our faces on our arms and our shoulders together, looking at each other, unable to distinguish anything but our mouths. I closed my eyes. The boat's soft rocking gave me the sensation of lying on the sea.

"The people at the shore asked what was going on between you and me," I heard Rafael say.

"What did you tell them?" I answered, with my eyes still shut.

"That nothing was going on," he said, and I felt his hand lightly caressing my back.

"Why?" I said, sitting up. "It doesn't bother me if they know about us."

The sun blinded me when I opened my eyes. Rafael was also sitting, with his legs drawn up to his chest and his arms around them.

"I don't want to start any gossip," he explained. "Celia told me our trip caused a scandal. They've forgotten it a little because of poor Uncle Manuel."

"How stupid," I said. "But I don't care. You can even tell them we've gone to bed."

"Don't be foolish," Rafael said, delighted, but then he kept quiet, staring at the sea.

"What are you thinking?" I asked him.

"That it's going to be strange to see you in Mexico City. But I wish I were there. Maybe it would have been better if I had met you the way Eduardo met Marta."

"I'm the same here as I am there," I said.

"I know. That's why you're different, even more different than Marta when she arrived. I like you this way."

"All that is very important to you, isn't it?" I asked.

"Of course," he said, "it's our life." He looked at me with happiness and added, "Don't listen to me. Nothing matters. Only you."

And he kissed me on the mouth. We lay on our stomachs again, next to each other; he left his arm on my shoulder. When I opened my eyes, the people on the beach were beginning to fold their umbrellas. Celia was waving to us from the shore and yelling something.

"Let's go and see what she wants," Rafael said.

The water was cold, but we soon entered a warm area again. Rafael swam next to me, without leaving me behind, and we got out together. Celia was about to go in and she wanted to ask me if the nanny should take the boys. I said that it was fine, and she asked Rafael if he was eating with them.

"No, come with me," I told him.

"Fine, we'll stop by later," Celia said, but Lorenzo stayed behind drinking another beer with us and asked me when I was thinking of going back to Mexico City. I answered that I still wasn't sure.

"Don't think I'm trying to get rid of you," he said.

Rafael laughed.

"She's always on the defensive," he said.

"And she's right," Lorenzo added, with a tinge of flirtation. "No, seriously, I think your being here is good for Marta," he said then. "As I told you yesterday, Eduardo is going to have a lot of problems from now on."

"Why?"

"Because of his father's business. His affairs must be a mess," he said.

I explained to him that in any case I had to go back to work in a few days, but he seemed to take it for granted that I would be staying indefinitely. He and Rafael sat under the umbrella, while I lay next to them, in the sun. Lorenzo started talking about all the activities in Mérida during the following months, after the end of the season, but by then I would be gone and it made me feel like an outsider. I knew it would be a long time before I would return, and again I thought about how distant I was from Marta. While Lorenzo talked, Rafael stretched out his leg and started rubbing my shoulder with his foot. Far off I saw the young man from the plane, with two girls even younger than he was. When they passed in front of us, he came over to say hello. He gave Rafael and Lorenzo a cold "Hi" and told me how sorry he was about Eduardo's father.

"My parents were at the funeral, but I couldn't make it," he added, as if he needed to apologize, with a ridiculous though charming seriousness.

Then he told me he would be leaving for the United States in a week and, if I was going to be in Mexico City, he would like to stop by to say hello on his way back. I gave him my office and home phone numbers. He shook my hand to say good-bye and ran to his friends, who waited where he had left them, watching us.

"Why did you give him your numbers? Do you really want to see him?" Lorenzo asked as soon as he left.

"Why not? He'll remind me of all this," I answered.

"You're crazy," Rafael commented.

"Not really," I said. "I'm sure you acted the same way at his age."

"Maybe," Lorenzo said. "In any case, you've made him happy."

And standing up, he announced that he was going home for lunch. With Rafael's help, he closed the umbrella and started gathering his things. The beach was almost deserted, and the sea was starting to get rough again, causing the boats near the shore to rock violently. The tiny sails of the fishing boats returning to the coast could be seen over the horizon.

"We're going to have a strong wind again," Lorenzo said, the huge umbrella over his shoulder.

Rafael walked me to the house and then said that he was going to change and would be right back. From the terrace I saw him run home, not turning to look back, the towel in his hand. The boys had finished eating long before and were in the back patio playing with the nanny. I went to my room to shower; when I came down, Rafael was already in the kitchen, helping the maid heat up the food.

"You'll see what a great lunch I'm going to fix. Are you hungry?" he said when he saw me come in.

He was shirtless and barefoot, as always. I thought I would remember him like this later on and his image would never leave me.

At the table, while the maid came and went constantly, the fact that we were alone made me feel strange and uncomfortable, though Rafael talked and behaved with absolute naturalness.

"You feel uncomfortable," he told me, when the maid left after serving us coffee.

"Yes, I think so," I confessed.

"Why?"

"I feel we don't have a place."

Rafael stood up and kissed my hair.

"I am your place," he said.

I kept quiet.

"Hasn't it been what you expected?" he asked me.

"Yes, of course," I answered, regretting what I had said before. "I like being with you. More than anything else."

"But you miss something," Rafael said.

"What?"

"To be able to be yourself completely, right?"

"That's up to you," I answered.

"Then there's no problem," he said, laughing.

Celia and Lorenzo arrived a little later; we played bridge, bored and with no desire to talk, because, as Lorenzo said, what we all really wanted was something else. The continuous murmur of the wind among the palms made me nervous and tense, and in spite of it the heat was more intense than ever. Celia, my partner, had a hard time restraining the temptation to reproach me for my mistakes.

"No one wants to play," Rafael said after the first game. "It'd be better if we went to Progreso."

"What for?" Lorenzo protested. "You always want to be somewhere else."

"Just for some ice cream," Rafael said.

"Yes, let's go. It makes me nervous to play like this," Celia broke in.

In Progreso we went to the same ice cream parlor I had gone to with Marta and Eduardo and sat under the arcades. With Lorenzo's help, Celia started telling me about Marta's first months in Mérida, while Rafael stayed aloof, his eyes wandering from the ice cream parlor's list of flavors to the people passing by, until Lorenzo asked him what was wrong.

"Nothing," he said. "I was listening to you."

"The thing is, he wasn't here when Marta arrived and it bothers him that he can't participate in the conversation," Celia said, for my benefit.

"I got here five months later. I don't see the difference," Rafael said. "Besides, Elena must already know all that. She and Marta used to write to each other."

"It's not the same," Celia said.

"In any case, I don't understand what you're trying to prove," Rafael went on.

"Prove? Nothing. I'm simply talking about Marta because I love her and remember how hard everything was for her at first, living at Uncle Manuel's. What's wrong with you is that you feel guilty. I don't know why."

My ice cream had melted almost completely, untouched, and I was playing with my spoon in it. I looked at Rafael and felt like protecting him. He called the waiter and paid the check, but when we got back in the car, instead of taking the street that led to the highway, he turned and drove toward the levee.

"We're going for a ride along the pier. It's too soon to go back," he explained.

The waves covered the beach almost up to the levee and the wind came whistling through the open windows, but on the other side, under the houses' arcades, people still sat on their rocking chairs and many children played on the nearby sand dunes. In front of us, the pier stretched out endlessly into the open sea, disproportionate and absurd. Two ships were unloading, and train cars lined almost the whole stretch. Rafael drove in silence. When we reached the pier's last esplanade, he opened the door for me. As soon as I got out, he took me by the arm and led me to the side, where one of the ships was unloading.

"I can't stand Celia's attitude," he said.

"Don't be silly," I answered. "I'm with you and I don't care."

The wind blew my hair over my face and made my skin feel sticky.

"I know," Rafael said. "But she doesn't have to pick on you because of me. They're against me, not you."

"Why?"

"Stupidities from long ago. But maybe she's right. It's my fault."

"What? When are you going to tell me?" I asked.

"It's nothing important," he answered. "I have to go to Mérida today, but we'll talk about everything when I get back the day after tomorrow."

"It has something to do with you and Marta, right?"

"Yes," he said.

"Why didn't you tell me before?"

"Because there was nothing to tell. We'll talk later. Trust me until then. Can you?"

"Yes," I said. "I knew it all along."

And I thought about Marta's return. Lorenzo and Celia hadn't gotten out of the car and they started honking. We went back. When he dropped me off, Rafael said he was going to change and would come back to see me before he left for Mérida. Celia asked me again if I didn't want to go with them to the rosary, but I answered that I didn't know if Marta was coming and I preferred to stay with the boys. Then I called the nanny and went out to the beach with her and the boys. Some people were still swimming, but there were fewer than usual; the whole time, behind us, the murmur of cars going back to Mérida filled the highway. I sat on the sand, depressed, not wanting to think about anything, looking at the inexhaustible ebb and flow of the waves, without paying attention to the boys, wishing I could talk to Marta to find out everything from her, but without resenting Rafael because of it, certain he had been sincere with me, knowing I didn't regret having been with him.

When Marta arrived I ran out to greet her, but she was tired and in a bad mood. She finished feeding the boys and went upstairs to put them to bed, while I stayed downstairs, not knowing what to do, feeling that after having missed her so much, her presence made me feel even more uncomfortable in the house. She came down, having changed from the black outfit into pants, and sat next to me, without talking. I asked her if she was tired; she shrugged her shoulders.

"Not too much. What I need is a drink. I'm beginning to sound more like Eduardo. Shall we have one?"

In the kitchen, while we were getting the ice, she asked about Rafael.

"He had lunch here and has been with me almost all the time," I told her.

"And how have you been feeling?" she asked me, her back to me.

She looked very attractive with her hair pulled back, in pants and a sleeveless blouse. Sure that each of my words would bother her, I didn't know what to say, because I still didn't know what she felt for Rafael, or if there had really been something between them that had ended because of me.

"Strange," I finally murmured. "Maybe because I feel closer to things."

"I don't understand you," she answered.

We went back to the living room and she lay on the couch, her glass in her hands, taking small sips once in a while with quick and nervous movements.

"In spite of everything, I loved Don Manuel very much," she finally said to herself, without looking at me. "I wish my father were with us. I feel an emptiness. You saw him before leaving; how is he?"

"The same as always. He hasn't changed," I said, when I realized that she was actually waiting for my answer.

"He's never seen this house. All of this was Don Manuel. It's unbelievable. I couldn't stand being in Mérida any longer, with my mother-in-law. Poor woman."

"Don't think about it," I said.

"But I don't want to think about other things either," she answered.

It seemed that in spite of everything, she was being unfair to me, and I kept quiet.

"Shall we have another drink?" she said then.

She went to the kitchen and came back with the bottle, water, and a bowl full of ice; after she served me and herself, she lay on the couch and started talking again, as if to herself, taking the same nervous sips from her drink. Though it was completely dark, we hadn't switched the light on, and the sound of the sea reached us clearly in the darkness.

"Do you know that Rafael and I talked about you in Campeche, when I still wasn't sure what he expected from you? Rafael is very strange. It's going to take a great deal on your part to really get to

know him. When I wrote asking you to come, we thought that . . .
I don't know what . . . Eduardo was very confused and so frightened.
I have to help him a lot."

I got up and went to sit next to her.

"I want to talk to you. I know I've hurt you. You should have told
me," I said to her.

"No, it's not exactly that," she answered, very quickly. "You are
you, I've always known that. We're just very different now. It's
natural, but I didn't expect it. On the other hand, without realizing
it, you've made me see a lot of things. What do you think about
Eduardo and me now that you've seen us? I asked you the same thing
the day you arrived, do you remember? Except that we never
continued the conversation. Now you can answer."

"He doesn't look very happy, and I knew before I came that there
was something bothering you," I said.

"But is anyone different?" she answered. "I don't know what we
want. All of us. Even you. At least now I know I love Eduardo. What
do you plan to do? Do you expect to get married, like me?"

"I don't know," I said, sincerely.

"We're lying," she said. "We should have dinner, don't you think?
I really don't want to get drunk. They must be praying the rosary in
Mérida. Is Rafael coming?"

I told her that he was going to Mérida but had promised to stop
by before leaving; she stood up to turn on the light.

"We're going to have to get him to stay. He shouldn't leave us
alone. Let's prepare something for dinner."

When he came in, we were in the dining room. Marta asked him
if he had already eaten and started talking very quickly, making jokes
and laughing at them herself, as she did when we were teenagers.
Rafael had his coat in his hand and his tie hung loose around his
neck. He told Marta he had to leave right away, but she insisted he
stay for dinner. The maid was listening to us attentively. Before
sitting at the table, Rafael asked Marta, for the first time, how
Eduardo was doing.

"You can imagine," she answered.

"Is he coming?" Rafael went on.

"No," Marta said. "Not until tomorrow or maybe the day after."

"And you're not going?"

"No. I can't take another rosary or the visitors all day long.
Eduardo is out all day taking care of things, and I have to be here to
look after the boys."

Rafael started eating in silence while Marta looked at him without touching her food, and I looked at her. She finally started eating, too, but after a few bites she set her plate aside.

"Do you think it's wrong for me not to go?" she asked Rafael.

"No," he said. "But Eduardo must need you."

"I know," Marta said, with an unexpected tenderness in her voice. "I could have gone with Celia and Lorenzo. Have they left already?"

"Yes, but it doesn't matter, don't worry," Rafael said. "I'm exaggerating."

I realized how close they were through Eduardo; but it didn't bother me, because Rafael talked with complete sincerity; nevertheless, when he finished eating, Marta insisted he stay, and when he refused, she turned to me.

"You ask him."

"He can't . . . ," I said, upset and furious.

"Don't be silly, Marta," Rafael commented, almost at the same time.

He stood up to pick up his coat; Marta followed and put her hand on his shoulder.

"I want you to stay. Really. We have to talk."

Rafael caressed her face lightly before answering.

"It's not important. Later."

She stayed next to him, and he turned toward me.

"I'll come back tomorrow if I can; if not, the day after."

"Fine," I said.

He started to reach out for me, but instead touched Marta's hair lightly.

"See you later. I'm going to see Eduardo."

Marta didn't move, but when Rafael disappeared down the hallway, she turned to me and, as if asking permission in spite of herself, in a painful manner, sad and angry at the same time, she said, "I have to talk to him. I can't take it any longer."

And she went after him.

It took me a long time to realize that I was alone and I had to accept that, somehow, I always knew this was going to happen if I went after Rafael and, nevertheless, I had done it; now what I felt also mattered, but I couldn't stop respecting that absurd right that from the beginning I understood Marta had over him. But I was jealous and the only thing I wanted was to talk to Rafael to find out everything, because it was also true that he was on my side. I had felt it that morning and continued to feel it now. Nevertheless, without moving from the living room, I heard the sound of his car starting, and I didn't go out to the patio until I was sure, from the time that had elapsed, that Marta had gone with him.

"They left together, miss," the maid told me when I passed by the kitchen.

"Yes, I know. Don't worry," I had to answer. "Marta doesn't feel well. She's very nervous. They went to Progreso for some medicine. You can go to bed."

"But Don Rafael didn't want her to go. I heard him," she added.

"Don't worry. He knows what he's doing. You can go to bed. I'll wait for them," I insisted.

"Don Rafael is very good," she commented to herself when I walked away.

In the patio the shadows of the palm trees shook inexhaustibly on the ground. I went out, dazed, and stood in the middle of the highway, staring at the darkness, until two cars sped by, one after the other, honking, forcing me to move to one side; then a group of people, from which several voices greeted me, stayed talking near the house across the street. I went inside the house again and sat to wait in the living room, without feeling lonely or being aware of the passing of time, with the sensation that nothing that had happened really concerned me, completely empty, refusing to think amid the silence, convinced that the sea had disappeared all of a sudden, but when I heard the sound of the car entering the patio again, I switched off the light instinctively, ran up the stairs, and stopped in the hallway to wait.

Marta and Rafael came in and turned on the light.

"Do you want me to call Elena? I'm sure she's still awake," she asked, in a calm, serene tone.

"No. I'll go up later. Everything's all right," Rafael said.

I was embarrassed to be listening, but I couldn't move.

"Sleep down here if you want. No one will know. It's past midnight," Marta said.

"It's not necessary. Don't worry. Everything's all right," Rafael repeated. "Go to bed."

"I'm ashamed," Marta said in a low voice.

"You shouldn't be. We both knew it," Rafael answered.

I could imagine his smile when he said it; the thought that he might be touching her made me jealous of Marta, then sorry for her, because now, in spite of everything, he loved me, but I refrained from going downstairs, certain it would have made things worse, not better. I locked myself in my room, from where, sitting on the edge of the bed, my hands on my knees and the light still off, I heard Marta coming up. I wished she would come in and at the same time I was afraid she might, but after pausing in front of my door, her steps faded, and I heard her enter her room. I knew Rafael was going to come up, and suddenly I felt I didn't want to see him, for my sake and maybe also for Marta's. I switched the light on and waited, unable to avoid feeling stupid, as if now everything had turned into an absurd game that had to end so everything could be the same again.

When Rafael knocked, knowing I wouldn't let him see me as he expected made me feel a selfish and secret pleasure. I let him knock several times, stronger each time, without responding, but suddenly, in my mind, I saw him behind the door, and against my will I got up and opened it.

He took my hand and led me out to the hallway, but I didn't let him go any farther.

"No, I don't want to go downstairs. Why didn't you tell me?" I asked him, unable to avoid it.

"I thought you already knew. And you did, didn't you?" he answered, in a low voice.

"Marta says it's very hard to get to know you," I said.

"On the contrary," Rafael said. "It's too easy. I love you. You know that."

He kissed me lightly, but I moved away immediately. The light coming out of my room was the only one illuminating the hallway, and once again I felt uncomfortable and angry at him. The sea seemed to penetrate the house through the dull and agitated murmur coming in through the open windows.

"How's Marta?" I asked him.

"She's fine. She always was. It was my fault," he said, calmly. He kept quiet for a moment, then repeated, "I love you."

I let him kiss me, longer this time, but without responding.

"I don't want to leave like this," he said then. "I need you. I want to clear everything up."

"You have to leave," I said, but added, "I love you, too. But I don't know if it matters now. I don't know. It's your fault. And you know it. Go away."

He looked at me, without touching me, resigned.

"I'll come tomorrow afternoon," he said. "Stay here. Don't walk me down, but think about me, please."

I went back into my room before he got downstairs. When I heard the sound of the car, I thought Marta must have heard it, too. I loved him, but there was nothing definite between us yet. I started waiting for him from that very moment, unable to sleep, feeling that I should have ignored everything instead of creating that distance by making him talk.

XII

In the car, alone with Rafael again, I discovered that the day spent with Marta came between us, over and above the wait. Somehow things were different, like the suddenly deserted beach, with its endless line of dead fish. After his "how are you?" when we were alone, he drove in silence toward the center of town, as if, before anything else, we had to get away from Marta and the boys. In the plaza people moved around the stands, the music from the cantinas mixing in the air as before, but there were no vacationers in sight. Rafael turned right, off the asphalt road and onto a street of firmly packed sand with dogs barking all around us, furiously chasing the car. I tried not to look at him, waiting for him to talk, but he would only turn once in a while and smile at me. The car bumped along, making Rafael drive slowly, zigzagging to avoid the deeper holes. From the doors of huts, children and occasionally a woman stared after us. I recalled the boy at the pier that morning and wondered where he lived. I was linked to the place in a different way because of him. Then we also left the huts behind when Rafael turned to the left to take a narrow road, threatened by the mangrove trees whose huge leaves and white trunks closed in from both sides. Beyond the trees could be seen the vast white clearing that announced the marsh. We turned again and drove onto it. Rafael stopped the car and left the motor running.

"These are the salt flats," he said. "Do you want to go farther in?"

"If it's possible, yes," I answered. "It's so strange."

"Sometimes the ground is soft, but there are paths. I hope we don't get stuck," he said.

He drove ahead cautiously between the plots divided by rows of poles stuck in the ground and finally stopped, almost in the center of the clearing. The place produced a strange feeling of emptiness. The sun was still setting and shone on it like a mirror, casting countless reflections; in the most humid parts, the white took on a pink tone, creating a marvelous play of unsteady planes in which the true distance disappeared entirely. The mangroves marking the beginning of the marsh seemed incredibly far off. We were enveloped by a pungent, penetrating odor, with an element of decay in it and something else as well, related to the purity of the sea.

Rafael remained still, with both hands on the wheel and his body slightly bent over it. Without taking my eyes off him, I leaned back against the door, raised my legs to rest my bare feet on the seat, and put my arms around my knees. He stretched out his arm and took my foot with his hand. The ritual gestures, I thought.

"What are we going to do?" I asked him immediately.

He let a moment pass without responding and also asked me, "Has anything else happened?"

"Nothing. I've hardly been able to talk to Marta. First, she was with the boys, then later Celia and Lorenzo came over. I haven't done anything but wait for you, wait and think of you."

"I've also thought about you," he said. "But in Mérida everything is different. I should be able to explain why to you; each thing assumes a different place. It wasn't good to meet you at the beach. Here we're too alone with ourselves; you exist for me and it seems to be enough. The same thing happened to Marta. Over there everything relates to something else, which also matters."

He let go of my foot and turned toward me, placing an arm on the backrest to face me.

"Last night, when I got to my house, after leaving you and thinking of you all the while I drove on the highway, something happened to me. I couldn't see you, neither you nor Marta; I could only think about Eduardo. But it was really a way of thinking about myself. Maybe it had to do with getting home so soon after everything that had happened. The house was totally dark, as if nobody lived in it. I realized that it had been so long since I had taken a good look at it that I wasn't really aware of it, as I was before, when I was a child, maybe. I've always thought I see things carefully. And nonetheless, there, in front of the gate, everything seemed new— well, not exactly new, but the opposite, as if it had moved away without me noticing and now had returned to make me see the fissures in what I had presumed was an invariable continuity. I think I told you already that as children, for Eduardo and me, my house and his were one house, like lots of other places. They were the world, like his parents and mine and the rest of the older people. A closed order in which we had a natural place. And I've always believed in that order. Do you understand? I went inside the house and through every room, turning the lights on and trying to find myself in them. It's been months since I've gone into any of them. It's absurd for me to still be in that house with my aunt. Celia should live there. Maybe then I could always see it that way, from the outside. But look, with you it's different again. This also reminds me of other things. As children we lived obsessed with the marsh and the salt flats, maybe because they never let us come here, or hardly ever. It was like another world, open. When I would go to spend my vacation in Campeche, with my aunt and uncle, I missed this place; its great distinction was the marsh behind the beach, while in Campeche there were only hills. The sea became land. They were perfectly separated and defined; here, on the other hand, they blend together. Once, Eduardo, Celia, and I came here instead of taking a siesta. I remember it clearly; they wore sandals and I was wearing shoes. At the most I was seven and Celia five. I hated sandals; as soon as no one was watching, I'd change into shoes. We came here and, of course, the first thing we did was go where the ground was the softest. After a moment we were covered with mud up to our knees and it itched, but it was an adventure. I had to take off my shoes, because they got horrendously heavy, and I don't know where or when I lost them. It must have been two or three in the afternoon. You can imagine how hot it was. The three of us started complaining that we were thirsty, but deep inside that's what made the adventure more attractive. We walked around here, close to the mangroves, until it started getting dark. I was in front and Eduardo helped Celia out of the mud when she sank in too deeply. Everything belonged to us! When we got back, they had been looking everywhere for us, and Eduardo and I almost got killed. They didn't touch Celia. That increased the pride we felt from being dirty and tired. Then we bathed and our skin began to burn terribly from the salt, mine more than anyone's, because I was barefoot. Nevertheless, I liked the idea that my shoes had stayed there and were already part of the salt flats. I guess I still think they must be somewhere around here, as witnesses."

He laughed, but he was far away from everything, including me, deep in himself, without even noticing how it had started to get dark, and somewhere far away, a dog kept barking. But before continuing, he took my hand and caressed it, absentmindedly, more than anything playing with it, as if it were an independent object.

"It's strange. Maybe back then Eduardo was closer to Celia than to me. I always saw them as one person, sometimes following me and then making me follow. Deep inside I was sure they'd end up married, like a natural extension, because I saw them the same way I saw my parents and his. Then, as a teenager, you never see the little girls you've grown up with, I mean, as women. Eduardo had thousands of girlfriends, but he never looked at Celia. He got along with her as he did with me and made fun of her boyfriends the same way I did. When I saw him with Marta, it seemed natural that someone else, completely foreign to his previous life, should be the one to marry him. Maybe now, I'm going to do the same."

He really looked at me for the first time since he had started talking.

"Something awful happened with Marta. For a while we thought we were in love. It was months ago. First we thought something was going to happen, but then it simply became the way things were. We knew it or we believed it, but we didn't even talk about it anymore. Until you got here. Both of us knew your arrival was going to mean something, because you'd be a witness. Something much more natural occurred. Don't you realize what goes on here? There are happy childhoods and miserable lives. We don't know what to expect from life. When I arrived and saw them, I mean Marta and Eduardo, I firmly believed everything was going to work out well for them. Marta was willing to do anything for him. If I fell in love with anything, it was their initial happiness. It made me feel close to her. But Marta was also looking for a ghost that wasn't Eduardo, the everyday Eduardo. But that one was good enough. And she was happy. I'm sure. Then something happened . . . time, I think. No, it's not nonsense. I'm talking about the everyday happiness and the problems, the everyday suffering. You already saw some of that. With all those things, they couldn't be themselves either. Here, no one is, they just endure. But Marta has never stopped loving the original Eduardo. That's why she sought me out. But between them there's a real union now that time has given them, and it's worth much more than all the ghosts. I found that out when you arrived. And now maybe she knows it, too. But you and I are different. Or at least, you're different. Maybe both of us."

With a sad serenity I realized that I felt closer and farther away from him than ever. The darkness was beginning to erase his features. There was a dull, constant heat. Rafael kept quiet and caressed my face intensely, attempting to truly reach me.

"It's been marvelous that you came. And not only for me. For Marta too, most of all, for Marta. I had lunch with Eduardo today. He's much better and has made some important decisions. All this time the most complicated issue has been that strange loyalty I have for him. I never felt I was betraying him. It was something else. As if I had something of Marta's that didn't belong to him, but, in exchange, he had the truth. I've kissed Marta only once. That's it. I wouldn't even be able to say exactly when everything started. We talked about it for the first time more or less a year ago. Maybe I knew before then that something was happening, but I didn't want to think about it. It began just like that. One day Marta told me that she thought she loved me. Then both of us started looking back for signs, not knowing why we were doing it. The bad thing about it is that I've hurt her so much. Especially during that period. But maybe it's also been good for us."

Darkness made the conversation easier. Now we talked, flowing in and out of ourselves, without either one of us feeling where we were or what was happening around us. Suddenly, however, I wanted to touch him, to have the Rafael of the previous morning, and for him to make me come alive. I put my feet next to his legs.

"It was different with you. You arrived and I saw you. From the first moment. I don't know why," he went on. "That's the way things happen. Maybe also, at the beginning, you were the Marta I hadn't known. But only at the beginning. Now you're just you."

He started caressing my legs and we kissed. I felt his hands unbuttoning my blouse and the whole conversation was left behind, forgotten, to allow only that first moment to exist and again the sea and the sun of that first morning.

Afterward, I rested my head on his shoulder, his arm around mine. Above, the moon had come out and the stars almost touched the ground. A murmur of flights, of secret movements, came from the mangroves.

"When are you leaving?" Rafael asked, kissing my hair.

"Why?"

"I've been thinking about it. The day has to come, doesn't it?"

"Yes. I want to leave soon. So you can come for me."

Rafael kept quiet. I moved away a little.

"What's wrong?" I asked.

"Would you like to come and live in my house?"

"I don't know. I still haven't seen it. And I can't imagine what it'd be like."

"Yes. It's hard to associate you with it. You're still not a part of all this."

"Neither are you."

"You're right, but in a different way, maybe. Because it's still strange to love each other. And because, I think, we don't know how to fool each other. You're not like Marta. You don't look for the same things. That I know. Not even at the end, when you know what to expect. What's your life like in Mexico City?"

"Very different. I'm alone."

"But you had . . ."

"Yes. But that's also different. That's why I can tell you I'm alone. He was a kind of companion, more than anything. What I thought I wanted to have."

"I can't imagine myself with you in Mexico City," he said.

"That's what I like."

Rafael drew me close again.

"We have to try it," he said. "But what you've seen isn't the other; it isn't the house in Mérida either."

"I know. That's what scares me. I can't go back in time like you. To me it would only be the present, everyday things. As a child I never felt anything was worthwhile; on the contrary. I always looked ahead, expecting to leave everything behind, to finally get to what was really important. We lived in a kind of private street. Do you understand? Several identical houses in a cul-de-sac, stone-paved, with grass growing between the stones. Its only charm was a tall fig tree, right in front of my living room window. Every time the figs came out I thought, one more year, and it made me happy, as if I was getting further away from something I didn't want. Maybe it was school. I hated school. All the girls were horrible, but I felt uglier than all of them. I didn't have any friends. If you had met me then, you would have been horrified. I was so ugly. With a hard braid that stuck out. The only thing I'm glad to remember is the park. I'd go there to jump rope. I could spend hours jumping rope. My father sat on a bench to watch me and said I would end up with legs like a soccer player. Always the same thing and I always laughed. That was long before I met Marta. Then, everything changed. It was marvelous. I only had an adolescence. Maybe that's when I stopped waiting."

Rafael drew me closer to him.

"I want to protect you."

"No, that's not what I want," I answered, without thinking what I was saying.

"In a way, that's what being married is all about," he said.

"Then I don't want to be married," I said. "I'm not Marta."

And I realized it was true. Nevertheless, I was with Rafael and felt that everything led me to him.

"I don't understand you," Rafael confessed, disturbed.

I hid my face on his shoulder, with my lips on his neck.

"Oh, Rafael, I only know I love you," I said, desperate and confused. "That should be enough."

"And it is enough, because it makes us accept everything else," he answered. "If not, it wouldn't turn out right."

The silence around us was awesome, and suddenly I had the feeling that we were in a dead place.

"There's something I haven't told you, about my aunt, the one who lives with me," Rafael went on. "You haven't met her because she never goes out. But there's nothing wrong with her legs, as I told you. She's crazy. Not exactly crazy, but a little disturbed. It's a kind of death. She's been the same for fifteen years, I mean, with the same face, without aging. She's completely peaceful. She just doesn't recognize anybody. She's the aunt I used to spend vacations with in Campeche. And she looks the same as she did then. Do you understand?"

"No. It doesn't have anything to do with us, does it?"

"Not with us—with the city, with my house, with me, maybe. It's very strange living with her, although she doesn't get in the way."

"We're talking too much," I said. "We both know what we want. It only has to be done. Would you come to Mexico City to get me?"

Rafael kept quiet for a moment.

"Yes," he said then.

"What about Marta? Do you think I should talk to her?"

"It's up to you. And her. I know you love each other the same as you always did."

"Yes, but something has changed, too. It'd have to be a new friendship. Not the one we had before. That one no longer exists."

"Don't say that," Rafael said.

"Fine. You don't have to understand it. Let's go. They must be waiting for us."

I kissed him before he started the car.

"It's been wonderful talking to you."

Rafael searched for my lips, but while I felt his mouth on mine I thought that in spite of him, I owed Marta a strange loyalty. Then Rafael turned on the headlights and the light disappeared in the enormous white surface, now with shades of yellow. I tried to imagine him there, as a child, with Celia and Eduardo, but it was impossible. I couldn't even really see his relationship with Celia, for example; on the other hand, and in a certain way, he continued belonging to Marta's world.

He turned carefully, avoiding the small wooden barrier separating one zone from another. The light revealed the mangrove trees hiding the path, and a little later we started moving between them, unable to avoid the holes, zigzagging from one side to the other. Rafael drove in silence, bent over the wheel. In the beam of the lights, a multitude of insects flew around, sometimes crashing against the windshield, even though we were moving very slowly. When we got to the first huts, Rafael turned to me.

"It bothers me to have to go back there."

I got close to him, put my arm around his back, and leaned my head on his shoulder.

"You know something?" I said, without knowing why. "I don't regret anything and I'm not going to forget you. Even if you go back to Marta."

"I won't forget you either."

I felt like crying, felt it terribly, but the tears wouldn't come. The dogs were already barking next to the car and once in a while they got in front of the headlight beam, running ahead of us. I didn't dare look toward the huts. In the plaza some of the stands were still lit, but hardly anyone was there; the dried, sandy garden had the same lonely appearance as it did on the night when Rafael, Marta, and I went to look for José; the same jukebox music disappeared in its empty space, and the sand rose in front of the church, forming shifting hills. When we reached the paved street, Rafael sped up. On both sides, every house was dark and no one walked along the highway as before. Eduardo's car was already in the backyard. The wind kept whipping the palm trees without pity, making them bend from one side to the other and moan, with a constant and wild murmur. I remembered what Marta had said that same morning: "You'll see how different it is from now on."

The House on the Beach

XIII

Eduardo, without the black suit, wearing one of the sport shirts he always wore and white pants, was fixing himself a drink.

"It's crazy to go to the marsh at this hour. You didn't get stuck?" he said.

"No," Rafael answered, patting him on the back.

Marta, lying on the couch, with her head leaning on the backrest, didn't move.

"Do you want a drink?" Eduardo said.

"Yes," Rafael answered, and turned toward me. "Do you?"

I went to sit next to Marta. She sat up and looked at Rafael.

"Celia and Lorenzo came looking for you. They were on their way to the rosary."

"What did you tell them?"

"The truth," Marta said, pointing at me with her hand.

"Very good," Rafael said. "What about you, how do you feel?" he added, turning toward Eduardo.

"Tired, but that's all. What I needed was to be here again. There are lots of problems, but not as many as I thought. Father left everything in order. Poor man. He never told me anything."

He handed a glass to Rafael, came to give me mine, and sat next to Marta. Rafael, standing in front of us, hesitated an instant.

"What about your mother? How is she?" he finally asked.

"You can imagine. Wanting to be alone and surrounded by people. We can only wait. She started arranging father's clothes and things. She cries all the time. But it's good for her."

"Yes, of course," Rafael said.

He took a few swallows of his drink, still hesitant, and then sat in front of us, leaning forward, his elbows resting on his knees and the glass in both hands, slowly turning it.

"I already told Marta about the house," Eduardo said.

"Yes? What do you think, Marta?"

"It's fine. At the beginning it's not going to be easy with Eduardo's mother, but we'll be more comfortable. It's a matter of readjusting. This was a false solution, anyway. We wouldn't be able to stay. Eduardito has to go to school and . . ."

"But are you happy?" Rafael interrupted her.

"Yes. It's going to be different." Then she explained to me: "We're going to Mérida to live with Eduardo's mother. This was our last summer in this house. You were lucky."

"They'll be much better off in Mérida, don't you think?" Rafael asked me.

"I guess," I said, feeling unable to respond.

"And much closer to each other," Marta broke in.

I asked when they planned to move, and Eduardo answered that it would be as soon as possible, but in reality it was as though something had ended and no one knew what was going to happen next. The four of us felt sentimental and uncomfortable. Eduardo and Rafael simultaneously raised their glasses to drink, and I felt that the scene had something ritualistic about it, although no one knew its significance.

"Well," I hesitated, "I guess I'll have to leave soon, too."

Rafael glanced at me but didn't speak.

"By the way," Marta said, "Eduardo brought a letter for you. It's there, on the table. And I got one from my father. He's coming to visit us this Christmas."

"Another piece of good news," I said, trying to smile.

"Yes, that one is," Marta answered.

That same night she came to my room. I was lying in bed, still smoking, unable to sleep; though it wasn't as hot as the previous nights, the wind had stopped blowing completely and not a single murmur could be heard. The four of us had dined together under the disturbing lights of a distant thunderstorm that rose up suddenly and then stopped without it ever raining, leaving a strange sensation of calm. The conversation never changed from the possibilities of moving to Mérida, the details of Eduardo's father's death, and the economic problems Eduardo would have to face and for which Marta, suddenly happy, always saw an easy solution within reach. Celia and Lorenzo stopped by on their way back from the rosary, taking Rafael with them, so we didn't have a chance to be alone more than a few brief moments. During the dinner he didn't take his eyes off me, and when Marta asked us what we were planning to do, he said he would come to see me in Mexico City, but I thought we had nothing else to say to each other and I almost felt relieved when he had to leave with Celia and Lorenzo, though the kiss he gave me on the cheek as he said good night made me want to be near him.

Marta appeared at my door and asked me if she wasn't interrupting me. I told her not to be foolish and sat up a little, glad she had come. She sat on the edge of the bed and took one of my cigarettes.

"When are you leaving?" she asked me.

"If there are tickets available, the day after tomorrow," I said, deciding that very moment.

"I wish you'd stay a little longer," Marta answered. "You could help me move."

"You know I wouldn't be much help."

"Yes. You're right," she said. "But I hate to see you leave. Everything seems to be going back to the beginning. I don't want to be alone again."

"Maybe I'll be back soon," I commented, with a difficult smile.

"I wish you believed it," she answered, "but I know it's not easy, even though Rafael loves you and maybe you're in love with him now. I realized it a little while ago, during dinner. You don't want to belong to this. It terrifies you, doesn't it? Eduardo agrees with me."

"I could get used to it. You did," I said, trying to convince myself she was wrong.

"You won't want to. Maybe because of what you've seen in me. I love Eduardo more than anything. He is truly my husband. When I wrote inviting you, I needed your support to convince myself it wasn't true and I was the same as before. But I'm not. And that makes me happy. I don't care about the problems; it's what I want and what I need. To me, Mexico City, I mean everything we can remember together, no longer exists. It's always going to exist for you. Maybe that's why I know you're not coming back, and I don't want you to leave so soon. I'm a little scared of saying good-bye."

She had the same look as when I saw her at the airport carrying her child.

"Tell me something, did you go to bed with Eduardo before you got married?" I asked her.

"No, you already knew that. But it's not important," she said.

"What's wrong with me, then?" I asked her.

"Nothing. You're different. It's impossible for all of us to be good at the same things."

"But I love Rafael. I like what he is and in just these few days he has come to matter more than anyone else. What am I good for? As I told you this afternoon, I feel like a whore."

She laughed.

"What did you talk about with Rafael?" she asked me.

"It was very strange. We talked about everything. About him, about me. And about you as well. But there was more to it. There's something between you two. I can't believe it doesn't matter to you."

"It does," she said. "I love him a lot. But what there is is precisely that something. I wouldn't know how to explain it to you. Maybe I've always known it, but I think I realized it when you and I were talking this afternoon and we were laughing, and especially when I saw him leave with you. He's like Eduardo and like me, only Eduardo's my husband and always will be. Do you understand the difference? Nothing would've changed. What we liked was that it was impossible. Both of us. But now Rafael has you. That can be a plus for me. It'd be good if Rafael could bring you back from Mexico City. It's up to you, though; that's why I don't think it'll happen."

We both laughed.

"It's like before, isn't it?" I said. "Maybe it isn't worth it. What's important is to know."

"What did your letter say?" Marta asked.

"Nothing important. It's from my mother. Your father called her to tell her what happened. She sends her regards and asks when I'm returning."

A little later Marta said Eduardo was waiting for her and she left. Without realizing it, we had started talking again about high school. I fell asleep immediately, without trying to figure out if Marta was right, happy with my decision to go back.

The next day the sound of the rain against the window woke me up; when I was finally able to shake off my sleep completely, I realized that for a long while I had been hearing it in my dreams, unable to wake up precisely because of it. The absence of the sun erased all sense of time. It wasn't cold or hot. I stood up and looked out the window. The sea had the same gray color as the sky and was very calm. The raindrops fell monotonously on it, creating some movement on its surface and forming small holes in the humid sand of the deserted beach. Only a few children ran in and out of the sea enjoying the rain. Seeing the abandoned beach, I felt I was somewhere else, but immediately the voices of Marta's children reached me, fighting about something, and then hers scolding them. I put on my robe and went downstairs for breakfast.

"What a change, isn't it? I was right," Marta commented when she saw me.

"Yes," I said. "What time is it?"

"Almost eleven. Eduardo's already left for Mérida, and these two are unbearable; you must have heard them," she said, pointing at the boys. "Sit down and have breakfast. There's nothing to do. The rain won't stop for hours. There's not even a wind to take the clouds away. It's so strange."

It rained until well past noon. While I was eating breakfast, Marta sat next to me; we stayed there talking for a long time about nothing, and I never quite decided to go up to change. When Rafael arrived he found me still in my robe. He sat with us and we continued talking. Instead of bothering him, the change brought by the rain put him in a good mood, but he wasn't able to convince us to go swimming. Then Marta made an excuse to leave us alone, and I told him I had decided to go back to Mexico City the following day.

"Do you have to?" he asked me, very seriously.

"Not necessarily tomorrow, but one of these days, and I had to decide, don't you agree? The sun's not even shining here anymore," I said, trying to diminish the importance of my decision, but he remained serious.

"Did something happen last night?"

"No, nothing. Everything's fine," I answered.

He didn't speak.

"I'm in love with you," he said then.

"I'm in love with you, too," I answered, sincerely.

"I'm going to be jealous," he said. "I thought about it last night and couldn't sleep. I need you all the time."

"Jealous of whom?"

"Of your friend in Mexico City."

"You shouldn't be. It'd be ridiculous. I'm going to wait for you. I love everything you are, nothing more. I don't care about anyone else."

He stood up and hugged me.

"I like seeing you in a robe," he said. "I'm going to remember you like this, like this and the way you were the first day, and in Campeche, and yesterday, when I arrived and you got up to greet me."

I kissed him and stood there hugging him.

"Come for me," I said. "Come. I want you to come."

Instead of going to Mérida, as he was supposed to, he stayed with me, with us; we spent the rest of the morning watching the rain fall on the beach and sea, and the few boys who, in spite of it, floated on the water or ran stiffly along the beach on the wet sand, while Marta's children moved around us, bored. When we sat down for lunch, the sun broke out timidly, little by little imposing itself until finally it erased every trace of rain on the sand, though the sea was still gray and choppy. A gigantic rainbow cut across the horizon and the three of us lamented that it was too late to go swimming.

In the afternoon Marta and I went with him to Mérida, dressed in black, to go to the rosary afterward. The sky, totally clear, looked so white that it was almost nonexistent, and the wind coming through the open windows smelled like wet grass, as it had on the road to Uxmal, but it was hot again. Before going to Eduardo's, we stopped at a travel agency to make my reservations. As we left, Rafael put his arm around my waist and drew me to him. I felt his desire and also desired him, desperately, regretting having gotten my ticket. The city looked different, with more traffic and the noise of the horse-drawn carriages blending with that of the cars. Although the clock had just struck five, a dull moon floated absurdly over the cathedral towers. We went to have some ice cream at the arcades in front of the thick laurels of the plaza and everything was almost as cheerful as it was the first day, in spite of our black dresses. But when we got to the house I realized it had been a good idea to get my ticket. His mother greeted us, her eyes swollen, and asked Marta when they were planning to move in. She started crying again, confessing that she couldn't bear the loneliness of the house. She seemed to have aged suddenly and looked smaller. Marta hugged her, touched, while Rafael and I watched in silence. I thought about Marta living in that house from then on, and the change seemed to reveal an absurd, relentless continuity, but she appeared completely calm as she made plans with Eduardo's mother. For a moment I discovered Rafael looking at her affectionately, admiringly, and I was jealous. When Eduardo's mother went to change for the rosary, the three of us stayed on the veranda, watching the shadows gradually fill the garden and listening to the distant murmurs emerging from the darkness. The beginning of the night never felt like this in Mexico City. Here it had something much more definite; it would suddenly envelop everything and take it somewhere else.

"This is your last night here," Rafael said.

"Yes. I would've liked to have seen the sun set at the beach."

"Does it make you sad?" Marta asked affectionately.

"Yes," I confessed. "But I can't fully believe it's the last. It's going to be strange being in Mexico City again."

Rafael took my hand.

Then Eduardo arrived. He kissed Marta and told her he was going to change, almost without looking at us. Marta told him we had picked up my ticket and I would be leaving the next day. He stood still for a moment, surprised, considering it, and then turned to Rafael.

"What about you?"

"I'll go to see her later," he said.

Eduardo kept quiet again, thinking. Then he seemed to change his mind, and told me, in a light tone, "It's too bad you're leaving so soon. We're going to miss you." He kissed Marta again and added, "I'll be right back. It's late."

Some relatives and old friends, looking tired, their faces shining with perspiration, began to arrive. Eduardo's mother walked out arm-in-arm with him and we went to the church. Though there were plenty of people, we looked lost in it. From the pulpit, with a microphone hanging in front of his chest next to the crucifix, the priest started to pray the rosary in a monotonous, empty voice. From the first moment I gave up following him and tried to think about something else, my skirt sticking to my legs and my back wet, slightly dizzy from the changing shadows the flickering candles projected, following everybody else's movements, kneeling and sitting alternately. The ocean and the sun were far away. Although Rafael was sitting in the same row, we were quite apart, and Eduardo and Marta had gone up to the first pew, next to his mother. The unrhythmic murmur of the voices answered the priest's progressively more extended hum; sometimes he would say the first part of the prayer and at other times the second part, breaking the rhythm of the response, until the notion of one or the other was lost. I felt as though we had slipped out of time, and only the flickering candle flames had a real, independent movement. Everyone was dead beforehand, living only for the moment or in the past, remembering the dead. Nevertheless, as soon as we left the church, the picture changed entirely. Small groups, talking in happy and lively shouts, formed a few steps away from Eduardo's mother, turning their backs completely on the previous action with a clear sense of cheerful community. Rafael asked me if I wanted to have dinner in Mérida or if I'd rather go back to the beach. I told him I preferred to go back and went to talk to Marta and Eduardo. They suggested that we go ahead while they took his mother home.

Alone with Rafael, I went for a ride around the city, passing again in front of his house before taking the highway. He showed me his grade school, Lorenzo's old house, now a hotel, and the park where he played as a child.

"Once we set fire to the dry grass and almost burned everything down. Eduardo's father had to get everyone out of jail and he almost whipped us to death."

Then he stopped at a refreshment stand under the trees, where people were served in their cars.

"I don't want you to forget this," Rafael said.

"No, I'm not going to forget."

On the highway, the stars looked incredibly low again. Rafael would turn every other moment to look at me and smile, as if he wanted to make sure I was with him. He looked very young. I sat as close to him as possible, caressing the nape of his neck with a strange tenderness that overtook me and left me weak. He put a hand on my legs; I started to desire him, losing myself in the reality of that touch, as before, on the trip to Campeche.

"I feel very close to you. I'm going to miss you a lot," he finally said.

"Me too," I answered, with a hoarse voice, and suddenly added impulsively, "I want you to sleep with me."

When Marta and Eduardo arrived, we were on the beach, facing the sea. Rafael had lit a fire with dry palms, but it had already gone out. Eduardo came up without us noticing his presence and said he had been calling us for hours. Marta had started preparing a special farewell dinner for me and, in spite of everything, she and Eduardo were happy. Before sitting at the table, the four of us drank too much and laughed a lot over Eduardo and Rafael's comments about our foreignness compared to them, but then Marta adopted a protective tone toward both of us that disturbed me and clearly made Rafael uncomfortable. After dinner she began to talk about Mexico City, accentuating the tone to advise Rafael about what he should and shouldn't do when he went to see me, talking about my mother and brothers—until Eduardo, a little upset also, told her she was drunk.

"Rafael should do exactly the opposite," he added, trying to turn it into a joke.

She looked at him with a surprised expression, and I had to laugh.

"We're giving it too much importance. We're too serious again," I commented.

"True," Eduardo said. "We can't help it."

I stood in front of the window, turning my back to them and trying to see the ocean. Rafael came to me and put his hand on my shoulder.

"I think I'm going to bed. You don't mind if we leave you two alone, do you?" Eduardo said.

"Of course not," Rafael answered.

Eduardo came and gave me a good-night kiss on the cheek.

"Do you remember the afternoon you got here and we talked? It was very pleasant . . . I didn't remember you that way and I liked you very much."

"Yes," I said. "You have to make things right. Take care of Marta."

"Of course," he answered. "Good night."

Marta kissed me, too, and smiled at Rafael. They went up with their arms around each other. Rafael and I became uncomfortable, not knowing what to do. We started kissing, but the nanny whom I had talked to the first morning on the beach appeared with some of my clothes. She said she knew I was leaving the next day so she had washed them that same afternoon and was now taking them up to my room. I felt that Rafael and I still had something to tell each other, something very important that would clear up a mistake both of us had made, but everything seemed pointless. Instead of talking we kept kissing each other, although the desire made me feel guilty, because it was a way of remaining silent. It brought us closer, however. We made love right there, without even undressing completely, and Rafael didn't go up to my room. When I walked him to his car, I was only able to repeat that I would have liked for him to sleep with me, but I wasn't sad.

Yet the next morning, I completely recovered the flavor of the previous days. Though the sea was still rough, the day was gorgeous. Marta served Eduardo and me breakfast, since we came down at the same time. He had to return to Mérida. He told me we would see each other at the airport, repeating with a tender, gentle look how good it had been to have me with them all that time. The boys, already in their trunks, were waiting for us to take them to the beach, and Marta was wearing shorts again, as she had the first day. Rafael came in trunks, too, and we spent the entire morning at the beach, under the sun, in and out of the water, unable to decide to return to the house now that we didn't have to arrange to happen on each other in order to be together; it seemed impossible that I would be in Mexico City that same night. I was jealous of Marta, who would stay forever and for whom, in the end, this summer would come to be one more season; it hurt me to think that if I ever came back, perhaps they would no longer have the house, there would be nothing to discover, and things wouldn't be the same, but under the sun, everything was too real. Only when Celia and Lorenzo, who had not come out to the beach because they were getting ready to return to Mérida, came to say good-bye, and I hugged them with real nostalgia, did I understand that I was no longer there; I had begun to return much earlier, and the morning had been a marvelous but fictitious epilogue.

From the terrace Rafael suddenly pointed out to me Don José's boat, returning to the beach under full sail, and I said I wanted to say good-bye to him. We went with Marta and the boys, walking along the shore up to the place where they unloaded the catch beyond the pier. From there we saw how he hauled down the sails just before he arrived. The boys were delighted watching the fish, among the people from the town, but Don José had to tend to his customers and he hardly paid attention to me.

Then all we did was wait for time to pass and we left for Mérida a little before five, in the blazing heat, so I would have time to say good-bye to Eduardo's mother. On the highway I just wanted to look at the scenery. She started to cry as soon as she saw me, repeating over and over that it seemed impossible that Don Manuel was no longer there to say good-bye to me. All the maids came out to see me off and remained standing, stonelike and silent, on the veranda next to her as we crossed the garden.

Rafael insisted that we go through the center of the city again so I could see the plaza; then, at the airport, his lips pressed tight, he seemed unable to look at me, although I didn't let go of his arm for one moment and tried to be happy to lessen the importance of my leaving. The boys were running all over, and Marta spent the last half-hour trying to keep them at her side. When the flight's departure had already been announced, Eduardo arrived, running, convinced it was too late, with the smile of an apologetic young man. As I was saying good-bye, amid the hurry and the confusion, after kissing Rafael, I felt a sad happiness when I saw him next to Marta, who again had the youngest boy in her arms. The last time I turned around to see them, Rafael was a few steps behind them.

After the plane took off, it made a full turn and passed over the city. I was surprised to see so many trees behind the closed walls of the houses. The person sitting next to me was a sweaty American, in short sleeves, who fell asleep right away . . .

This book is set in Berkeley Medium, with Zeal dingbats.

Printed on 60 lb Glatfelter Natural and bound by
Edwards Brothers, Ann Arbor, Michigan.

Designed and composed by Ellen McKie on a Macintosh
in PageMaker 4.2 for the University of Texas Press.